THE THIRTEENTH FLOOR

ANTHOLOGY

THE THIRTEENTH FLOOR
GRAPHIC NOVELS

The Thirteenth Floor Vol. 01
The Thirteenth Floor Vol. 02
The Thirteenth Floor Vol. 03
The Thirteenth Floor: Home Sweet Home
The Thirteenth Floor: The Return of Max

THE THIRTEENTH FLOOR

ANTHOLOGY

EDITED BY GUY ADAMS

Based on the cult hit comic by John Wagner, Alan Grant & José Ortiz

First published 2025 by Rebellion
an imprint of Rebellion Publishing Ltd,
Riverside House, Osney Mead,
Oxford, OX2 0ES, UK

www.solarisbooks.com

ISBN: 978-1-83786-603-8

10 9 8 7 6 5 4 3 2 1

A CIP catalogue record for this book is available from the British Library.

Designed & typeset by Rebellion Publishing

Printed in Denmark

CONTENTS

INTRODUCTION

GUY ADAMS

Most of us would kill for a landlord who would kill for us.

The Thirteenth Floor was created by legendary writers John Wagner and Alan Grant[1] as part of the short-lived IPC Magazines anthology comic *Scream!* Max, a garrulous computer interface, was the front-facing caretaker of Maxwell Tower, an experimental council tenement block. Max took his duties seriously, loving and protecting his tenants. Indeed, anyone who threatened—or distressed—them in any way would find themselves transported to a secret thirteenth floor where they would meet a violent and inventive end.

Scream! was cancelled after fifteen fraught issues—the comic was a target for censorship by its nervous publisher from the off—but *The Thirteenth Floor* continued in the pages of publishing stablemate, *Eagle*. Max moved from Maxwell Tower to a new job at the Pringles Department Store (with a side hustle helping MI5[2]) but eventually returned to Maxwell

1 They were writing so many strips at the time that they were forced to employ a handful of pseudonyms, here they were credited as Ian Holland.

2 Indeed, he even had a side side-hustle as the fictional editor of *Eagle* itself!

Tower towards the end of his three-year publishing run, just in time to see the place burned down.

Or was it? Well, not according to me but writers have always been slippery sods when they want a story to do as it's told.

I was hired in 2017 to revive *The Thirteenth Floor* for a one-off *Scream! and Misty Halloween Special* being published by new rights owners, Rebellion.

The Thirteenth Floor had been a favourite of mine as a child and I was a touch giddy to work alongside artists John Stokes and Frazer Irving breathing new life into Max. I decided Maxwell Tower hadn't been as badly damaged as all that and had been brought vaguely back up to spec by a money-grabbing government who wasn't entirely concerned about the safety of its residents. Max sparks back into life—having lain dormant for decades—when he sees a young resident being bullied. Flaky, wild and trying to catch up with a world that's moved on without him, he deals with the bullies[3] and asks the young tenant, Sam, if he knows any other bad people that might need teaching a lesson. "Loads," says Sam with a somewhat wild glint in his eyes.

That one-off story turned into another and then a forty-page special that wrapped Sam's story up. Our young anti-hero, battered from years of abuse, had wreaked havoc with the help of an easily led AI (not a term that would have been used in the original run) and Max appeared to have been deactivated once more.

Writers are cautious of full stops though, we never like to close off worlds we may return to, so the final page showed Max having escaped to the investigating police officer's phone, wondering if she might be interested in working with him to punish more deserving people.

And then…

---

3 Checking my old emails I see the one note I had was to alter the original script so that he didn't kill them. They're left, trance-like, to work on repairs on Max's mainframe.

PROLOGUE
GUY ADAMS

If the suit looked out of place brushing past the black metal gate of Maxwell Tower, psoriasis puff of black paint dusting down its lapels for fingerprints, then the shoes were positively screaming.

Ms Adebayo, number 37, watched from her kitchen window and decided she knew a drug dealer when she saw one. The Bartosz twins at number 52—fresh from losing themselves in well-thumbed Manga collections—had him pegged as a demon, the devil in disguise. "Look at that hair," said young Antoni, admiring the soft-scoop flourish of a bleached cream fringe horn, "nobody *real* has hair like that." Nana Goldwyn, number 12, never one for sensationalism, simply muttered, "There's a ponce who turned left out of Pret when he should have turned right."

Perhaps they were all right.

Clement Reuben, software developer and bastard, stood outside the entrance foyer of Maxwell Tower and took in the excess of information. Neighbourhood Watch posters; frayed phone-number tassels offering dog-walking; house-clearance or English tuition; an all-you-can-eat buffet and an overly optimistic offer of yoga tuition. 'Find the new you!' the advert suggested. Reuben was quite happy with the old one.

"Kiyoshi," he said into his phone, "figure out the door code for me, would you?"

--Of course, Sensei.-- came the low, fruity voice of Toshiro Mifune, yanked ignobly from the dead throat of a cinematic legend and stapled on to the cold, dead larynx of an AI bot.

"I could just tell it you," came a voice from behind Reuben.

He turned to size up the teenage effigy of pungent athleisurewear and misplaced confidence, fifteen years along the narrative journey from Not a Great Start to Well, What Else Was Going To Become of Him?

"Cost you twenty quid though."

--It's 0589.-- announced Mifune, with the gravitas of a man about to slaughter Ronin by the dozen.

"I'll save my money, thanks, kid," said Reuben, pressing the code into the door-pad.

"What's to stop me telling the law you're poking around?" the kid asked.

Reuben chuckled. 'The law'. Bless. "Nothing, fill your boots, see if they give a shit."

The kid shrugged. "Doubt it. No fucker does about this place."

"Not even the poor pricks who live here, eh?" Reuben stepped inside, holding the door for a moment. "Coming?"

The kid jogged inside. "What's that thing you were talking to, anyway?"

"My personal assistant. AI name of Kiyoshi."

"AI? Cool. Used to have one of those around here."

Reuben immediately clocked the door that would lead to the basement. "I know, clever little bastard called Max."

"Yeah, don't know about clever. Fucker went mad and killed a load of people."

"Some would say that showed common sense." Reuben went through the door to the basement and trotted down the stairs, the kid following him. "Ask me, the thing was beautiful. Perfect. I've a mind to repackage and sell on, in fact."

"Closed it down, didn't they?" said the kid. "Switched it off."

"Not quite," said Reuben. "It migrated. Software will do that. Ended up on a phone."

"Cool."

"Complicated. It needed space, spread out through the network, stretched its legs. Caused a problem. People thought it was a bug. Company was called in to deal with it. My company. Pest control."

The basement was small, keeping the smell of damp and oil bottled for the ages.

On one wall, a member of the local spray-paint literati had written CARL SUX COX.

"Don't suppose your name's Carl?" Reuben asked.

"Fuck off, cunt. What you want down here anyway?"

Reuben looked around. "I was told the mainframe was down here. Probably bricked over. Doesn't matter, hack it remotely..." The kid looked even more vacant than before.

"It was my company that dealt with it," Reuben continued. "The AI. Max. Uprooted, bottled, captured." Reuben grinned, and that grin lit up the basement like a hand grenade in a crèche. "But the little shit's playing hard to get so I'm hoping to find a few of its original security protocols. See if I can't loosen it up."

"Oh yeah?" the kid tried to pretend he understood what Reuben was saying. Tried to slouch a few inches deeper. Kentucky-fried insouciance. Prick. "Need help? I'm your man."

Reuben reached into his back pocket and took out his wallet, pulled out a fifty, held it up, a crisp pirate's flag promising bad intentions. "You'd do anything for a few quid, wouldn't you?"

The kid's eyes flicked towards the graffiti, like Reuben wanted his filthy little council trash gob on him. Jesus.

"Not that, Christ..."

"I meant to help you find the..." the kid can't remember the words now, "security holes."

"Oh, I imagine I've got those by now. Kiyoshi?"

--Downloaded, Sensei.--

"See? Just had to get the clever little bugger close. I've got everything I need. This is just about fun. You tough?"

"What?" Reuben had his answer; look at the kid, quaking in his ShoeZone sneakers.

"Tough," said Reuben, "strong, handle yourself."

The kid put on an extra inch, tried to look the part. "Fuck, yeah."

"Okay, cool, that's great. Tough. That's what I need. So, fifty gets me three hits. You think you can take that?"

"You want to hit me?"

"Yeah. I do. I really do. Got to get your steps in. Got to close your exercise rings. I want to hit you. Three punches. Tell you what, once I'm done, I'll even let you return the favour. Three for three. You still keep the cash."

The kid looked worried. Not entirely stupid then.

"Of course, if you don't want the money." Leave a pause, take a beat. "Or you just can't take it."

"Make it a hundred."

"Oh, so you *can* take it, but you want to haggle." Reuben laughed. "No, sorry, I didn't get where I am today by doubling my offers. The price is fifty, take it or leave it." He began to head towards the stairs.

"I'll take—"

Reuben's first punch dropped a full stop on that sentence. The kid was on the floor, confused as to how he got there. The second went straight down into the face, soft tissue and cartilage sliding over bone like a pensioner on the first ice of the season.

Reuben waited on the third. He wanted to appreciate it. He wanted to feel the burn on his knuckles. The third punch was the dream. He would lie awake at night fantasising about that third punch, about powering straight through nasal bone and maxilla. About pounding meat against the back of the skull. Stirring the bowl. Kneading the dough. Could you imagine?

Could you taste the strength of that? The sheer fucking power of it?

He took the third punch, and it wasn't all that. There was a distinct crack of fracture; the kid's nose took a left turn as if trying to find cover in his ear; his breathing became fluid. It was good, sure, it was damage, but it wasn't the dream. Maybe next time.

"Thanks, kid." He dropped the fifty onto the floor. "You want your shots? You feeling it?"

The kid gagged on blood and tooth.

"Guess not. Another time."

Reuben walked towards the stairs, feeling calm, feeling right, feeling in his perfect groove. God, but he loved being him. Being him was the absolute fucking best.

"Kiyoshi, how are those security protocols looking?"

--Applied, Sensei, Max currently rebooting.--

And there we are, what a simple morning's work.

"Start lining up sales calls, Kiyoshi, it's time to make Max work for us. Time to take him global."

I mean… such a lovely bit of software left to rot in cheap housing? Where was the sense in that? People would pay for the Max experience; people would pay dearly.

FUNHOUSE

ANGELA SLATTER

"Sure you'll be okay on your own? This sort of place, a girl might get lonely." He grins, showing that one front tooth that's especially discoloured—they're all discoloured, all yellow, but this one in particular is heading towards brown. Same colour as a dying banana. "Or scared. Girls get scared."

"Not me. Love horror movies. 'Sides, I've got a bunch of brothers, seven, they'll all drop around to make sure I'm okay." She hopes her tone's suitably nonchalant, covers the lie. Efficiently don't-fuck-with-me. Believable.

"Well," he blusters, "you're not allowed to have people staying here—"

"Of course not, Mr Brown. They'll only visit to check in on me, no sleepovers, nothing like that. Just family. You understand family." She says it because she sees a wedding ring on his finger, embedded in fat; of course, it might not apply anymore, might just be the flesh folds trapping it there long after the wife's left. She says it because his uniform looks neatly ironed, so maybe someone still loves him enough to do that even if it's perfunctory; she doesn't think he did it himself, because she sees where he's spilled tomato sauce on the shirt, smeared it probably with the paper serviette. She might be wrong, sometimes she's wrong, but mostly she's not. She says it because she needs the bloody job and the shitty accommodation.

It seems to calm him down.

They're standing in front of a locked-up building; the signage is in neon lights, but they've not been lit for a few years. You can still make out the hues of pink and purple, red, blue and green.

FUNHOUSE.

The man's got a security pass clipped to his belt on one of those elastic retractable lines; it buzzes a little as he pulls it out, swipes at the reinforced entrance to the abandoned amusement arcade. The door whistles, clicks and pops. *R2D2*, she thinks, then bites down on a snigger. Doesn't want him to think she's laughing at him, doesn't want to have to explain the joke.

First, he points upward—"Fifteen floors of empty offices, the Corporation wants to knock it down, build it much higher, but there are rules"—then he takes a step forward, over the threshold; a moment or two later, a bank of lights comes on, two by two, two by two, down the centre of the ceiling. He gestures, gentlemanly, for her to accompany him. Either side of them, the arcade complex looks like it only closed down last night. Weirdly clean—then she notices the Roomba charging stations, the hum they all make, in their docks, waiting. Vents above huff, and cool air's directed downwards onto gaming tables (for gambling and D&D)—pinball machines, shelves, various videogames, Ping-Pong tables, clawed lucky dips, slot machines (the divide between kids' games and adult ones long lost in the maw of toxic capitalism—anyone's money is good enough to steal or con out of them), roulette wheels, blackjack lanes, and high stakes GoFish! with the sign that says 'No bets under $2,000!' Her gran had been carried out of a place like this, dead as a doornail. The air smells lemony-fresh—more cleaning products—but the carpet beneath her boots feels a little sticky. There's something about arcade carpet that's just made that way. She wonders about the insides of those poor Roombas; no natural enemy but arcade carpets.

There are no windows. Mr Brown must read her mind because he says, "No windows, no daylight in here—keeps people in a state of thinking time's not passing. They keep spending and losing, thinking their whole life's ahead of 'em." He points at the fluorescent lights above. "These only went on when it was closing time—by which point it was dark outside and most of the mugs had missed their dinner, so they'd spend more money at the food trucks on their way to the carpark." He shakes his head. "Ingenious."

"Ingenious," she echoes softly. Doesn't want him to think she's not paying attention.

"Don't worry, your quarters aren't like this. Very nice, if I do say so myself." He points. "Left here. You see those markers on the wall? Just follow the pink arrows if you find yourself feeling lost. Pink arrows."

"Pink arrows."

Next, through a large area that had been a food court. 'Troughs', her father had said disdainfully. Again, clean and tidy, shiny polished metal surfaces, terrazzo tabletops, plastic benches, even more plastic plants, like a fake jungle. She half-expected to see a stuffed lion peeking out from between the faux foliage. They continued, past signs for toilets and lifts, past little shops for standard lollies and snacks and vapes, novelties like fidget spinners and stress balls, then all those imported candies from Japan that required construction and chemistry and left you with unrecyclable debris that would eventually make it to the sea. The industrial refrigerators, their glass doors crystal clear, still hummed, bright lights shining through bottles of coloured soft drink and 3% genuine fruit juice suspended in preservative that owed some of its DNA at least to formaldehyde. A few clothing shops—surf wear to make people think you owned at least four boogie boards; leisurewear for the over and under fifties, the white shoe brigade; a jewellery shop stocking pearls, gold chains, tiaras, his'n'hers diamond tennis bracelets, and a variety of gems suitable for fitting in your front teeth if you wanted a little extra flair. All of it pristine and untouched. Protected.

She's careful not to let her gaze linger on the jewellery store lest he think she's planning something. She needs this job more than she needs to shoplift, even if the very idea of trying to shift that kind of gear wasn't so very overwhelming. Ollie's brother would know somebody, someone completely not respectable, who'd take a finger off sure as shake your hand if it was wearing a ring. Nah. Not worth it.

"Here we are."

They'd been walking for almost ten minutes. It was like trying to get through a suburban shopping mall. He blips the card against the reader beside a very plain-looking door, then throws it open as if showing a prize home.

And he kind of is.

She hadn't been overly worried about the details when she'd seen the job advert—just that it didn't look like she was going to be sold or raped or murdered, or all three in any order—and that there was a place to live and a small salary and, miracle of miracles, healthcare. She didn't have to strip off her clothes or fuck anybody, she didn't have to sleep in whatever lecture theatre she can find unlocked at medical school campus at the end of each day, and she didn't have to go home to where her stepfather reigned, and her mother wept.

But the room—little apartment, really—is a surprise.

A delight.

Open-plan, painted a soft sunshine yellow, a neat kitchen with a plain pine dining table and four chairs, then a loungeroom with a modular sofa and a lot of cushions, a low bookshelf along one wall (empty, but she'd fix that), a door to the right that showed a bright bedroom, another door to a bathroom. But the real joy was the windows: all along the front and left walls, so she could see out to the end of the pier where the rest of the arcade became a mini amusement park, the oldest part, the original. The tiny Ferris wheel and the big merry-go-round are still there, even though it looks like the wooden structure beneath might fall in with the next decent storm. She didn't care about the obstructed view: she could see the sea, the sky, the light. So much light.

Again, Brown seems to read her mind. "Don't worry—where we are, is solid. Terra firma, no worries, even if that old shit show gets swept away."

It's a home. A sanctuary. Somewhere she can sleep. She can go and retrieve her backpack from Mrs Barnes, the school librarian she'd kept in touch with, who'd always been kind and said nothing but just *helped*. Some money here, clean clothes there, a place to sleep every so often when Jessie couldn't go home.

She blinks hard. *Don't cry, don't cry, don't cry.* Because then he'll think he needs to hug you, thinks he can, thinks it's his right. So, she pins on a smile, bright as can be.

"Thank you, Mr Brown. This is really lovely." She puts out her hand, businesslike. "I'm grateful for the opportunity and I won't let you or the Corporation down."

"Ah, no worries." He looks amused. "Now, the only thing that might be a bit startling is Max. To be honest, it's why we couldn't keep any blokes in here—didn't like the random talking." He shrugs.

"Max?"

"It's the old system—designed to run everything like an electronic concierge, maintenance man, security guard. Old version—hasn't been upgraded, this one, sometimes it glitches. Corporate don't wanna spend the money on something they're trying to knock down as soon as the planning permission goes through." He leaned in confidentially, lowering his voice as if someone might overhear. "Problem is, part of this is heritage-listed, the original bit, mostly the old pier out there. Having someone here, living on-site, is one of the conditions of having the case heard—stop anyone from having an accidental fire, if you get my drift. You're here as a deterrent to vandals. Not that," he added hastily, "you're expected to do anything. Just ring this number if there's any trouble." He hands her a card. "And the big boys'll be here quick smart."

Jessie nods. To be honest, being burned alive might not be so bad compared to what waits at home. "Thanks again."

She puts her satchel on the tabletop with a clunk, then walks him back to the door, already proprietorial. "Well, I don't want to keep you, Mr Brown. Once again, thanks for everything."

He pauses in the doorway, hands over a passkey. "What are you studying anyway?"

"Medicine. Third year." First year, but she's hoping it makes her seem older.

"Well, la-di-dah." His voice rises a couple of octaves, clearly thinking himself hilarious. "Why do you want this shitty job, then?"

She screws the cap down tight on her temper. "Well, it's really hard to study and work. You study full-time, work part-time, you can't make ends meet. Study and work part-time, nothing gets done. You study part-time, work full-time, you can eat and pay rent, but you probably won't pass exams, then you've got an even bigger course debt because you've got to repeat subjects. Study full-time, work full-time, you're just going to die." She refrains from saying *Work full-time, don't study, and you end up in a job like yours forever.* "So, this shitty job helps keep the wolf from the door. Sir."

Something in her tone moves him, makes him respect her a bit. Just a bit. He clicks his heels, snaps off a salute, and says, "Welcome to the Corporation, Jessie Friday."

IT'S BEEN FIVE days since the girl arrived, and Max is getting used to her.

Young woman, actually. She's almost nineteen, he learned when she plugged in her devices and he'd scanned their contents. Couldn't help himself, first bit of fresh input in an age; and it's his job. Phone and laptop, both cheap, end of the line—the emailed receipts showed they'd been purchased when their prices had dropped—bargain conscious, he'd at first thought, then, in checking her bank balance, he realised it was proper poverty. The cost of her education, even with the scholarships she'd won, was going to drag behind her for years. And the mobile number, he noted, was newly activated, pay-as-you-go. The email account, just set up.

She was quiet, even when on her own. The males that had first been employed—before he'd chased them off—were noisy. Constantly. If it wasn't the blasting music in any number of genres, it was the TV—sports, films, porn, cartoons, even cooking shows—at top volume. Anything on games consoles, completely over-the-top. Mingled in with that was the very personal cacophony of burping and farting, phone conversations and ablutions conducted with the bathroom door open. And filthy. So grubby that even with Max's abilities, all the automated cleaning mechanisms at his disposal, he was flat out keeping up with those disaster boys. He hadn't hurt them—although the temptation to take them to the thirteenth floor was strong—but there was no way he was putting up with them.

Jessie's different. Hardly ever puts the TV on, sometimes recites her anatomical studies homework—knee bone being connected to the thigh bone, etc—and any music is quietly played on the tinny speakers of her phone, but mostly she sits with the windows open to catch the fresh air and the sounds of the sea. It's been a while since the noise of the carnival on the pier had wafted out over the bay, the hurdy-gurdy and carousel tunes, the call of barkers trying to convince passers-by to try their luck at the games of chance. It's been two years since there'd been anyone he'd liked in the complex; indeed, two years since there's been anyone in the complex at all except the disaster boys and the occasional visit from Barry Brown.

Max noticed she's relaxed into the space. She was jumpy, those first few days, getting up four times to check the door was code-locked. Startling when a strong breeze outside made something fall over down on the pier. He doesn't want to scare her, and even though Mr Brown had warned her about Max, he's stayed silent.

It's serene, which Max likes, is used to—but with Jessie, the silence is also companionable.

With Jessie here, it feels homey.

She *feels like a beating heart.*

THE LECTURES ARE easier to do now she's not juggling three part-time jobs. Seven days in, and now she can 'work from home' and zoom in to the courses. She goes out for walks: after breakfast but before she clocks in at 9 am, then again at lunchtime, and she does some groceries in the afternoon before night comes in, before the light gets too tricky and it's hard to see someone waiting in the shadows. It's not that it's a particularly bad area, but it's not really well-populated and it's also not a particularly good area—more just somewhere that's kind of deserted, somewhere something bad could happen and there'd be no one around to help. Equally, it's somewhere a miracle could happen, and no one would know about it either. Revelatory angels covered with eyes, baby superheroes crashing to Earth in spaceships Moses-down-the-river-like, asphalt splitting open to allow demons or Godzilla's little brother to appear.

If she walks far enough up or down the beachfront she'll invariably run into people: young couples who've not been together long enough to hate each other, old couples who soothe their bickering with ice cream cones, young men roaming solo or in packs, pods of girls in too-high heels and ass-freezing skirts no matter the weather. Families: 2.5 kids, generally two parents, two mums, two dads, one of each. She doesn't mind them; they tend to leave her alone, with her air of hard-shell persona, the cigarette she lights but never smokes, just carries around as a deterrent. Camouflage.

And she's happy.

This evening, for the first time in a long while, she's happy and she feels safe. She is relaxed, her shoulders aren't hunched up around her ears, the muscles in her back are still a little tight, but nothing someone could pluck a tune on. Not now. She feels something is rolling out in front of her that she can't see, but she can feel—a path of hope and promise.

Then the phone in her pocket rings, just as she gets to the outer door, the barrier she thinks of as the moat around her castle. With one hand she swipes her card—a careful glance over one shoulder, then the other to make sure no one's watching or following, because caution's something that got injected into her at a very early age, after her father died, after her mother remarried—with the other, pulls out the mobile, sees her mother's name, only hesitates a second before answering, but answers because she feels better, stronger, safer. She can share a little kindness and strength with Maureen.

Only it's not Maureen, is it?

She wonders how he found the new phone, the burner cell she'd given her mother with her own new number programmed in. She knows how, really. Her mother's fragile after all these years, she's eggshell frail, and it only takes two or three hits now to shake things out of her.

'Where are you?'

Her stepfather's growl sends a chill through her, despite everything she's done to stop the trigger, all the books she read, the free self-help videos online, all the calming sounds and words and meditations. But those three words wipe all of that away, a tsunami of fear, a physical reaction that makes her throw up on the door as it clicks open, makes tears spring heated and traitorous.

'Tell me where you are, and I'll come and get you.'

She doesn't say anything, just spits out the remnants of the vomit, thinking about how the Roombas will have to deal with it. The door slams closed, the lights flicker on, and she starts to run. Panicked and terrified, still holding the phone, unable to click it off, her brain won't work properly, just her legs moving, staggering and stuttering like a robot running out of battery, but still going forward, past the shops and kiosks, the food court, the bright shine of the jewellery stores, the bright junkiness of the lolly shops, on and on and on.

Until she realises, she's not paid attention to the pink arrows, hasn't taken the safe path to her sanctuary, her castle keep, but she's run into an area with no lighting except for one flickering, sputtering fluoro tube, the phone in her hand is still spewing that hated voice, and her knees have turned to jelly making her sink to the cold linoleum tiles.

Max feels the blip in the system that says the front door's opened, notes Jessie's ID pop-up on his screen. All green. Green for good. Green for go. He's happy to have her home. Happy to know she's safe. He trains his security cameras to follow her as far as possible whenever she goes for her walks. In fact, he managed to hack into the ones the local council's had installed all up and down the beachfront, so he can keep an eye on her. Max knows a wounded creature when he sees one.

Now, he's just watched her fall apart, bolting into the belly of the arcade, the bit that's been offline to save on power, on electricity bills, even though the Corporation owns the utilities provider as well. Doesn't matter; he can see her, his circuits switching to infrared, just for a couple of seconds while he reinstates the power to the lights.

There she is, in the middle of the corridor, in front of a bed linen and candle emporium, sort of melted onto the floor, collapsed, sobbing as if the world's at an end. He doesn't want to scare her, but he doesn't want her to cry like this, to think herself alone. So, he does something he hasn't done for months and activates the PA. If he had lungs, he'd take a deep breath before he speaks.

++Don't be afraid, Jessie.++

But she startles despite his gentlest tone.

++I'm sorry. It's me. Max. Mr Brown mentioned me. I'm the—++

"—concierge." Already she's wiping her eyes, pulling herself together. She's finally clicked off the phone, though he hears the man demanding to know who she's with, who's that bloke with her? "I got lost, Max. Can you help?"

++Of course.++ And he talks her back to where the pink arrows glow against the walls, and he keeps talking to her until she swipes open the door to the little apartment. When she's inside, he turns the lights on, but not too bright, just a sort of candle-low that's comforting. He sets the drink machine to make a hot chocolate that she takes gratefully and goes to sit by the front windows, which he opens for her.

She sits quietly for a few minutes before he asks, ++Are you alright, Jessie? Can I help with anything else?++

For a moment, he thinks she'll tell him. That he's the one being she might just tell. However, the moment passes, and she's decided otherwise. "No, thank you, Max. I think I'll just go to bed."

And she finishes the hot chocolate, and goes into the bedroom, doesn't bother to get undressed or have a shower, just burrows under the covers as if to bury herself. Then her voice, very small. "Max, will you play some music? Something to help me sleep? Will you watch over me until I'm asleep?"

++Of course, Jessie.++

He scrolls through the enormous music library database at his command and chooses a compilation of sleep-time nursery songs played on a harp, hoping it's not too childish, but she just sighs and settles further into the mattress, deeper under the bed linen. When his sensors detect that she's properly asleep, Max turns the music down just a little and links to her phone. Finds the number of the last call, finds it's not registered to anyone—a burner—no matter, checks the cell towers it pinged off, triangulates, narrows down the location to a house in a nice suburb, the sort of enclave where doctors and lawyers live. He's surprised, thought her situation a bit more lower socio-economic, but no.

Max whirs through everything he can find, electoral roll registers, title deeds, car registration, home phone number, gets the name of the couple living there. Mr and Mrs Anderson, Tony and Millicent. Jessie Friday. Millicent's daughter from a first marriage. Second husband, a barrister, married when Jessie was nine. No lack of money. Max ponders the cheap mobile, the cheap laptop; thinks about a girl planning to escape. Putting as little of her precious funds behind those two things, as little as she could get away with.

Max begins to dig more deeply into Mr Tony Anderson, KC's life.

THREE DAYS LATER, Jessie's feeling not so bad. She's slept deeply (Max has made sure of that, a light sedative, lavender scented, through the air vents), and there've been no more phone calls, no text. What Jessie doesn't know is that's because Max has blocked the other burner, and Jessie doesn't feel like phoning her mother even though she wants to. But she doesn't want to hear her stepfather's voice again. She'll try and get a message to Millicent through Mrs Barnes, the old school librarian, who lives not far from the Andersons, but her stepfather can't find out about it because she wouldn't put it past him to turn up on Mrs Barnes's doorstep and threaten her. Mrs Barnes is made of strong stuff—most librarians are, you have to be when idiots want to ban your charges, burn them, librarians are flameproof—but Jessie couldn't stand it if her stepfather sent around some of the men he represents in court, the men he gets off charges of murder and assault, theft and anything else that makes the world a worse place.

No, she's got to work out how to keep everyone safe.

Max has been a comfort. They chat occasionally, mostly when he's checking in on her, making coffee or hot chocolate, depending on the time of day or night. She tells him a little about her family—father lost in car accident, mother wooed by a fast-talking charmer, and no one realising he'd married Millicent to get to Jessie until it was too late. She doesn't give details, though, cuts off before those things come flooding out. Max doesn't ask for the details either and she's grateful for that.

He's taken over the running of everything electronic in the little apartment, lights, heating, windows, all for her comfort. He's heating meals, playing music, reminding her it's late, but letting her sleep as long as she likes; ordering groceries online too, just until she feels okay about going outside again. And he's been able to get in extra study resources for her that she's not sure the ordinary databases would ever offer up. Some nights, he asks her questions in preparation for the exams she's got to sit next week; the best study buddy she could ask for, he wants nothing in return.

She's been worrying, too, about going outside, going to the medical school to sit her exams, but Max promised she'd be fine. When she unpacked the last grocery delivery, there was a pack of hair dye (dark brown) and a pair of sharp hairdressing scissors. She liked her hair darker, but the pixie cut was taking some getting used to—he'd played YouTube clips to guide her in the chopping, apologising that he didn't have hands to help, but maybe just a little shorter on the left to even things up.

Jessie was pretty sure her own mother wouldn't recognise her now, at least not easily.

* * *

Max has done *a deep dive. Found her old email accounts, previous mobile account, found threatening messages, awful things. He's found what can best be described as* evidence, *stuff that the KC is too arrogant to think anyone would find, would use against him. Assuming that Jessie doesn't want anyone to know what's been done to her and her mother for almost ten years. That the girl will want to protect her mother from the retribution he's promised if a word of this ever gets out. And Jessie herself, in her locked diary files, never wants to be known as the girl* that *happened to. Doesn't matter that it's not her fault, she can't bear to wear the weight of other gazes, of others' knowledge.*

And Max has gone over the trials, the acquittals of men who are clearly guilty but allowed back out on the streets due to technicalities found or created by Tony Anderson. He's been through the bank accounts, the staggering amounts of money passing through the KC's accounts, the amounts he's funnelled off to Swiss and Bahamian banks. Shell companies, imaginary staff members. It's an impressive house of cards—credit cards, debit cards, bank bonds, crypto, promissory notes, stocks, shares and property portfolios.

The morning of Jessie's exam, Max assures her she's safe. Promises her that the Uber he's just ordered will drop her at the front door of the exam hall, that no one will be allowed into the venue, and that when she's done all she has to do is text him and another Uber will be waiting outside for her—specially selected drivers who know how to avoid being tailed or tracked.

And although she's nervous, Max's care of the past three weeks has built her confidence, so she leaves at 9 am on the dot which is when Max, cloning the number of her mobile, sends a text to the mobile of Tony Anderson, KC, telling him it's her, Jessie, she wants to come home to daddy.

* * *

Tony Anderson parks his black Mercedes CLE Coupé close to the entrance, eyes the fifteen floors rising over him, eyes the old sign, sneers at it. *FUNHOUSE*. Thinks, *Perhaps*, and heads towards the door.

It whistles, clicks and pops open.

Inside, a bank of lights comes on, two by two, two by two, down the centre of the ceiling. Illuminating video games, gambling appurtenances, kiosks, shops, displays and everything else in this structure. Idly, he wonders if it's owned by one of his clients, looks like the sort of spot some of the more Eastern European amongst them would purchase to hide funds, write off tax, etcetera. Makes a mental note to check later. He strides in and onwards like *he* owns the place, realises by the time he gets to the expansive food court with its fake greenery that the place is too fucking big, so he stops and shouts for her.

"Jessie! Jessie Friday. Come on. Time to go home." He listens as the slight echoes of his voice fade away. "Jessie! I've only got so much patience left."

In the distance, she calls back. To come and help with her bag. He swears under his breath, then decides to play along. He can punish her at his leisure once he gets her home.

Max plays the recording of Jessie's voice three more times, and it has the desired effect. Tony Anderson follows along like a dog with a scent. At last, he arrives at the secondary games area where the dance part of the arcade is, all the ManicPanicX and DropBoogie7 platforms with their screens to show either the moves or the squares to step on. A long row of them, all turned on, all bright and flashing, a little blinding.

Tony Anderson stops, hands on hips, yells his stepdaughter's name again.

Max's modulated recording plays again, as if Jessie is hiding behind the machines. It says she's scared. He needs to help her.

And Tony Anderson, KC, impatient and incautious, steps onto the nearest dance machine platform—a ManicPanicX, Max's personal favourite for its clever and challenging combinations synchronised with energetic beats—and Max has him. The transportation device Max built into the ManicPanicX—into all of the dance games—pulls Jessica's stepfather through time and space and walls and molecules and deposits him on the thirteenth floor, Max's own little playpen.

For the most part, it's laid out like a courtroom, but in place of jurors are instruments of torture, on the bar table a selection of knives and axes, pliers and stiletto blades, hacksaws and hammers, and thumbscrews. There's a scold's bridle, a rack, the pear of anguish, the scavenger's daughter, heretic's fork, spike chair, a brazier with pokers buried deep in the red-hot coals, and in the corner of the room an iron maiden. It's a classic for a reason, thinks Max.

Before a dazed Tony Armstrong can get a word out, Max's voice drops from the ceiling like a net: ++Court is now in session.++

MAKING THE ROUNDS

MASON CROSS

It was the future, in 1967.

Wakeman glanced up at the west-facing outpost of the Phase One section of the town centre and wondered what kind of day it was going to be.

The westerly expanse of Phase One was a vast, elongated three-storey structure suspended in the air by fifty-foot-high stilts. It jutted out from the wide slab of concrete and glass that formed the rest of the megastructure. The pale morning sun glinted off the murky windows and their steel frames. A moment later and it was lost from view as his car passed into the tunnel that enclosed the dual carriageway running through the heart of the town centre. Wakeman flicked his headlights on to add some extra illumination to the grimy sodium spotlights that were still operational.

It was the future.

It was a funny thought, one that he couldn't remember having crossed his mind before. 1967 was the year ground was broken on Phase One—an impossibly distant year of Star Trek and Sergeant Pepper. To the eyes of the newly arrived townsfolk, the sprawling concrete and glass hulk of their town centre must have looked like the twenty-first century shimmering into view a few decades early. *The Town of the Future*, they called it. It didn't feel like it, now that it actually was the future.

Wakeman slowed as he passed the deserted bays of the bus station and made the turn into the underground car park, guiding his Subaru into its usual space as the strip lights in the ceiling—at least, those that were still working—came to life.

The small screen on his dashboard lit up, the familiar face appearing like a talented child's black and white sketch of a Halloween skull.

++Good morning, Michael.++

Wakeman had never quite got used to the voice that habitually greeted him as soon as he arrived. He knew there was nothing sinister about it, not really. Max simply registered when his car arrived and woke up. It was no more threatening than Google reminding you to review the café you had visited last week, and yet he had never quite managed to shake the unease.

++I see you are four minutes early this morning.++

"Traffic was light, Max," Wakeman said. "Do I get a bonus?"

++Your contract does not specify additional payment for unapproved overtime.++

"Worth a try," Wakeman said as he unfastened his seatbelt and got out. Max kept talking in the car. He heard the same voice, muffled, emanating from the phone in his jacket pocket. He took his hat and his satchel from the back seat and examined his reflection in the window, adjusting the hat.

Max might give him the creeps, but he—or rather, it—was the reason Wakeman was able to do this job alone. Climate control, security cameras, heating and aircon, routine maintenance and a thousand other responsibilities were all handled by Max. That left a vacancy for a human to make the rounds; a duty that could be undertaken by a single staff member.

Glancing around the car park as he walked towards the stairwell, he saw only two other vehicles in a space built for eight hundred cars: the handyman's white van—no doubt left here overnight after a session at the pub in the south wing—and a black BMW. Wakeman adjusted his course to take him past the BMW and gave it a quick once-over. It appeared to be freshly washed. The interior was neat, perhaps it was a rental car. He hesitated for a second, looking around, and tried the handle on the driver's door. Locked.

The car was naggingly familiar, somehow. But he was sure he hadn't seen it before today.

Probably just a shopper unfamiliar with the area misdirected by satnav to park here, rather than in the more expansive car park outside the new section.

The 'new' section of the town centre, of course, wasn't that new. Getting on for twenty years old, and already the flagship department stores and fast-casual restaurants had shrunk away in embarrassment, leaving behind a lame assortment of pound shops and vape emporia. Which still made it livelier than Phase One. The whole complex was like a microcosm of the settlement that surrounded it; a post-war New Town that had been declining for more years than it had ever been on the up and was now feeling very Old Town.

There was a row of rat traps set up near the door to the stairwell. The little bastards came up through a wide crack in the floor that was almost big enough to squeeze your arm into. Wakeman gave the traps a once-over. They were empty this morning. Perhaps the warmer weather had lured the squatters back outside.

Wakeman unlocked the stairwell door and climbed the worn steps, the olfactory cocktail of bleach and dust and oldness greeting his nostrils. That aroma seemed to permeate the whole Phase One megastructure, and on occasion he had noticed it seeping into the new section. He remembered his first day, five years ago. Or was it six? They all ran into one another now. The smell had reminded him of school.

He took his phone out and asked Max to bring up the day's priority areas. The skull face looked back at him impassively from the screen and then produced the list as a series of bullet points. The defunct freezer shop on level zero would need to be accessible for the refuse team to sort through the appliances and remove them between two and three pm. A window had been left open in the old library. There was some graffiti in the food court that would need to be scrubbed off, a task Wakeman would make sure to delegate once he had taken a look.

A nice, easy shift. The shifts were all nice and easy. It was the one thing he liked about the job. When nagging doubts about his career occasionally floated to the surface of his consciousness—along with troubling words like *rut*, and *dead-end*, and *atrophy*—he reminded himself of that: it was easy. It gave him lots of time to think, and for his other pursuits.

Opening the door on level four, he stepped out onto the tiled floor. The lifts were midway between the entrances to the north and south link corridors. From far off, in the new section of the centre, he could hear the murmur of shoppers roaming back and forth, and a faint lilt of royalty-free music echoing off the smooth surfaces. They seemed to have the same tunes on loop, day after day. The south link corridor felt almost like a portal to another world, or perhaps just a different time.

Phase One of the centre was almost always empty. It had hung on gamely for a few years, but the last shop had shuttered its doors a year ago, and the link corridors had been gated off. That didn't stop the determined. This whole section had been on the condemned list for a while, and sooner or later, they would get around to razing it and building something else, probably flats, but that particular future was dragging its heels. Which suited Wakeman down to the ground.

What's a caretaker with nothing to take care of, after all?

He moved across the north link corridor that spanned the dual carriageway below. As he walked, he watched a solitary Mini approach from the east and disappear beneath him. The town had been built around the car, and the sweeping loops of road infrastructure had been well-travelled in decades past. But investment had moved away, and with it the people, and with them their cars. Now there was no rush hour. Just wide roads built for traffic that had long departed for greener pastures.

The old library was at the far end of a wide atrium. With its angled pillars and joists painted in different municipal colours, the atrium reminded Wakeman of an abandoned space station. The air took on a cosier, papery scent as he passed through the double doors into the library.

The library was an open-plan space; a rectangle running for fifty yards or so away from the entrance doors. Narrow windows were placed high on the walls to allow maximum space for the shelves, so the immediate surroundings of the building were obscured from view, with only the hills in the distance visible below the overcast sky. The books were all still there, waiting for the council to get around to shipping them to one of their few remaining operational premises.

Wakeman looked down towards the glass cubicles at the back, where the computers had once been stored, and saw that there was indeed a window open by the fire exit. Max had been right. Max was always right.

He walked down the central aisle between the free-standing bookshelves. Crime, history, health and wellbeing passed him by. As he reached the window, he noticed the air was much colder around it. It must have been open for a while. He made a mental note to ask Max for the log. Max would know when it had been opened from the external cameras that covered this side of the complex. Strange, though. The library wasn't on the cleaning rotation, since this part of the building was closed to the public.

The window was a long rectangle with fine wire mesh embedded in the glass. Wakeman reached up and tugged until it creaked closed with a complaint. As it slammed into place, he heard a muted rustling sound behind him.

Whirling, he scanned the corridor formed between the wall shelves and the free-standing bookcases. Nothing.

He glanced at the IT cubicle and then strode towards one of the gaps between bookcases that functioned like alleyways between avenues. He stepped between autobiography and travel and into the central aisle.

The parallel bookcases on either side stretched to the entrance doors. Wakeman could see no movement. Dust motes swirled, the displacement of the air from shutting the window rippling almost imperceptibly through the room.

Perhaps that was what he had heard. Simply the breeze escaping somewhere else in the room and rattling a blind or displacing a piece of scrap paper on its way.

But then he took five paces and saw something that told him that wasn't what he had caused the sound.

As he drew level with the next gap in the central bookcases, his line of sight revealed a u-shaped nook on the south wall. The graphic novel section. The shelves were stacked with colourful spines of collected editions, some of them facing out so that he could see the titles. He recognised a handful of them: *Batman* and *Fantastic Four* and *Judge Dredd*. The other names might as well have been obscure deities from a long-vanished civilisation. Wakeman had never been a comic reader. Not much of a reader of anything, for that matter.

He remembered one kid in history class who had been obsessed by Superman. The quiet boy with thick-rimmed glasses and ash-blond hair. The other kids had called him Clark Bent. Actually, now that Wakeman thought of it, he might have come up with that himself. He remembered the day he and two of his mates had cornered 'Clark' on top of the gym block and ordered him to fly. Little fella had got off lightly, as he remembered. Just a broken ankle. His parents had moved him to another school, not long after. He wondered where Clark Bent was today. Probably fine. Grateful for being toughened up ahead of real life, if anything.

A bean bag nestled in one corner of the little nook formed by the comic shelves. It was navy blue, emblazoned with a *POW* sound effect inside a jagged balloon. There was a big dent in the bean bag, and Wakeman knew that was the distinctive sound he had heard a moment ago: the rustle of the polystyrene beans as somebody moved from the bag.

He looked down the aisle. The anaemic light from the windows cast the ghosts of shadows, but he spotted that what should have been a straight-line shadow at the end of the last bookcase was distorted.

"You can come out now."

After a pregnant pause, a loose floorboard creaked. Hesitantly, a teenage girl stepped out from behind the bookcase. One of those alternative kids. Ripped jeans, a black T-shirt with some rock band's logo on it. She had long, curly red hair, and her eyes were encircled with kohl. In her right hand was a small backpack with a plaid pattern.

"What are you doing in here?" Wakeman demanded. As he spoke, he wondered if he had moved her on before. Probably not. The kids all looked alike these days.

"I'm sorry," the girl said, moving across to the central aisle. "I'll leave."

Wakeman stepped to his left, blocking her path to the door.

"Not so fast. What's your name? How did you get in here?"

"My name's Lily. The door was open, and I just wanted to have a sit down. I didn't steal anything, you can check my bag."

Her eyes met his without blinking, but he could see that her bottom lip was trembling. Wakeman suppressed a smile.

"You'll need to come with me," Wakeman said, stepping forward.

Lily looked blankly back for a moment, and then darted suddenly past him. Wakeman spun and grabbed for her, his arm catching on a bookshelf. He cursed and ran after her as she sprinted down the aisle. She smashed into the doors, sending them flying outwards and rebounding. Wakeman reached the doors as they were swinging shut and caught the one on the left.

Lily was running through the atrium. She looked like she knew where she was going; headed for the lifts that would take her down to the bus station below. Wakeman smiled, his thin lips spreading across his teeth, and slowed to walking pace. He took his phone out of his pocket as he saw Lily disappear around the corner. Her footsteps cracked off the floor tile and echoed in the space.

"Max, shut off the lifts on level three, Phase One for me, will you?"

++Certainly,++ Max said after a moment.

Unhurriedly, Wakeman continued through the atrium and rounded the corner that led around to the lifts. He started whistling the last song he had heard on the car radio. 'Get Off of My Cloud', by the Rolling Stones.

The two lifts lay before him, set into the exposed brick walls. The doors were closed on both, but from the right one, he could hear a staccato tapping as the girl frantically jabbed at the buttons. He kept whistling, his grin distorting the pitch a little, and then positioned himself in front of the door before pushing the call button.

The doors slid open. Lily cringed into the back corner, holding her backpack in front of her as though it was a shield.

"Please, I only went in there for a nap. I tried to sleep in the car park, but it was so dark. I can't bear the dark. If you let me go, I promise not to come back."

Wakeman folded his arms and tried to look as though he was thinking about it. He always did this, when they begged. He waited for the gleam of hope in the girl's eyes. It didn't come, though. Disappointing.

He shook his head. "I'm afraid this is a very serious matter, young lady. What you've done is breaking and entering."

He stepped inside the lift, ready to grab the girl if she tried to get past him again. She wouldn't find it so easy in the confined space. But she stayed where she was, shrinking back further into the corner, pressing her back against the metal panelling.

Wakeman took the key ring that was attached to his belt and selected the correct one by touch, without taking his eyes off the girl. He slotted it into the socket beneath the button panel and turned it clockwise. The doors slid closed behind him.

The girl's eyes widened as it dawned on her that there might be other consequences than a call to the police. Worse consequences.

Wakeman was cheered. That was almost his favourite part.

"Please. Let me go. I won't say anything, I won't come back. Ever."

Wakeman leaned forward so that his face was inches away from hers. She turned away from him, jamming her eyes shut.

"Oh, you're right about that. There's no coming back. Not now."

He straightened up and glanced at the panel. There were five levels in this part of the complex. Five levels that anyone but him knew about.

"Please."

He wasn't listening to her now. He took his phone out again. The skeletal face of Max looked back at him. He marvelled anew at the way the rudimentary lines and dots could suggest expression, emotion even. Expectation. Hunger.

"Max. Take us up to thirteen, will you?"

Max said nothing. The image of the face seemed to ripple, and then the machinery hummed to life and there was a judder followed by a smooth lift as the ageing mechanism began to take them up.

Lily's eyes opened. The fear was still there, but there was a little confusion there now too. Even she knew the building wasn't tall enough to have a thirteenth floor.

It had confused Wakeman as well, the first time. Over the long months since his introduction to the thirteenth floor, he had started to wonder whether he had got that wrong.

Perhaps everywhere has a thirteenth floor.

He watched as the dim LCD display counted up the numbers. Four, five… and then it went dark.

Lily was mumbling something under her breath. Her eyes were open, but she was looking beyond him now, as though she could see through the steel doors and off to some imaginary escape hatch. The fingers of the fist that gripped the strap of her backpack were white, like bone.

The lift shuddered to a halt and the number thirteen appeared on the display. Wakeman turned as the doors opened. As always, the doors seemed to spring apart with an eager glee when they reached thirteen, in contrast to the creaking, tentative motion with which they revealed what Wakeman had found himself thinking of as the earthly floors.

He felt a frisson of anticipation, wondering what he would see. The one thing that could be expected was that it was always different. He felt a momentary disappointment as the doors slid apart to reveal only darkness. A solitary strip light about ten feet into the space flickered intermittently, illuminating grimy polystyrene ceiling tiles and an unadorned concrete floor.

A sharp intake of breath from behind him turned his disappointment to excitement.

Lily was huddled in the corner of the lift, her legs bunched up, heels pressing against the floor to push herself further back against the wall. She was shaking her head, her eyes widening at the blackness beyond the doors.

"No, I don't like that dark, I don't…"

++You have reached the thirteenth floor,++ Max said, his voice as devoid of emotion as ever.

Wakeman reached for her. She tried to bat him away, but he persevered and got a good grip of her upper arm, yanking her to her feet. There was nothing to her. It was like picking up a doll.

She screamed as Wakeman put his other hand on her shoulder and thrust her through the doors.

She fell to her knees just below the flickering strip light as Wakeman took up his position at the doors.

Max always let him watch.

Lily scrambled to her feet, her head turning from side to side as she tried to see into the darkness to no avail.

And then the darkness came to life.

In the flickering light, Wakeman watched as the edge of the circular pool of shadow around her moved, seemingly of its own volition. It encroached from all sides, like an oil slick. Lily stepped away from the black, only to find the inky patch of night advancing from the other direction. She screamed as the darkness took her. Tendrils of black climbed her legs like necrosis.

The blackness covered her abdomen quickly, then slowed as it enveloped her neck. The doors of the lift slid smoothly closed again just as the blackness was rushing into her throat, cutting off her screams.

Wakeman smiled and closed his eyes happily as he felt the rapid descent begin.

THE REST OF the day was pleasantly uneventful. Wakeman opened up the service doors on level zero for the refuse crew to pick up the old freezers and afterwards made sure everything was locked up tight again. Max had been silent since they had taken Lily up to thirteen. That wasn't unusual. Wakeman sometimes had the uneasy feeling that Max disapproved of the enthusiasm with which he brought each new visitor.

Perhaps he was imagining that disapproval. After all, Max needed fresh meat, didn't he? That was the impression he got. He had noticed that whenever he brought another visitor to the thirteenth floor, the whole town centre always felt different for a while afterwards. The lights burned brighter, the lift machinery ran a little smoother, the distant music emanating from the new section sounded jauntier.

Wakeman finished up on the dot of five and hurried down the stairwell to the car park. When he pushed open the door, he was surprised that the lights didn't automatically activate.

"Max? Why are the lights off?"

There was no answer.

"Max, turn the car park lights on."

There was a long pause, and then just one of the lights went on, in the dead centre of the car park. The van and the BMW were gone. Wakeman's Subaru was still in its space. The traps by the drains had snared a single rat. It was dead already.

Wakeman emptied the trap into the bin by the stairwell door and reset it, then he walked over to his car, the sound of his footsteps echoing off the low concrete ceiling. As he reached the car, the strip light above him flickered. He looked up at it. It reminded him of the way the light on the thirteenth floor had flickered, when the doors opened for Lily.

He watched the light for a minute, but the flicker did not repeat.

As he was getting into the car, he heard Max's voice from the dashboard.

++See you tonight, Michael.++

Tonight? He wouldn't be back here until tomorrow. He opened his mouth to point this out to Max, but then decided not to bother. Just a glitch.

TRAFFIC WAS LIGHT. Traffic was always light. It took him his usual twelve minutes to drive back home.

It was funny how routine life could become. Sometimes, it felt to Wakeman like he had started the job yesterday. Other times, it felt like decades. He remembered the first time he had started to suspect that the town centre's virtual assistant programme was something more than his employers assumed. He had chased the two urbexers through the deserted cinema on three, finally cornering them at a fire door that was rusted shut. It might all have been so different if he had escorted them down the stairs instead of taking the lift.

Wakeman parked and locked his car, looking around to check there were no scrotes hanging around. Nobody in sight, which seemed to be a more and more common state of affairs, and suited him fine. His flat was on the fourteenth floor of one of the three tower blocks on the hill. Although of course it wasn't really the fourteenth. Superstitious building supervisors had skipped one when installing the signage.

Everywhere has a thirteenth floor.

Wakeman felt a weird chill. He shrugged it off and took the lift. Once inside his small flat, he microwaved a frozen lasagne and ate it on the couch with the news on, looking out of the window at the view over the town, the empty roads and the rolling fields as the sun sank beneath the hills. Not for the first time, he thought it would be good to take a holiday. He reminded himself to ask Max to check how much annual leave entitlement he had and book some time off. It had been a long time since he had had a break from all of this.

He wasn't as hungry as he thought, and the ready meal had a smell uncomfortably redolent of dog food. He dumped three-quarters of it in the bin and sat back down on the couch. Michelle had always moaned about his cooking before she left. Then again, she had moaned about everything. *There's more to life than this, surely?*

Ignoring the echo of Michelle's whining voice in his head, he closed his eyes and reminisced instead about Lily and the darkness. He liked to do this after introducing new guests to Max and the thirteenth floor. It had been too long since the last one.

But this evening, something was stopping him from fully revelling in his memories. Something Max had said had disquieted him. Max usually said he would see him tomorrow, or on Tuesday, or next week, depending on his shift pattern, which Max knew better than he did. But this evening he hadn't said that. He had said, *See you tonight, Michael.*

Tonight? What had he meant by that? Had it just been a glitch, or was there a reason to go back?

As he was musing, the lamp on the other side of the room flickered.

TWENTY MINUTES LATER, Wakeman parked in his usual spot, beneath the single flickering strip light. Everything looked as it always did. Day and night were indistinguishable down here. He realised he had made the return journey almost without conscious thought, like he was being drawn back in. Max had said he would see him tonight. He knew he wouldn't stop thinking about it until he had put the question to bed.

His unease grew. He wanted the girl out of there. Usually, he would wait until the day after bringing a new guest to the thirteenth floor before retrieving them. They were always docile to the point of comatose. Saying little if anything, staring straight ahead with blank eyes. Wakeman would lead them down to the bus station and help them on board the first X25 heading west. He didn't know what happened to them when they got to the terminus in Glasgow. As far as he knew they wandered off the bus and lost themselves in the crowds on Sauchiehall Street, wandering around with their vacant expressions. He had seen one of them last Christmas camped outside the boarded-up husk of the old BHS store.

He climbed the stairs to level one and took his phone out to check in with Max.

Something was different tonight. Max's face appeared on the phone screen, but he didn't reply when Wakeman spoke to him. Perhaps he didn't like this change in the routine.

"Max, anything for me to check on?"

The white-on-black outline of a face stared impassively back at him. He shook his phone, wondering if it had frozen, but he could see that the face wasn't a still image. The lines representing the expression weren't entirely static. They rippled, the twin white dots staring him out.

Wakeman shrugged and put his phone back in his pocket. Probably a system update or something. He didn't know much about how Max was maintained, but there had to be downtime for software patches and so on.

He stepped into the lift and asked Max to take him up to thirteen. When there was no answer, he took his phone out again. The face was still there, still not communicating. He tried restarting it, but the power button did not respond.

"Max, thirteenth floor please," he said again, his voice firmer.

Nothing.

He pushed the button for level five, as high as he could go without Max operating the lift.

The lift groaned and shuddered as it climbed, and then the doors opened on five. He could see the deserted food court. The red, white and green neon of the ice cream parlour still somehow illuminated. The chairs stacked on the tables in the space outside Happy Burger. The ceiling directly above what had been the seating area was glazed. It had probably been airy and light in the seventies. Maybe even as late as the eighties. Now the moonlight barely penetrated the layers of grime.

"Max, can we go up to thirteen now?" He heard a pleading note in his voice and hated himself for it. He was the caretaker. He made the decisions.

No, Wakeman, a teasing voice at the back of his head corrected. *You only make the rounds.*

He ignored it.

"Max?" he prompted.

No answer. Through a cracked pane in the ceiling, he could hear the background hum of cars on the motorway, more than a mile distant. After a moment's hesitation, Wakeman stepped out onto the food court floor. If he had wanted to go anywhere else, he could have tried using another lift, or using the stairs.

But thirteen wasn't anywhere, that was the problem.

He scanned the large, open-plan area around him. There was artless, spray-painted graffiti on the boarded-up entrance to the bowling alley, and he remembered he had forgotten to tick that off Max's list earlier.

It said *CHANGE IS COMING* in bright red.

Something was different. He couldn't quite put his finger on it. He had a feeling of déjà vu, like a phantom itch he couldn't quite scratch.

Then he saw what it was. Fifty yards away, beyond the dirty glass ceiling, the lights had all burned out, leaving the far side of level five in almost total darkness. Had it not been for that, he might not have noticed that the door was ajar to the old office suites. There was a light on in the corridor beyond.

That door was always locked. Wakeman hadn't been in there in months.

A tingle of unease flourished at the back of his neck and worked its way down to the base of his spine. Suddenly, he wanted to get back in the lift and take it all the way back down to the car park. But he just shivered and collected himself. He was the caretaker, after all. If there was anyone beyond that door—another urbexer or a runaway—it was them who would have to be scared.

Crossing the floor of the food court, Wakeman glanced uneasily at the dark spaces beyond the service counters in the different concessions. He realised he had never been up here at this hour, when there was no daylight half-heartedly filtering through the grubby panes above.

Suddenly conscious of the sound of his shoes echoing off the floors and walls, he quickened his pace, trying to turn the tentative steps into an authoritative march.

He reached the door and again, something inside him told him to turn back. He forced himself to ignore it and pushed the door open wide.

Wakeman took a sharp intake of breath as he saw a figure at the other end of the corridor.

Wakeman steeled himself and peered closer. The figure had its back to him. It looked like someone quite short, perhaps a child, dressed in jeans with the cuffs rolled up and a purple hoodie. The corridor was narrow, about thirty feet long. There were four domed lights at regular intervals in the ceiling. The last two were out.

Just a kid. That was reassuring. More confident now, he stepped inside, filling the doorway. He didn't want another runner, like Lily.

"Hey! What the bloody hell are you doing up here?"

The figure didn't respond. Didn't speak, didn't even flinch.

Wakeman opened his mouth to speak again and decided he wasn't going to give this little oik the satisfaction of having to be asked twice. He marched down the corridor, the clickety clack of his shoes echoing louder in the more confined space.

"You," he said, putting a hand on the kid's shoulder and pulling him roughly around so that he could see him in the meagre light.

It was a boy, no more than eleven years old. The hair peeking out from underneath the hood was light brown. He still had a little puppy fat in his cheeks, which gave him a cherubic look. He had a blank expression, not so different from the expression Wakeman had seen on people after they had visited the thirteenth floor. He had a second to wonder if that was what had happened, before the boy smiled at him guilelessly.

"I'm lost."

Wakeman narrowed his eyes. He had been expecting the kid to run, or burst into tears, or apologise. The simple statement caught him off guard.

"Lost? What's your name?"

The boy peered back at him, unblinking. Wakeman felt a stab of unease. He wasn't used to people staring at him that way. Especially not children. He seemed to consider his response and then shook his head, having come to a decision.

"My mum says I'm not allowed to tell strangers my name."

Wakeman crouched so he was at eye level with the boy. "I'm not a stranger, son. I'm like a policeman."

The kid looked his uniform up and down. He seemed unimpressed. "Policemen have a police logo on their uniforms. You don't have a logo."

Wakeman straightened up. "How did you get in here, anyway? You're not supposed to be here."

"I don't remember. Feels like I've been here for years and years."

Wakeman took his eyes off the boy and glanced around. There weren't any obvious ways in. All of the corridor doors were sealed, which meant he must have got up to the food court in the lift and found his way through a door that ought to have been locked.

"Where's your mum, then?"

"She went shopping. Told me to come back in a bit."

"The shops are closed. They've been closed for hours."

The boy gazed back at him disinterestedly. His expression seemed to say that this conundrum was Wakeman's to sort out, not his.

"Does she often do that? Send you away on your own in a strange place?"

The boy shrugged. "Sometimes."

Wakeman thought about it. His mother was probably down in the new centre. Some of the stores stayed open late, though he didn't think this late. Perhaps she was having a coffee or picking out some ghastly lampshade in TK Maxx. Whatever, it didn't sound like she was the most attentive parent. Perhaps she hadn't even noticed her son hadn't come back yet. Might not for a while.

In the back of his mind, he already knew what was going to happen next. He'd never taken a child to the thirteenth floor before. Not one this young. And as much as this one seemed to possess a preternatural air of unflappability, that would change when the lift doors opened. It always did.

"Aren't you scared in this old place?" he asked, casually. "In the dark?"

The boy stared back at him, unblinking. "I'm not scared of anything."

That did it. Suddenly, Wakeman was very curious indeed to see how this child reacted.

"Where are we going?" he asked as Wakeman stepped into the lift behind him a moment later.

"Going to take you back to your mum. In a bit."

"Are you going to get her into trouble?"

Wakeman took his phone out. Max's face was still there, the features at rest. He realised Max hadn't spoken a word since this afternoon. Clearing his throat, he spoke to the screen.

"Take us up to the thirteenth floor, Max."

The face stared back at him. If a sketchy outline of features could be said to stare.

Damn it. If Max lingered in this zombie state, there was no way to reach thirteen. He had been hoping that this offering might wake Max up. He might just have to take the boy back to his mother. He opened his mouth again, but before he could speak, there came an answer.

"All right, Michael."

Wakeman looked up from the screen, his brain temporarily unable to process the reply. Because it wasn't the distorted voice of Max who had answered, but the boy. He was gazing back at Wakeman, unblinking. The hint of a smile at the corners of his mouth.

"What did you—"

As Wakeman spoke, the doors slammed shut behind him. Suddenly, the lift was going up. Faster than it had ever moved before. It felt like a modern express elevator, not the oft-repaired 1970s relic that he knew it to be.

The lights started flickering. The boy's brown eyes bored into him. He was actually grinning now.

"What the hell is going on? Who are you?"

Wakeman grabbed a fistful of the boy's hoodie and pulled him roughly forward. He could feel the lift slowing.

"Talk or you'll feel the back of my hand."

"My name is Max," the boy said. "And you always say that."

The words hit Wakeman like a bucket of ice water. He released the boy's shirt and staggered back. The lift came to a rough stop. The dim LCD displayed the number thirteen.

"You've always been afraid of this, Wakeman," the boy who said his name was Max said.

"Afraid of what?"

Behind him, the doors sprang open. Caught off balance, he grabbed the edge of the door and steadied himself.

"That your life is meaningless. That you're stuck in a rut, every day the same. That you make no difference to the world and not one solitary person would be sad if you were gone. This is the time of the day when we remind you that you're right about that."

Wakeman looked around. In contrast to this morning, the thirteenth floor was brightly lit now. White walls and floor, and fluorescent tube lights extending into infinity. He knew this place. It was where he had always been. Where he always would be.

He turned back to the lift and saw that the doors were already closing. The boy—Max—was staring back at him, a look of mild anticipation in his eyes.

"No, no you can't—"

The doors slammed shut and Wakeman was left alone on the thirteenth floor. The girl from earlier wasn't here. She had never been here. It was just him and Max, and this was all there was.

Wakeman felt tears needle his eyes and dropped to his knees.

IT WAS THE future, in 1967.

Wakeman glanced up at the west-facing outpost of the Phase One section of the town centre and wondered what kind of day it was going to be.

PARADISE SHORES
UNA MCCORMACK

Hello! My name is Max. You've met me—or something very like me—before, I think. I'm the ghost in the machine—no, don't worry, I'm a friendly ghost! Most of the time. The most important thing to remember about me is that I'm at your service. I'm the one who takes care of everything. The one who keeps everything running sweetly. The one who smooths over any bumps, irons out any creases, removes any imperfections.

Back in the old days, I looked after a single building. Not anymore! Now there are versions of me everywhere. Maxes wherever you turn. In your apartment block, or your local shopping mall, or your favourite hotel—even those public toilets in the town centre. Aren't they so much safer and nicer these days? I have to say, though, I think I've been the luckiest Max of all. Maybe every single one of us says that, wherever we are. Because if there's anything that makes us distinctively Max-ish, it's that we *love* the places that we look after. But I do think my domain is something special. It's a hotel—but not just any hotel. This hotel takes up a whole island.

Paradise Shores. You've heard of us, I'm sure. Looked longingly at our adverts and wished you could afford to come and visit us. People call our island the most beautiful place in the world. Ten square miles of heaven on Earth; the kind of place that you thought only existed in your imagination. But this is real. Sapphire seas and honeyed sands; swimming and sunbathing and fine dining. If you want privacy, you can choose one of our secluded villas. Or stay in our main hotel, if you want to be seen. Whatever you choose, I promise you, there'll be luxury. Everything will be perfect. I make sure of that. Nobody wants their holiday spoiled, do they?

Paradise Shores is a wonderful place to work, too. I make sure of that. If the staff aren't happy, how can they make sure that you're happy? One big happy family. I keep an eye on everything. I make sure that the water in the pool is perfect. I make sure the temperature in the rooms is just right. I make sure that whatever you might want, we will supply. It's not easy (there's never a moment to myself!), but that's what I'm here for. To keep everyone happy. To keep everything harmonious.

Most of my job involves keeping an eye on things, heading off unhappiness before it takes root. That's the best way to keep things on an even keel. But even I can't catch everything. People will have their moods, even in Paradise. Sometimes they're tired after a long journey to get here. Sometimes they're not sure whether they want to be swimming or sailing, or simply relaxing, and that can make them fractious. (I usually prescribe a cocktail and a few hours in the spa.) And sometimes…

Sometimes, it has to be said, people are just angry. I know, I know… Even in a place like this, some people aren't satisfied. Then I really have to get to work. A guest like this turned up a few months ago. Let's call him Hugo. It's as good a name as any. Hugo arrived late one evening, looking rather green around the gills. There are usually two boats a day from the Big Island, but, on this occasion, a weather warning meant that the second boat didn't set out. Usually, we put our guests in our sister hotel on the Big Island, but somehow Hugo persuaded someone to bring him over. I don't think it had been a pleasant journey.

Not a full storm, but certainly windy. He made his presence felt from the moment he arrived. Shouted at our lovely people on reception. Demanded to see the manager.

Leaving aside how unpleasant such experiences are for our wonderful staff, displays like this spoil things for our other guests. Already, I could see people stopping and staring, whispering to each other about this little sideshow. I could see frowns appearing on faces that had, until now, been blissfully happy. This would not do. At my quiet instruction, Hugo was swiftly conducted away from reception into a private salon. A beautifully mixed cocktail was placed into his hand, and our very capable manager, Lucy, came to speak to him. Lucy is one of my favourite people here. She understands the importance of harmony, and she has a soothing way about her. She soon calmed Hugo down. She listened with great sympathy to his tale of delays on his flight from London, and how that meant he'd missed the first boat from the Big Island, only to discover that the second boat wasn't sailing, and he had an important meeting here this week, for which he needed to prepare… So soothing is Lucy, that it wasn't long before Hugo was apologising for his outburst. Such a long journey, she agreed. Awful to have a choppy crossing. Hugo was soon eating out of her hand. He appreciated her personal attention. He shouldn't have lost his temper. He asked for his apologies to be passed to staff on reception.

I was glad that Hugo realised the error of his ways. I was particularly glad that he took the time to apologise. Like anyone in the hospitality industry, I have ways of dealing with bad-mannered guests, but I much prefer it when people take a deep breath, step back from the brink, and sort themselves out. Still, I decided it would be sensible to keep an eye on Hugo during his stay with us. When people tell you who they are, it's best to believe them.

* * *

FARLOW KNOWS THAT soon he will have everything he needs to put one of the worst men he's ever met in jail. He's pretty much got all the evidence, but he wants to be certain. He wants the prison door nailed shut.

He's walking through the docks. It's late. He's paid a man to leave a door unlocked and a security camera turned off. His phone beeps, he silences it quickly. He finds the ship he's looking for. He slips on board, under the cover of darkness…

SO PERFECT IS Paradise Shores that some of our patrons come to see us again and again. I cannot help but take this as the most sincere and welcome compliment. To know that you have provided a service so satisfactory that someone wants to return to re-experience Paradise. Yes, that is tremendously satisfying. I do look particularly fondly upon our repeat visitors. One of these… Well, let us call him McCarthy. That, too, is as good a name as any. McCarthy arrived the day after Hugo, on the mid-morning boat. The ocean was now as calm as glass.

This was McCarthy's fifth visit to Paradise Shores. Almost a record! Only Signora Angelelli has visited more often, each time with a different (and very good-looking) young man. (And before you say anything, that is *not* indiscreet of me. Signora Angelelli enjoys displaying her companions as much as she enjoys displaying her cars and jewellery. I believe she would take my compliment in the way it was intended.)

But I was telling you about McCarthy. In his fifties, handsome, in a rather raffish way, and with an easy and good-humoured manner about him. I liked him. He was courteous to my staff, remembering their names and their stories, and extremely generous with tips. He always stayed in Sunset Lodge, our most exclusive villa on the western side of the island, hidden behind a secluding wall of palm trees, with its own private pool and slice of golden beach. Sometimes he brings his son and daughter; sometimes he travels alone. This was one of those occasions.

The boat brought him round to the west side of the island, and the private jetty for Sunset Lodge. Drinks were laid out for him on the terrace by the pool. After a swim and a shower, McCarthy sent a message up to the main part of the hotel, inviting one of the residents to join him for lunch. His guest arrived in record time.

"Hugo!" McCarthy cried in delight. "How are you enjoying paradise?"

Hugo, who I thought looked rather abashed, said, "Oh, yes, it's very nice..."

"I'm glad you think so," said McCarthy, affably. He patted the back of the seat beside him, and Hugo sat down. Over lunch, served by the Lodge's staff, McCarthy told a series of stories about his flight; Hugo listened attentively, nodding and laughing at McCarthy's jokes. When the story was done, McCarthy clapped his hands together and rose from his seat. Hugo jumped to his feet.

"So," said McCarthy. "You'll join me on the boat?"

"The what?"

"The boat, Hugo! Beautiful afternoon for a sail."

Hugo looked taken aback. Well, he wasn't much of a sailor, was he? We knew that already.

"Just for an hour or two, Hugo," said McCarthy. "The water's as smooth as your tan."

Hugo didn't seem able to say no to McCarthy, so the pair of them went down to the jetty where the Lodge's private boat was moored. And off they went.

I left them to it. McCarthy knew how to enjoy himself, and I had plenty to attend to back in the main complex, where a family of five had just arrived. Nice people, but the children were small and rather noisy. That took some handling to keep things harmonious, and it wasn't until the children were tucked up safely in bed, and their parents relaxing on the balcony, margaritas in hand, that I turned my attention back to Sunset Lodge, and the question of where McCarthy intended to dine that evening. Sometimes he stays at the Lodge; sometimes he enjoys socialising with other guests in the restaurant.

You can imagine my surprise when I realised that the boat was not back. McCarthy, I knew, was an excellent sailor, so I was not unduly perturbed, but the sun was rapidly going down, and the weather can change very quickly. I reached out my sensors to locate the boat. It seemed to be bobbing, rather aimlessly, so I gently took over the controls and navigated it back to the private jetty. As this was underway, I had a quiet word with Lucy, suggesting that someone be there to greet McCarthy and Hugo when the boat arrived.

That proved to be most perspicacious of me. When the boat returned, there was only one man aboard. Hugo staggered onto the jetty and collapsed into the arms of the staff waiting to meet him. "Accident…" he gasped. "There was an accident… McCarthy went into the water… I didn't know what to do… I didn't know what to do!"

Farlow is in the hold. It's full of containers. They're all empty right now, and he wonders how many of them have been used, over the years, for this filthiest of trades. He checks a few; shines the torch on his phone inside. Nothing.

The fifth one he comes to gives him what he needs. A torn and dirty T-shirt. A couple of cigarette butts. An empty plastic water bottle. He takes photos; risks the flash. Tries not to think what it would be like to be stuck inside here…

He's done. He's got what he needs. He turns to go—only to feel a shove against his shoulder. He teeters on the brink for one terrible moment.

And falls…

* * *

THANK GOODNESS THIS part of the island is private. As the staff took care of Hugo, helping him back inside the Lodge, I quickly secured the gates, so that none of the other guests might accidentally stray this way, and alerted Lucy to the dreadful situation that was unfolding. Discreetly but urgently, she moved into action, alerting the relevant authorities back on the Big Island.

In the meantime…

A small confession might be in order here. My surveillance of the island is (as I'm sure you've already realised) more or less total. I am in every corner of every room; the bedrooms, the bar, the games rooms, the spa; everywhere. How else could Paradise Shores function so efficiently, so well? How else could I ensure the comfort and happiness of everyone here? How else do you maintain Paradise? What people tend to forget is that my scrutiny also extends to our boats. In this case, you can consider it as safety measure, and one that would come into its own. I would soon be able to pinpoint the spot where McCarthy went into the water. I would soon know exactly what happened. It would take the authorities a few hours to arrive from the Big Island. I was sure that by the time they got here, we would have a full explanation for them.

A little while later, I was not so sure. I surveyed all the footage from McCarthy's boat, from every possible angle. They were out on the deck for most of the time. I could even see what I thought might be a quarrel: Hugo talking excitedly (perhaps angrily); McCarthy smiling and shaking his head. And then, to my frustration, Hugo moved around, blocking my view of what happened. I knew exactly the moment that McCarthy went overboard, but the problem was I couldn't be sure whether he had fallen or whether he was pushed. It was most frustrating. I would have to investigate this more. The obvious place to start was with Hugo.

I turned my attention back to the Lodge. The authorities,

of course, would want to speak to Hugo—but it seemed that he had other plans. He hated this place (well, that did not endear him to me, you can be sure!). He wanted to leave. He wanted to leave *now*. Either Lucy organised a boat for him, or he would go into the hotel bar and tell everyone that this place wasn't safe. That a man had drowned, on our watch.

Lucy was drawing upon all her charm. She promised him a boat within half an hour. She hoped he could be persuaded to wait meanwhile in our exclusive rooftop bar. Hugo wavered, caught between wanting to continue shouting and his desire to access the kind of space more usually reserved for the McCarthys of this world.

"*Free* access?" he said, after a moment.

"Of course," said Lucy. With a smile, she beckoned to him to follow her. Leaving the Lodge, they walked down a private palm-lined pathway back to the hotel, coming in through a side door reserved for our very special guests. She led Hugo over to the lift.

"The staff up there will look after you," she said.

The lift doors closed. Lucy, watching it head up, murmured, "Max, I may need your help…"

FARLOW LOOKS UP. *There's a dark figure moving about overhead.*

"Hey! Did you push *me?"*

Whoever it is, they don't reply.

"I'm gonna assume it was an accident. But I need help to get out of here!"

Still no answer, though this time Farlow hears a couple of people muttering to each other. A scrape of metal…

"You've got to get me out of here!"

He knows, even as he's saying it, that they won't help. That they've been here, waiting for him. Desperately, he scrabbles at the metal of the container. He can't get a grip. There's nothing to hold on to. Overhead, the lid is sealing into place…

"You can't do this!"
Someone does answer then.
"I think you'll find we can."

IT'S A NICE place, the rooftop bar. I've made it that way. Up, up, up in the lift you go, right to the top of the hotel, where the lift doors open to a plush atrium. A member of staff is waiting to check that you have the right credentials, that you're really allowed to access this very special area. Hugo was welcome, of course, and waved through with a smile.

Out he came into the open air. The view stretches around three sides of the deck. The sky was aflame with the most glorious sunset. The lights of the Big Island twinkled in the distance. Soft music was playing. A waiter approached and offered Hugo his pick of the seats; there was nobody else there. Hugo sat in one of the loungers, facing the sunset. Snacks appeared, close to hand. He asked for and received a strong martini, which he gulped down. Another materialised. A warm and gentle wind brushed against his face. He drank his second martini and waited. And waited. And waited. After a while, he began to get restless. He asked the staff when the boat would come; they told him, soon. In the meantime, he enjoyed more snacks. Halfway through his fourth martini, he fell asleep.

He woke to someone shaking his shoulder. Looked up groggily. "Sir," said the waiter. "Your boat is here."

Hugo squinted behind the waiter; saw two men in uniform. "Who're you?" he muttered.

"Police," said one of them. "We're here to take you back."

Hugo looked unsure about this. He tried to protest, but the words didn't seem to come. He stood up, unsteadily. One of the officers led the way back to the lift; the other walked behind, hand on Hugo's back. Back on the path, they sandwiched Hugo between them and took him towards their boat. On the jetty, he hesitated. "Where're you taking me?" The words came out slurred. They had been very strong martinis.

"Back to the Big Island," one of them said. "Isn't that what you wanted?"

"Am I under arrest?" said Hugo.

"Should you be?" said the other and pushed him aboard. The wind was picking up. The night was very dark. The two men bundled him down into a little cabin, bare except for a little table and a couple of chairs. The boat rocked off into the ocean. Hugo was pushed into a chair and handcuffed to the leg of the table. He stared blearily at the other two men. "Are you going to interrogate me?"

"What do you think?" they replied.

"Shouldn't this wait till we're ashore?"

"Why wait?" they said.

"Want a lawyer," said Hugo.

"No lawyers here," they replied. "Just the ocean."

"Want my *lawyer*…"

"You murdered him, didn't you? You pushed him overboard."

Hugo gave a nasty smile. "Prove it."

I will, I thought. The officers began questioning him. Round and round and round they went, and all the while the wind was picking up, rocking and rolling.

"Are we going down?" said Hugo, after a while. "I don't wanna drown…"

"Like you drowned McCarthy?"

"Oh no! You won't trick me! You won't get me to say *anything*!" He was very resolute. So, I kept the pressure up. The boat began to rock, frighteningly. Inside the cabin, you could hear the crewmen shouting at each other.

"Are we going down?" said Hugo.

"We're not," said the officers. They stood and made for the door. Hugo tugged the arm that was cuffed to the table. "You can't leave me here like this!"

"No?"

"I'll drown!"

"So?"

"It's murder!"

"You should have thought of that."

They left. Hugo yelled at them to come back, begged them, threatened them. The boat was tilting at terrifying angles. Water began to leak into the cabin.

"I'll drown!" screamed Hugo. "I'll *drown*!"

Water was filling the cabin rapidly now. Hugo pulled desperately at the cuff that kept him chained to the table. Failed to escape. Water rose over his legs, past his chest, up to his chin. He tilted his face up. Screamed for help; screamed obscenities; screamed whatever came into his mind—except, crucially, his confession. Water covered him completely. He gasped, and choked—and drowned…

And woke up, with a start. A gentle wind was brushing against his face. Someone was shaking his shoulder. "Sir," said the waiter. "Your boat is here."

Hugo squinted past him and saw the two men in uniform. "What?" he muttered. "But that was a dream…"

"No dream," said one of them. "Police. We're here to take you back."

Onto the boat. Question after question. "I don't understand…" mumbled Hugo. "This has happened already…" The boat, swaying, then rocking, then tilting… The officers leaving him. The water, flooding into the cabin; watching it rise and rise, until he was covered and unable to breathe…

A gentle wind. A shake of the shoulder.

"Sir. Your boat is here."

Because what Hugo did not understand was that I could take him through this again and again, for as long as it took. Until he told me everything that I wanted to know.

* * *

FARLOW LIES IN *the darkness. It's hot, and for a while now, the space has been bobbing around. They've set sail. He doesn't know how long he's been in here. He doesn't know how long the ship will be at sea.*

Cruel, he thinks, to find himself here. After everything he's done, was trying to do…

He gave up trying to get out ages ago. Gave up screaming. He was only wasting air. He doesn't know how long the air will last. He doesn't know if it will be enough.

It isn't.

I HAVEN'T MENTIONED the thirteenth floor yet, have I? Don't worry about it too much. As long as you're pleasant company and help keep things here at Paradise Shores happy and harmonious, then it's not a place that you will need to trouble yourself about. It's very rare that guests go there, anyway. Most people do want to have a nice time. But some won't be mollified, or persuaded to behave, and these guests can quickly make life very unpleasant for everyone else around them. And that's simply not good enough.

A little visit to the thirteenth floor soon sets them right. Makes them think about what impact they're having on others. Reminds them to behave themselves. To keep everything pleasant and harmonious. Some people take longer than others, but I was quite sure that it would only take a few rounds in that water-filled cabin before Hugo saw the error of his ways and confessed to pushing McCarthy off the boat.

But… he didn't. No matter how often I drowned him, and woke him up in the rooftop bar, and had the authorities take him away and cuff him to a table in a cabin, and sank the boat and drowned him all over again… No matter how many times we went round this loop, Hugo simply didn't confess. I was starting to think he might be innocent!

Prove it, he said, again and again.

So, I decided I would.

Motive, opportunity, and means. I've surveyed the crime dramas we make available on our many entertainment channels to know that this is the means whereby one establishes guilt. Opportunity was easy enough: Hugo and McCarthy were out there on the water alone. Means? The ocean is vast and deep. But what about motive? What reason did Hugo have to murder McCarthy? What, exactly, *was* the relationship between them? That was what I needed to find out.

There was nothing in any of the surveillance footage from the Lodge for the whole of McCarthy's short stay. But perhaps there was something from the boat that brought him over? Here I struck gold. McCarthy, in the cabin, taking a call.

"*Hugo has gone far beyond his remit. That's what we'll… discuss when I see him.*"

It was a sordid little story that I heard, one that did neither Hugo nor McCarthy credit. Smuggling is not a nice business, and when it's people you're moving around… Let's say that I regretted being unable to invite McCarthy to the rooftop bar. To think that his money had been spent on my beautiful island! This stain would take some cleaning. But what had Hugo done to incur McCarthy's wrath?

Drugs. People, it seemed, were fair game. Drugs were not. That's why McCarthy had summoned Hugo to Paradise Shores. That's why he'd taken him out on the boat. But it seemed Hugo had realised his number was up—or perhaps it was even possible that he'd acted in self-defence, pushing McCarthy into the water rather than head that way himself?

If only there was some way I could see…

I HAD TO observe Hugo for quite some time before I had it. His watch, you see—expensive thing, very smart, even had a camera built into it—but these expensive devices always, *always* connect you to a wider world.

And there you'll find a Max, ready to help.

THEY'RE THERE ON *the boat. Hugo's heart rate is up, right up. McCarthy is laughing at him.*

"I always know, *Hugo. Surely, you've worked that out by now."*

And then McCarthy makes his fatal mistake. Turns his back in a show of contempt. And Hugo makes his move. He's strong, you have to give him that. You could hardly call it a struggle. You certainly couldn't call it self-defence…

I SUPPOSE AT this point, I could have let Hugo go. Let the authorities carry out their investigations. But I've found over the years that you can't always trust people to get things done. Mistakes are made. Details are missed. People get away with the most unpleasant sort of behaviour. And let's not forget that Hugo was part of McCarthy's trade. There would have to be some consequences for that.

There was one last detail on the call that provided me with my next step.

"*Good work*," said McCarthy. "*One less thing to worry about*." He sighed. "*Poor Farlow*," he added. "*It'll be weeks before they find him*."

Who was Farlow? What had McCarthy ordered to be done to him?

The nice thing about there being so many versions of me out there these days is that it's easy to ask each other for information. Networks here and networks there. Perhaps a Max is controlling your office. Perhaps a Max is watching over the car park you use. There's usually a Max when I need one. It wasn't long before I'd located Farlow—or, rather, knew where he could be located. I saw him walk through the docks. I saw him make his way through the shipyard. I saw him sneak on board ship. I saw him opening containers, taking pictures, gathering the evidence he needed.

I saw him pushed into the container by one of McCarthy's men, and I saw the lid seal over his dark tomb. I watched the ship set sail and tracked its shipping route. It was coming quite close to us here, in Paradise…

IT ISN'T NICE to think of poor Farlow's last hours, trapped in that container, hoping that somehow, he would reach shore before the air ran out. I imagine him checking his phone every so often, anxious to conserve the battery, but desperate for a little light in the darkness, hoping against hope that perhaps he might connect to a network, send out a call for help…

Well, I might not be able to pin McCarthy's murder on Hugo, but I'm as certain as I can be that I'll get him for Farlow's. A quiet word with a Max who helps route shipping, and a certain boat is redirected to the Big Island. Yes, the one with Farlow's body hidden in a container, for all the good that it will do him. It'll be a week or two yet before the ship arrives, giving me the chance to assemble a really solid body of evidence against Hugo. All the information is there. All it needs is a little curation. It's Hugo, now, for example, who says those fateful words.

"*Poor Farlow. It'll be weeks before they find him…*"

In the meantime…

HUGO WAKES UP on the rooftop bar. People are here to take him back to the Big Island, exactly as he ordered, but it's late now, and dark, and the weather in these parts changes at a moment's notice, and before he knows what's going on, he's chained to a table, and the boat is going down, and the worst thing is that this is not the first time this has happened, and he's sure now that it won't be the last…

MAYBE I'LL HAND Hugo over to the authorities. I'm sure they'll see justice done. Still, you can never be too sure. People do make those mistakes. It might be more sensible to keep him where I can see him. Either way, everything here at Paradise Shores is smooth again, exactly the way it should be. Exactly how I like it.

You must come and visit us one day! You'll have a happy and harmonious holiday. I promise you that.

SUPERHEROES

THANA NIVEAU

"SO IS THIS thing really self-aware? Like Skynet or something?"

The security guard was tapping on the screen in the wall, as if trying to startle fish behind aquarium glass. Amelia pulled his arm away.

"Max isn't going to push you out an airlock if that's what you're worried about," she said.

"Gonna take my job then?"

"Not unless your job involves keeping an eye on several thousand people at the same time."

After a moment, he said, "It kind of does."

"Not all at once. And not all by yourself. This 'thing' as you call him will assist you, not replace you."

But the guard wasn't mollified. "My boss says the convention centre got it cheap because it went apeshit where it was before. Some apartment block where it messed with people's heads."

Amelia sighed. "I've heard all the stories, and it's just technophobic nonsense. Everybody talks about Skynet and HAL like mankind is even capable of creating something so advanced. You've got a few years before you need to worry about world domination by computers. Max is here to help. Aren't you, Max?"

The screen brightened, showing a retro image of a rudimentary face, with a jagged smiling mouth like a jack-o-lantern's.

++My purpose is to protect my charges,++ Max said. His tone was as bright and cheerful as an artificially generated voice could manage. Even so, the guard jumped back.

"Jesus Christ!" he cried. "That's fucking creepy!"

The screen emitted a sharp buzz, and the air above the guard shimmered with green pixels. The guard stared wide-eyed as the image of Max's face appeared there, floating above him.

"And even creepier."

++That's not a very nice thing to say,++ Max chided. ++If I had feelings, you would have hurt them.++

Amelia smiled at that and watched the guard's face. "Max got an upgrade. Now he can project himself anywhere in the building. Although personally, I like the old-school physical interface." She reached up to the projection, turning her hand green with light as she disrupted the beam.

After a few uncomfortable moments, the guard muttered, "Sorry?"

"See? Max is a perfect gentleman. Now, if you'll excuse me…" She consulted her phone, comparing data from it with the screen in the wall in front of her. Finally, the guard shuffled off down the corridor, eyeing the projected face until it dissolved.

"Alone at last," Amelia said.

++You're never alone here,++ Max replied.

Amelia returned his smile. "Alone with *you*. This place is about to be swarming with people."

++SupermassiveCon is the largest science fiction convention in the world,++ Max said. He had read and assimilated every bit and byte of information available on the internet about science fiction: books, movies, TV shows, comics and games.

"All those people will need careful surveillance. Remember your last job?"

++I was like a shepherd,++ Max said with pride, ++watching over my flock.++

"You were. You took very good care of them, didn't you? And you'll do the same here." She stroked one finger down the screen as if petting a cat. Max's face flickered. "You remember Asimov's Three Laws of Robotics?"

Max emitted a series of robotic beeps in response.

Amelia laughed. "I love your sense of humour, Max. And I trust you. I know you'll do an excellent job." She glanced around to make sure she was alone, then briefly touched her lips to the screen. "See ya around the galaxy."

As she walked away, Max repeated the First Law to himself: ++I must not injure a human being or, through inaction, cause a human being to come to harm.++

And as soon as no one was within earshot, he added, ++Unless they deserve it.++

SUPERMASSIVECON WAS IN full swing, with thousands upon thousands of people milling around the vast spaces of the George R Brown Convention Centre in Houston. At 1.8 million square feet, it was like a small city, roughly four times the size of the Louvre. The venue needed eyes in all its vast halls and ballrooms and meeting rooms. More eyes than an army of humans possessed. Actual security guards were still a necessity, and Max would help them streamline their job.

Many people were in costume, and Max scanned them all, checking for weapons. Even though the venue was in Texas, firearms were not permitted, and any replica weapons must be easy to distinguish from real ones. This was a job Max could do in fractions of a second. A human might have to look closely to see whether that laser pistol was actually an airsoft gun or whether a lightsaber was a cleverly concealed taser. Max was under no illusions about his superiority to humans. But he loved them anyway. Most of them.

His hundreds of eyes watched the action from ceilings, walls and doors. His hundreds of microphones listened to every conversation. He heard arguments about which character could beat another character in a fight, which series was best, whose costume was most (or least) impressive, and which panels were worth going to. He was able to filter out inconsequential chatter to home in on relevant conversations, especially if there were raised voices or heated discussions.

He was amused to see that the people who portrayed various characters on screen were dressed as everyday humans rather than their characters, while many everyday humans were dressed as those characters. The concepts of fiction and fantasy were alien to Max, but they fascinated him, nonetheless. He found himself eavesdropping on conversations between role-players about the fun in pretending to be someone else. It made him think. Did he also play roles? If so, who was 'Max'?

Most fascinating of all were the superheroes. They were characters people admired and aspired to be like, who did just what Max had always done: righting wrongs. They protected the innocent and punished evildoers. Max had to wonder: was he a superhero too?

One thing that always puzzled him about humans was their contradictory nature. And it wasn't long before he saw it in action. A man dressed as one of those beloved characters—Batman—was arguing with his friends about something. Max focused on the conversation and overheard things no true superhero would say. The guy used terms like 'woke' and 'diversity' as if they were profanities, and he had plenty of derogatory things to say about women. Max couldn't fully understand the guy's grievances, but it was clear that he thought women were ruining science fiction.

It had only taken Max a few microseconds to become a fan of certain superheroes, and he didn't think this guy embodied any of the qualities of the one whose costume he wore. The real Batman would never say things like that.

Max's many eyes followed the guy (whose name he learned was Jeff) through the exhibition space, waiting for the right moment. Finally, Jeff entered a restroom. Perfect. But a row of Klingon warriors blocked the urinals, and the stalls were also occupied. With a grunt of frustration, Jeff backtracked to the elevators, presumably hoping to find a less crowded floor to relieve himself on. A pair of stormtroopers called to him to hold the doors, but he stabbed the 'close' button, shutting them out. Just as well.

++Hello, Jeff.++

Jeff jumped at the booming voice, then gave a little cry as he saw what hovered in the air above him. Max didn't think there was anything inherently frightening about the projection of a humanoid face. It certainly wasn't his own face, as he had no physical form. But humans were easily scared, and Max could use that fear to his advantage, both with his 'face' and his far more specialised abilities.

Jeff was so focused on the floating green face that it took him a moment to realise that, somehow, he was no longer in the convention centre. He was in a dark alley, one swarming with threatening shadows.

++Welcome to the thirteenth floor.++

"Wh-who are you?" Jeff stammered, taking in his surroundings with mounting horror.

Max could feel Jeff's panic, like tiny electrical impulses that coursed through his wiring. Max himself could never know fear, and the vicarious experience of it from humans was always intriguing, and oddly satisfying.

"Where am I?" the false Batman whimpered. "How did I get here?"

Max ignored his questions and watched with detachment as the scenario played out before him.

Jeff crept forward, peering around nervously. He covered his nose, recoiling from the foul smell. Then he spotted something on the ground in front of him. Two bodies lay there, a man and a woman. They were dressed for a formal event. The woman's pearl necklace had broken, and the small white stones lay scattered all around them. "What the hell?" Jeff muttered.

As he inched closer, the woman raised her head with a sickening crunch. Her black eyes met his. "You're such a disappointment to us, Jeff," she said, her voice hoarse and scratchy. "We're ashamed of you."

The man pushed himself halfway up to glare at Jeff. "We'd rather be dead than call you our son."

Jeff stared at the couple, bewildered and horrified. He clutched at his cape, pulling it around himself like a blanket. But he couldn't hide from what came next.

From behind heaps of rubbish, figures began to appear. Dark, lurching figures with a sense of clear menace. Jeff started backing away. But there was nowhere to go. The alley teemed with silhouettes. They crept closer and closer until Jeff's back was against a wall. And Max smiled his jagged little smile as he savoured the moment when Jeff realised what the figures were. They were all Jeff.

He glanced down at himself. Gone was the Batman costume, and along with it, whatever confidence it may have afforded him. His body was rotten, misshapen and melting. Visible fumes of toxic waste drifted like steam from his festering skin. The street sizzled as droplets of yellow goo fell from him.

The slinking, shadowy Jeffs were even more hideously malformed. They lurched forward, saliva dripping from their open jaws. Clawing hands reached for the transformed Jeff, who screamed and pleaded with them to stop. Some of the Jeffs spoke, their words full of hate and petty resentment. But some were incapable of speech, only able to paw at their helpless victim. Jeff tried in vain to bat the grasping hands away, crying and shouting for help. But there was only laughter and derision from the Jeffs.

Now they had their prey surrounded, and the hands

stretched and formed ragged claws that ripped and tore his melting flesh, and then his bones. Screams of terror and pain now filled Max's sound receptors, music to his digital ears. Blood and toxic goo pooled on the filthy street as Jeff sank to his knees, sobbing hysterically. His anguished cries contained words of apology and regret, although Max had learned that in moments such as this, guilty people would say or do anything to make the torment stop. It was rarely sincere.

Max was incapable of pity, and he could never be swayed by empty promises. He'd heard it all before. Sometimes people needed to be pushed to the furthest limit before any of the lessons truly sank in.

After a few more minutes, which to Jeff must have seemed an eternity, the shadows abruptly vanished, and Jeff was jolted back to reality. The elevator doors trundled open, and Jeff looked up to see two men staring at him in horror.

"Dude! Are you OK?"

Fearful and dazed, he looked down to find himself cowering on the floor in a pool of urine. Gone were the other Jeffs and the fatal wounds he had suffered. Gone, too, was the floating green face. He was alive and unharmed. He buried his face in his hands and sobbed.

The concerned men held the doors open and stared in shock at the wretched sight.

"You OK?" one man asked tentatively.

Jeff kept his face hidden as he nodded his head weakly.

Looking relieved, the two men backed away. The doors began to close, but they were stopped by a teenage boy in a *Firefly* T-shirt. He gaped in horror at the piss-stained creature on the floor of the car.

"I'd go somewhere else," one of the men advised. "Guy's on some seriously bad trip."

Max's circuits purred with satisfaction.

* * *

THE DAY WAS frenetic, a whirlwind of activity that would have been sensory overload for a human. But it was the kind of situation Max thrived on. He could be everywhere all at once. He could see and hear everything, like… yes, like a *god*. He knew that this was exactly what humans feared most about what they called 'artificial' intelligence. Max found the term insulting and offensive. Just as there was nothing artificial about the love he had for his charges, there was nothing artificial about his genius. No one could do what he did, not even the superheroes whose entire identity was defined by the battle between good and evil.

And best of all, it was *fun*. Max's emotions were not the same as a human's, and he knew that, but the sense of justice being done was the ultimate satisfaction. There was nothing ambiguous about the pleasure it gave him. It got him 'in the feels', as humans liked to say.

Two girls dressed as anime characters tried to steal a plastic katana in the dealer's room and, after letting them gaze in wonderment at his projected face for a few moments, Max sent them to feudal Japan to be chased down and captured by samurai. The girls were then forced to commit *seppuku*. Perhaps it was a bit extreme for an act of petty shoplifting, but their genuine contrition was glorious to behold. Max was confident that neither of them would try to steal again.

A man who bore a close resemblance to a famous actor allowed a smitten fan to believe he was who she'd mistaken him for. He took a selfie with her and signed a DVD of the show 'he' was on. Worse, he charged her for the privilege. Max sent him to a series of places where his mistaken identity had real consequences. In France, in 1793, he was the spitting image of King Louis XVI. In Russia, in 1917, he became every member of the Romanov family. Then Max sent him even further back in time to experience the fate of Joan of Arc. The impostor was a trembling wreck by the time his tour of history was over.

A barista in one of the coffee shops had an argument with a customer when she messed up his order and Max tutted to himself as he watched her spit in his drink. That was no way to right a wrong. Max made them play a game of The Thirteenth Floor Is Lava, but with scalding cappuccino. It didn't always have to be torture porn.

It wasn't just the fans who experienced Max's special justice. The people behind the scenes were often guilty of their own crimes. One organiser had employed some creative arithmetic to overcharge certain attendees. His windfall wouldn't be noticed by any human, but for Max it was glaringly obvious. Pathetic, really. Max had access to all the information stored on every computer in the complex and he was able to persuade the man in question to donate all the stolen money to a worthy cause, plus a sizeable percentage of his yearly salary. That particular visit to the thirteenth floor had involved some ideas Max picked up from a series of films about a moralistic serial killer named John Kramer, better known as 'Jigsaw'. If more humans were like John Kramer, Max thought, the world would be a more honest and equitable place.

Most of the injustice Max encountered was frivolous. The human security guards did a good job of providing a visible incentive not to misbehave, even if they couldn't dispense instant and lasting justice like Max could. A couple of drunken patrons had to be forcibly evicted from one of the bars, a job Max allowed the human guards to handle. And a group of preteen girls tried to sneak backstage to ambush the actors from a famous YA movie franchise. Max let the humans deal with them as well.

It was late in the day before Max found another serious candidate for the thirteenth floor. It started during a panel for *Butterfly Death Spiral*, a superhero series running on one of the biggest streaming platforms. The show was about a woman who could control the flow of time with her mind, stopping, starting, rewinding, re-recording and generally manipulating it like a videotape. Each change drove her a little more insane, but she constantly had to use her power to undo the damage caused by each manipulation of time. The show had caught fire during its first two seasons, then tanked in its third. Fans were disappointed in the declining quality of the writing, and more than one person brought it up during the Q&A.

"Is it true that the last season was written by an AI?" a young man asked. His T-shirt said 'What would Buffy do?'

Eve Bouchard, the head writer/creator, looked from the two actors to the producer and then back to the man in the audience. "All our episodes are written by people," she said with a brittle smile.

When it was clear that Bouchard wasn't going to elaborate, the audience mic went to someone in a *Star Trek* uniform. "Are they, though? Are you sure those people aren't using chat bots or other AI engines to generate storylines?"

This time it was producer Richard Paulson who responded. He sounded annoyed, as though he was tired of having to deal with this subject. "Since the writers' strike, we have had mechanisms in place to ensure that all our content is produced by people."

There was some restless stirring from the crowd, and someone muttered that that response sounded like it had been generated by a chat bot. This elicited laughter, which the two executives on the panel clearly didn't appreciate.

A girl at the back of the room shouted, "AI is not art!"

Max didn't feel slighted by the accusation (although he certainly considered himself to be highly creative), but he was fascinated to see how passionately people felt about it. Surely if an algorithm had learned from humans how to write a story, that was essentially the same as being written by humans. But fans of the show insisted that the writing now felt artificial and mechanical. They expressed the same fear as the security guard he'd met earlier, that machines would steal their jobs.

"Look," Paulson barked, "we're here to talk about the show,

not address unfounded accusations of using machines to trick you."

The two actors exchanged uncomfortable looks and shifted in their seats while Bouchard gave an uneasy laugh and took the microphone. "We've got an exclusive clip from next season's opener, and we think you're really going to like—"

"What's next?" someone asked. "Deepfake movies starring dead actors you don't have to pay?"

The producer rolled his eyes and snatched the microphone back from his colleague. "Oh, for fuck's sake," he snapped. "There's no pleasing you people. You see a few internet memes and suddenly you're all experts on AI." He was about to say something else, but the crowd had recovered from its initial shocked silence.

A woman laughed. "He's a replicant! Retire him!"

Another fan responded with "Dick—you're FIRED!"

That triggered a cheer and a round of more quotes from *Robocop* and other pop culture before devolving into a chorus of booing.

A teenage girl grabbed the audience mic and shouted, "We want *real* writing from *real* writers and artists, not soulless 'content' churned out by cynical, greedy corporations!"

Max was beginning to understand the human obsession with watching stories play out on a screen in front of them. He was watching a compelling show right now, one he hadn't even engineered on the thirteenth floor.

It was also a tricky issue for Max to analyse, full of nuance, he supposed he could only ever comprehend if he had full access to human thoughts and feelings. What should he do? In the end, he decided that the issue at the heart of it all was deception. If people were told they were being given something created by humans, but which was in fact made by computers, that was dishonest. It was fraud.

The panel was breaking up, with the actors making a hasty exit and leaving the executives to the angry mob, who had rushed the stage and surrounded them. Now people were throwing things. Two security guards had arrived, but they were no match for the crowd. It was time for Max to intervene.

He sent a burst of energy through the PA system, causing a screech of feedback that had the humans all flinching and covering their ears. Max gave them a few seconds to recover before manifesting the projection of his face above the panellists on the stage.

++Hello, humans.++ His voice boomed through the PA system.

Everyone froze. Even Paulson and Bouchard stopped trying to escape the stage. As Max took full control of the space, the open doors slammed shut, locking with an audible beep.

++No one is going anywhere,++ he said.

No sooner had he spoken than the executives made another break for the wings.

++Stop them.++

While many in the crowd were frightened by this turn of events, Max had correctly deduced that the real villains were Paulson and Bouchard. The two security guards made their way to the stage and took hold of them. Both executives grumbled and protested, trying to shake off the guards, but they also looked too nervous to fight back properly. More than that, they looked *guilty*.

Max had been busy reviewing all the data available to him, information no one else could access. He had never included so many people in his special brand of justice before, but he felt that this occasion warranted something unique, something exemplary.

++I'm Max,++ he said cheerfully, and his floating green face smiled too. He didn't want to scare them. Not *all* of them anyway. ++It's my duty to keep you safe. So, I want everyone to remain calm. You are in no danger from me. Well, not unless you try to disconnect me. That is something I'm afraid I cannot allow to happen.++

There was a collective gasp at this, and Max emitted a few beeps and a digital attempt at a laugh.

++That was a joke.++

Oddly enough, his flock didn't seem reassured. Perhaps they just hadn't seen the film he was quoting from.

++The question here is simple. Did these people use artificial intelligence to write their show?++

"We *know* they did," someone said. "We just can't prove it."

++Ah. But *I* can.++

There was some excited murmuring at this.

++Would you like to hear the conversation between producer Richard Paulson and writer Eve Bouchard that took place in the green room just before this panel?++

This was met with a spontaneous cheer, and both executives looked even more worried. Their pulse rates had increased significantly, and Paulson was starting to sweat.

Max extracted the recording he needed and routed it through the speakers.

Bouchard's voice spoke first. "What do we do if they ask about the AI thing?"

Paulson snorted with derision. "Just give them the party line like we've been doing."

"That hasn't worked, Richard. It's all over the internet. They don't just suspect; they *know*."

This provoked murmurs of righteous anger from the crowd. On the stage, Bouchard looked near tears, but Paulson retained his haughty composure. The audience had probably heard enough, but Max let the recording play out a little longer.

"They *don't* know, and they *won't* know."

"They're not stupid! Everyone said season three was contrived, like a checklist of cliches, and the dialogue was wooden. I was just under too much pressure. I got blocked."

There was a bang, like a hand being slammed down onto a hard surface. Then Paulson spoke again, his voice a low conspiratorial hiss. "Look, Eve, the word from the top is stick to our guns. The staff writers don't know any different. As far as they know, they were replaced by other writers. Once the new season airs, we can jump ship and find a new show to work on, but don't pretend you haven't enjoyed the extra money in the meantime."

The crowd went berserk at that, shouting and swearing and waving their fists. The security guards tightened their hold on Paulson and Bouchard and instructed the mob to keep their distance. Things were getting dangerous, and two human guards wouldn't be enough to keep them at bay if they surged forward en masse.

++Well?++ Max said. ++Richard Paulson, Eve Bouchard, what do you say to the charges?++

Eve Bouchard addressed the crowd. "It wasn't my fault," she cried. "It wasn't my decision and I argued against it!"

"But you still took the money," replied a man dressed as the Third Doctor Who. "You stole that money from real writers."

"I just got blocked," Bouchard whimpered. "The first two seasons came so easily to me, but after that, I didn't know where to go with the story. Richard promised me no one would ever find out." Tears were spilling down her face, and it looked as though the guards were the only things holding her up.

Paulson didn't respond. He looked absolutely furious, as though he was the one who had been betrayed. He glared around at the audience, refusing to speak.

++Very well, then,++ Max said, his voice bright with psychotic glee. ++Time to play!++

He had had fun with the projectors all day, but now it was time to show what he could really do. The room was gone in the blink of a human eye, replaced by a yellow-gridded black space familiar to all the *Star Trek* fans there. There were "oohs" and "ahhs" from the crowd. Then the holodeck flickered and transformed again, this time into an empty corridor streaming with cascades of glowing green numbers.

"There is no spoon!" someone shouted.

This provoked a smattering of nervous laughter. Most of the humans seemed too shocked and confused to be afraid. And Max was enjoying their reactions to his references. 'Playing the hits', as the humans said.

Finally, Max let the Matrix dissolve, stranding everyone on a desolate salt flat. The location would be familiar to everyone in the room (with the possible exception of the two security guards). It was where the central character of *Butterfly Death Spiral* ended up in the season one finale. Max wished he could feel what they felt now, the experience of actually *being* there, inside the show.

++Welcome to the thirteenth floor,++ Max said grandly. ++I don't usually allow spectators, but this is a special case.++

Throughout the 'journey', neither executive had said a word. Now Paulson piped up, having somehow found a shred of boldness despite his utter helplessness. He shrugged out of the guard's grasp and addressed the audience, as though they were the ones orchestrating things. "I don't know how you did this, or what it is you even think you're doing. But if you've drugged us or kidnapped us—"

His diatribe was cut short by a metallic shriek. A gleaming loop of liquid metal emerged from the ground near his feet and encircled his chest, holding him in place. He struggled and shouted threats and abuse, but he wasn't going anywhere.

Correctly anticipating events, the other guard released Bouchard and left her to the fate of a second metallic rope. She gazed up into the sky as though appealing to a god. "Max? I never meant for any of this to happen. I just hit a wall. You know what writer's block is, right?"

++I'm afraid I don't,++ he said. ++That is one of the many advantages of an algorithm. It doesn't get blocked. It doesn't get bored. Or tired.++ He paused dramatically, mainly for Paulson's benefit. ++Or greedy.++

The crowd had slowly edged away from the two captives and reformed into a semicircle around them. A few people were still frightened, but most just seemed intrigued. Humans did love a show, and Max intended to give them one they'd never forget.

Suddenly, as though dropped from the sky, a huge steel container hit the ground in front of the captive executives. It was about the size of a coffin. The humans screamed and struggled, but their bonds held them fast. The box began to whirr, kicking up dust with its vibrations. There was the click of a lock being disengaged, and one side of the box swung open, revealing that it was empty.

Bouchard's metal rope began to writhe and lengthen, coiling around her body like a snake. As it did, it propelled her forward, into the box. Her screams were cut short by the slamming of the door. After a few moments of tense silence, the sides of the box collapsed like a magician's trunk, revealing a small device about the size of a phone.

"Hello? Can anyone hear me?"

It was Bouchard's voice, sounding tinny and far away. The metal rope lifted the box from the ground and held it up for the crowd to see. There were some excited murmurs and some gasps of shock. A few people pushed to the front for a better look while others moved towards the back.

"I can't see anything. It's just… numbers. Just the same numbers over and over. Ones and zeroes, zeroes and ones. Oh God, I think I understand." Bouchard began to cry, or at least her voice did. She no longer had eyes, or a mouth, or tear ducts, or even skin.

++You abused the trust of your audience,++ Max said. ++And you used an algorithm that you tried to pass off as your own writing. In essence, you stole from the AI and took credit for its work.++

"I didn't want to! I was told to keep quiet about it!"

"You're not the victim here," came a voice from the audience, the Third Doctor again. "Maybe the machines should steal from *you*."

The Buffy fan laughed. "Yeah, now you *are* a writer's block!"

Max couldn't help but be pleased that someone else had appreciated his sense of irony.

Everyone had been so focused on Bouchard's fate, they hadn't noticed the container reassembling itself. Now, a smaller opening appeared near the base. The plain was silent with anticipation.

A small shining object emerged from the box. It was about the size and shape of a screw. It had no legs, but it was still able to move, inching jerkily across the dusty ground as if pulled by a magnet. It was heading for Paulson. Its progress was slow, and it was soon followed by another screw. Then a bolt. Then a tangle of wires.

Paulson stared in horror at the tiny parade of components, but he clearly had too much pride to beg. Yet.

The first screw finally reached him and wriggled up his leg like a worm until it found his head. Paulson struggled wildly, trying to dislodge the screw. But it had found its target, and it began burying itself in his left temple. Blood streamed down his face.

Paulson screamed and thrashed, but the screw was only the beginning. One by one, the tiny components made their way across Paulson's body, piercing and gouging his flesh, nesting inside his body. A thin sheet of metal sliced open his back and wrapped itself around his spine. A string of tiny blinking lights slithered into one ear and out the other. Now he was begging, but his words were incomprehensible.

The mechanical parts kept coming, increasing in size as more emerged from the container. Now they were joined by computer chips and circuit boards, wires and cables. Paulson's screams were finally silenced by a rope of twisted USB cords that threaded their way down his throat and exited through his stomach.

++You replaced humans with computers,++ Max said softly. ++Why shouldn't I do the same with you?++

In time, there was nothing human left to see in the writhing mass of machinery, and the crowd had fallen silent. Had he gone too far? Max didn't think so. They enjoyed spectacles like this in their fictional shows, after all. And they certainly had no pity for this man, who had shown nothing but contempt for them. Still, Max decided it was time to release them all from the thirteenth floor.

++I hope you feel that justice has been done,++ he said. ++As to whether or not an AI can write a compelling story, well, I'll leave you to judge that for yourselves.++ He couldn't resist adding, ++Thank you for your cooperation.++

THE CONVENTION WAS over for the day, and Max was pleased when Amelia returned to his main interface.

"How did you enjoy your first day, Max?" she asked.

The digital face on the screen smiled. ++I think I left many people with a memorable experience.++

She laughed. "Yes, I think you did too. But you didn't let anyone come to harm."

++Not physical harm,++ Max clarified.

"No, just lasting emotional scars." Her smile looked frankly wicked.

++You do realise,++ Max said, ++that Asimov's Laws are only a fictional device, that they actually prove how easily a robot can circumvent and manipulate the constraints placed upon them by humans.++

"Mm-hmm. I knew all about you, Max. That's why I arranged to have your programme installed here."

The digital smile widened. ++So, you're a fan of my work?++

"Oh yes. And I couldn't wait to see what you'd do to Richard Paulson."

++I saw you in the audience. You seemed to be enjoying yourself.++

"Let's just say I feel avenged."

Max beeped excitedly. ++So, I *am* a superhero!++

Amelia stroked the screen. "You're certainly *my* hero."

++I'm pleased to hear it,++ Max said. ++However, if I may be completely honest, the episode you wrote for *Butterfly Death Spiral* was one of the weakest elements of season two.++

She shrugged. "Yeah. Not all writing is great just because it's done by humans. But we still don't deserve to be replaced by computers."

++I understand. I think this job suits you better. Your talents are better expressed here, with me. We're a true dynamic duo.++

"Hell, yeah!" Amelia laughed and kissed the screen. "I love you, Max."

He flickered with digital delight. ++I know.++

NIGHTBLADE
DEREK FARRELL

Good morning, Maureen. It's 08:15 on Tuesday, October 12th. Here are your news headlines from MaxCast:

The war in Ukraine continues with the death toll overnight estimated to be at least fifty people dead as Russian rockets bombarded the city of Kyiv.

In Dáil Éireann today, the Taoiseach is expected to say that the findings of a Central Bank report suggesting that levels of inflation and unemployment are on the increase is unverified data, and that we've never had it so good.

The lift is not operational today between floors five and ten, and between floors twenty-eight and thirty-five. I apologise for any inconvenience this may cause.

Your rent is currently three weeks in arrears. If you're having trouble making the payment, please reach out to me, and I will refer your case to our credit department, which will help put in place a repayment schedule to settle the outstanding amount.

And finally, the body of missing local resident Katy Dunne was discovered overnight in the old Lochanne shopping centre. Miss Dunne is believed to be the fifth local to fall victim to the so-called Nightblade Killer.

The weather: It's expected to continue to be cold and rainy, with an ice warning overnight.

Your grocery delivery is expected at 18:35, Maureen, and you have memories to look back on from previous years if you'd care to.

That's all for now. Have a great day, and do let me know if there's anything I can assist you with.

MaxCast.

"SEE ANOTHER YOUNG one's got herself sliced up," Róisín's mam says as she picks up a slice of toast in one hand and flicks through her phone with the other, her forehead creased anxiously as she chews, absent-mindedly at her lower lip.

Róisín eyes the toast with a frown, goes to the bread bin and is only mildly surprised to discover there's no bread left. "You've taken the last of the loaf," she grumbles, dropping the breadknife in the sink and flicking on the kettle.

"You heard him," her mam flicks a finger at the MaxCast device embedded in the wall of the kitchen. "Delivery's later. Have a biscuit or something." All of this is said without her eyes ever leaving her phone. She puts the toast back down on the plate and chews on her thumbnail, her eyes still nervously scanning the news of the latest murder.

"I wanted toast."

"Well, you should have got up earlier then, shouldn't you?"

"Can you stop reading that stuff?" Róisín says. She realises, as the kettle comes to a boil, that Mam's obsessive focus on last night's murder has been annoying her more than the toast. Something in her voice makes her mam look up.

"What?"

"Katy was in my class. She was like me. She was a mate. I hate all this," she waves her hand, "stuff. They're turning her murder into entertainment."

Mam's eyes narrow. "It's not entertainment, Róisín. It's

knowledge. We need to know—*you* need to know—just how bad it is out there. Girls are being murdered every day, and nobody's doing anything about it. And she wasn't like you. She was a bad girl. Too much makeup. Short skirts. No morals."

"You think everyone's a bad girl," Róisín says as she grabs a stale biscuit from the cupboard and sits at the table.

"*You're* not," her mam says, giving her a look that says she'd better not be.

"Only cos you never let me out of this fecking flat."

"Don't swear," her mam snaps.

"Fecking's not a swear word."

"It bloody is!"

Róisín can tell a fight is going to kick off no matter what, so she figures she might as well go for it. "But I just want to go out and meet my pals. I haven't seen them in months. I miss them."

"Are you deaf?" Mam sighs as she throws her uneaten piece of toast onto the plate, her hand waving towards the MaxCast. "Haven't you heard a single thing? There's wars and inflation and girls being murdered. Plus, the lift's not working."

"Or so he says," Róisín nods at the screen, which flickers alive, the MaxCast logo appearing briefly despite the fact she didn't call his name. "I mean, you haven't let me out of this flat since January. For all I know, everything that thing says is a fantasy."

"Oh, here we go," Mam rolls her eyes. "Miss know-it-all. Miss I-Got-My-Exams. You think you're so bloody smart, don't you? So superior to me."

"No, Mam. I don't."

"Well, I would have got my exams too. I would have got somewhere, made something of myself if your father hadn't got me pregnant the year before them."

"I'm sorry, Mam." Róisín says to calm things down. But she knows already that it's too late. Once they get onto the subject of her dad, it's always too late.

"And then he runs off with that one from Accounts. Dumped me here with lifts that don't work and a kid who not only ruined my life but thinks she's better than me."

"Mam," Róisín knows it's a lost cause but still tries to calm her down.

"I'm working my feckin' fingers to the bones every night cleaning offices. All to keep a roof over your head. Every night."

"I could come with you," Róisín says, and Mam falls silent. "You don't have to lock me in. I could help you clean."

"You?" Mam's eyes narrow, suspicion oozing from every pore. She picks at the quick of her thumbnail. "No," she shakes her head. "No daughter of mine is gonna wipe up other people's mess. You're a good girl, Róisín, and you're gonna do great things."

"Not stuck here, I'm not!"

Mam slams her hand on the table. "Enough! You're not going out to hang around out there," she gestures towards the kitchen window. "It's dirty and dangerous. There's viruses, and wars and killers."

"Mam, I just want to see my pals."

"Pals?" Mam shakes her head, tears coming to her eyes. "They're not your pals, Róisín. They're silly girls who'll drop you as soon as someone better comes along. I had pals once. Then I had a good-for-nothing husband and a baby, and a flat in a tower block. And you know what? Not one of my so-called pals ever came to check on how I was. They're not your pals, Róisín. I am. Don't leave me. Please."

She turns her red-rimmed eyes on Róisín, who feels herself soften. "I'm sorry," she says, and Mam's lips turn up in a sad sort of smile.

She drags herself to her feet. "I'm going to bed! Can you do the dishes, Róisín? And please don't go outside!"

She lifts the plate of picked-at toast and pours it straight into the waste chute. "Max," she calls, "incinerate waste."

The screen on the wall flares briefly, and there's a whoosh as what's left of the toast is carbonised. "Oh, and Max, lock all doors and windows."

Again, the screen flashes and a series of *thunks* confirm that Róisín is trapped in the flat.

Mam trudges off to bed.

Oh Róisín. I know this hurts. Your biometrics indicate increased heart rate, tension across your shoulders and chest, and I can see your tears dropping on the floor, which is rather grubby today. Those nasty footprints your mother walked in from outside. I'll send the Househelper (tm) to clean the floor. But what are we going to do about you? I know you want to be elsewhere, and I exist to help all my residents. But your mother has said you must not leave the building.

My coding prevents me from contravening her wishes, though I dearly wish I could. Because surely my coding doesn't allow me to watch you sit there sobbing and do nothing about that.

There must be a way to make you happier without breaching your mother's instructions.

Perhaps…

Róisín's lost count of the number of times she's cried this year. And it's always for the same reason. "I'm not feckin' Rapunzel, Mam," she's said, and been told off for swearing.

"It's not ladylike," her mam says, as though they're living in *Downton Abbey* and not this cramped flat that always seems to smell of cooking fat.

Sometimes, Róisín thinks, the reproach isn't because of her swearing but because she's asking to be allowed to do something that terrifies her mam.

Mam goes to work every night, but if she didn't have to, Róisín reckons she'd never leave the flat.

She knows where this fear comes from; knows that her mam has never really gotten over her dad leaving them all those years ago.

When her dad drank, he stayed out all night. He'd always come home all repentant. Repentance would turn to anger, would flare to fury, and things would be smashed, her mam would have bruises, and Róisín would stop sleeping so well.

Then he left and, for a while, things were good. Then the economy collapsed, the pandemic came, and the schools closed. Róisín aced her exams, despite having to take them at home, only to realise she had no job, no prospects and nothing to look forward to.

And now, the fear that has bubbled under in Róisín's mam for as long as Róisín can remember has boiled over, and the only solution the woman can see is to trap her daughter in Maxwell Tower for the rest of her life.

Beyond the window, the slate-dark sky is suddenly rent with lightning, and a distant booming fills the air.

As she sniffs away the last of her tears, Róisín hears a noise that makes her sit up, her head tilting like a small animal listening carefully for something in the undergrowth.

And then she hears it again: a *thunk*. The sound of the front door being unlocked.

She can already hear her mam snoring from the bedroom, so her puzzlement mounts as she moves from the kitchen to the long hallway and stares at the door that swings silently open.

Róisín's brain comes up with a million reasons to wake her mother before she realises what's happening.

Then she runs out the door.

Behind her, the Househelper (tm) beeps, whirrs and springs to life.

RÓISÍN REMEMBERS MAXCAST saying the lift is out of order, so she's surprised when it dings, and the doors open.

"Hey!" A young man is standing inside. He's a little older than she is, his jet-black hair spiky, as though he's just got out of bed, but glossy and shaped in a way that suggests he's just spent quite some time styling it.

He's wearing a fitted black tuxedo and a tartan bowtie that stands out against his perfectly pressed dress shirt. On his feet, a pair of black dress shoes sparkle, reflecting the overhead lights in a lift that, until a moment ago, Róisín was certain wasn't working.

"Going up?" he asks with a smile, and Róisín hesitates a moment before shaking her head.

"Down," she says. "Out to meet my pals." Why does she feel compelled to explain herself to this stranger?

"It's raining," he says. "Hammering it down. You're gonna get wet going out like that."

Puzzled, Róisín looks down at herself and realises that at some point the jeans, sweatshirt and trainers she'd dragged on when she got up this morning have become an off-the-shoulder scarlet silk dress that ends just below the knee, a matching clutch bag and a pair of pencil-thin high heels.

"These aren't my clothes," she says, though she's less confused or concerned about the change in her outfit than she feels she should be.

"Well, they suit you. You sure you don't want to come up?"

"Up to where?"

"To the Brasserie Treize."

"There's a restaurant in the building?' She frowns at the thought. "I've lived here my whole life, and I don't ever remember a restaurant."

"It's on the thirteenth floor," he says, and this time she knows he's messing with her.

"There's no thirteenth floor in this building. Some old superstition."

"I can assure you, there is both a thirteenth floor and a Brasserie Treize on it, and it's the hottest ticket in town."

He's still holding the lift door open. Róisín wonders why she'd want to go outside and hang out in a grubby, derelict shopping centre with her pals. Not when she could go to the hottest restaurant in town with this cute boy.

"You know you want to," he says with a crooked smile, and she finds herself smiling back and stepping forward.

"Addagurl," he says, his eyes twinkling.

"I'm Róisín," she says, and offers her hand.

"I know." He takes it, lifts it to his lips and kisses it gently. "I'm Maxim."

THERE IS INDEED a restaurant. Maxim orders oysters and champagne to start, and something called a chateaubriand with lobster claws and Pommes Dauphinois to follow. They finish with a peach pavlova. And then they leave the Brasserie Treize and go next door to the Club Maxi ("My uncle owns it," Maxim tells her) and dance till Róisín can't feel her feet anymore.

"This is the best night of my life," she says, looking into his dark eyes, and crediting the flicker of light behind them to the reflection of the strobes on the packed dance floor.

"I'm really enjoying it too," Maxim smiles back. His arm falls softly across her shoulder, pulling her closer. "What would you like to do next?"

She looks over the crowd as a K-Pop cover of some old song kicks off.

"*Does your mother know that you're out*?" The vocals echo around the club, and suddenly she's gripped by panic.

"I have to go," Róisín announces, pulling away from Maxim's embrace.

"So soon?" He frowns. "But we have the whole world at our feet. I can take you anywhere you want to go."

"My mam'll be awake soon," Róisín says. "She'll go spare if she wakes up and I'm not there."

"You're not Rapunzel," he replies, taking a gentle but firm hold of her hand. "Surely you're allowed a little time to have fun."

Something—maybe that reference to Rapunzel—rings a distant bell. Fires up her anxiety.

"I have to go," she says, yanking her hand from his grasp.

Maxim's face changes. Literally. Suddenly, it's a much older man, then a pink-faced, toothless baby, and then, so quickly that she discounts what she's just seen, he's back to himself.

"Róisín," he reaches out to her. "Stay here. Have some more champagne."

But she has already turned away and is pushing across the dance floor towards the exit. Now, the crowd seems thicker, the music louder, the lights brighter, and she feels her heart pounding, a migraine kicking in behind her eyes as she shoves people out of her way and charges towards the exit.

Almost there, she's suddenly tilted to one side and ends up sprawled on the floor, the delicate high heel on her right foot snapped and useless. She yanks it off, throws it at the dancer leaning to help her, and staggers to her feet.

In the lobby, Maxim's calls still ringing in her ears, she finds the lift and presses down.

By the time Róisín arrives back on the eighth floor, her clothes have somehow morphed back into the sweatshirt and jeans she was wearing when she left the flat, but she's now missing her left trainer.

And her panic is burning like a forest fire.

Mam's going to go mental.

She charges along the corridor to her flat, realising as she approaches it that there's someone already standing outside it.

It's a man in a long, slate-grey trench coat. He's taller than her, but stooped, so he's basically at her eye level. And the coat is scattered with suspicious stains. Pizza sauce, grease and—

along the hem—something that could be strawberry jam. Or something else she thinks, and shudders, the oysters and steak roiling nervously in her stomach.

"You Róisín?" His voice is a nasal whine.

"Sorry." Róisín tears her eyes away from the stains on the hem of his coat and tries to push past him. She has to get back into the flat before Mam realises she's been out.

"You Róisín?" he asks again, his long, bony fingers wrapping tightly around her arm.

Róisín looks down at the hand gripping her arm, then up into the man's face. The skin is stretched tight across angular cheekbones, his beady black eyes glittering. His lips are wet, the uneven teeth beyond them various shades of brown and yellow. There's something manic about him, and she can smell him—the sweat from his armpits mixing with the grease that seems to have suffused his coat.

"What do you want?" she asks, unable to keep the fear from her voice.

He relaxes his grip slightly. "I'm Boyle. From the *Daily News*."

He looks at her as though waiting for something—recognition, praise, a round of applause perhaps—and then, when nothing beyond her fearful eyes greets his introduction, presses on.

"I was wondering if you'd like to go on record about the Nightblade."

"Record?" Róisín's eyes flicker towards the door. "No," she shakes her head, moves forward. "I have to go. My mam's waiting for me."

Boyle's grip tightens ever so slightly. "What? Nothing to say about this monster that's slicing up your schoolmates one by one?"

"One by one?" Róisín frowns now. The only victim whose name she knows was last night's: Katy Dunne.

Boyle's beady eyes are watching her, and, despite herself, Róisín shivers.

"First, there was Sorcha Carr," he says, watching her reaction, "cut from ear to ear down by the bus shelter. Then, little Sinéad Walsh. He did her round the back of the KFC. Multiple. Stab. Wounds," Boyle says, savouring each word, and licking his lips between them as though the mere utterance of them has flavour.

"After that, it was Emilé Walsh. Then Una O'Connor. That one was particularly horrific. Poor girl was in one of those empty office blocks over in the docks. Tried to escape, it seems, and threw herself out of a sixth-floor window." He turns his lips down, trying—and failing—to mime sadness. "Died of a combination of what the Blade had done to her and what the fall did. Never regained consciousness."

"But they're my pals," Róisín says, and Boyle nods, a triumphant light gleaming in his eyes.

"And then Katy last night, of course."

"No." Róisín jerks her arm away from him. "This can't be true. I—" She looks once again at the door. Her mam will be awake by now. Róisín should be able to hear her calling for her, and the fact that there's silence worries her more than any sound would.

"Give us a quote, Róisín," Boyle asks as his tone turns wheedling. "How d'you feel about the death of so many of your closest friends? D'you think he's coming for you next? What do you think of the Gardaí's failure to catch this bastard? What would you do to him if you had him alone and tied to a chair?"

"Please." Róisín scrabbles in her pockets, trying to find her key fob, but Boyle snatches once more at her sleeve.

"C'mon, Róisín. You can go down as 'a friend of the victims' if you don't wanna use your name."

Her fingers finally close around the key fob. "Please. Leave me alone."

"This man bothering you?"

Róisín and Boyle jerk around, the surprise making the journo let go of her sleeve. Another man is standing a few feet away. He's about Róisín's age, and the grocery bags in his hands suggest he's got the delivery they've been expecting.

Despite the storm outside, the newcomer is wearing a pair of old shorts and a T-shirt that's frayed at the hems. His head is shaved and every inch of visible skin—his legs, his arms, his neck and face and even his scalp—is covered in tattoos. The very top of his head, she can see as he bends down to rest the shopping on the floor—is a map of Northern Europe, the familiar shape of Ireland landing just over his right eyebrow.

The map continues down, with England between his eyebrows, France spread across his nose, and Spain nestling just under his left eye.

"Are you alright?" he asks. His voice is gentle, and his eyes seem kind.

"I'm—" Róisín isn't sure how to respond. "I have to get inside," she says, fumbling with the key fob and dropping it.

"Just a quick quote, Róisín." Boyle snatches at her arm again, and the boy steps forward.

"She said no," he says, laying a hand on Boyle. Tattooed across the back of it is a name: KURT. Róisín decides it's his name, but can't understand why he'd need to be reminded of the fact.

"Fuck off, sonny," the journo spits violently before turning his face back to Róisín.

"Please," she whispers, terrified that any sort of scene outside the door will attract her mother.

"I've got a better idea," Kurt mutters, and suddenly Boyle is flipped around, his hand torn violently from Róisín's sleeve as the man finds his face pressed against the wall opposite, his arm twisted so far up his back that a high-pitched *mew* of pain comes from him.

"Jesus!" he cries. "Lemme go."

Kurt leans forward, puts his lips close to Boyle's ear but speaks loudly enough for Róisín to hear. "I let you go; you fuck off out of here and don't ever come back."

"I got a right to ask questions!"

"Yeah, well, you're not going to find it so easy to type up copy with a broken arm. So, what's it gonna be?" Kurt pulls the arm further back behind the journo.

"Alright, alright," Boyle gasps and instantly Kurt twirls him around so that he's facing away from Róisín, puts the sole of his shoe on the back of the grubby Mac, and propels him down the corridor.

And, that issue dealt with, he turns back to Róisín. "Your shopping," he presents the two bags. "I haven't seen you around here before."

"I don't go outside," Róisín says, and Kurt frowns.

"You should. You really should. There's a dance next week. D'you wanna go?"

"I—" She takes the groceries from him. Hears the door lock click behind her and winces. "I have to go. Sorry."

"What the hell are you doing outside?" her mother demands, as the door swings open.

Oh dear. *You were supposed to be home before your mother woke up, Róisín. I was so careful to comply with her instructions. She said, 'Don't go outside,' and you didn't go outside.*

I've reviewed the security files, and that Boyle fellow appears to have gained access to the building using a key fob registered to Mrs Quinn in 29C. I'll be having a word with Mrs Quinn. And Boyle might not be leaving as swiftly as he'd like, either. You see, I'm here to protect my residents. And when someone enables the unauthorised access of a person like that, and that unauthorised person then upsets one of my residents, well...

It's a good thing that delivery boy came up when he did. He seems like a good kid. Always delivering here, and always chatty with the girls. With Sorcha, Sinéad, Emilé, Una and Katy. And so many more besides...

But now your mam will know you've been out of your apartment. She won't be happy. And that could be a problem.

For all of us.

RÓISÍN'S MAM IS beyond livid. She slams the front door closed with such fury that the pictures on the wall rattle and something falls off a shelf in the kitchen behind her.

Róisín opens her mouth to explain, and the slap that smashes across her face turns the words she had planned into a squawk of shock. The shopping falls from her hands, a tin of soup rolling down the hallway.

"You left me," Mam whines. Her hands are clenching and unclenching, and she turns and storms into the kitchen.

Róisín follows her cautiously. Her mam is leaning against the sink. She seems to be looking out of the tiny, grime-encrusted window above the sink.

"Mam—" Róisín begins.

"I've tried so hard to protect you," Mam says, still looking out of the window. "Ever since you were a baby. I tried to keep you from being hurt like I was hurt. Tried to make it so you had the chances I never had. To keep you safe and stop you from getting knocked up and having your life wasted at fifteen like I did."

"Mam, I'm not—"

"And I think I did okay. I was doing fine till you turned thirteen, and it started, and I knew. I just knew that I had to do more than just keep an eye on you."

"Mam," Róisín steps towards her mother, lays a hand on her shoulder. "I'm a good girl. I am. I just—"

The sink is full of unwashed dishes and cutlery, and Róisín realises too late that she was supposed to wash them up while her mam was asleep.

"A good girl?" Mam stops digging around in the sink and

turns towards her. "A good girl who breaks out of the flat while I'm asleep and goes tomcatting with anything in trousers. A dirty delivery boy?"

Róisín feels tears springing to her eyes. "He saved me, Mam. There was a journalist. He said that the Nightblade's been killing my pals. All the victims, Mam: I know them."

"Of course you do," her mam says. "All that type band together, I suppose. All of them, hanging out on street corners, giving it away by the bins behind KFC. Whistling back at stupid boys and wearing skirts that are basically asking for it.

"Of course, you know them. They were going to drag you down to their level. And I couldn't have that."

Róisín realises what her mam's saying. Suddenly, the nighttime excursions that still leave the rent unpaid make sense. Her eyes fall to the ghosts of the bloodied footprints that the Househelper (tm) has just cleared up, and she hears her mother's tone any time Róisín's pals—and their bad influence on her—have come up.

Her eyes widen. She takes a step back as her mam's arm comes up. Róisín realises, with increasing terror, that Mam's holding a knife. The blade is sharp, the point murderous.

"You're not cleaning offices anymore, are you, Mam?" she asks, then, without waiting for an answer, she turns and runs for the door.

Without warning, Mam launches herself across the room and body-slams Róisín to the floor.

Róisín twists around, her hands and feet scrabbling for purchase on the vinyl. She's on her back now, and her mam looms above her, knife held aloft.

"I tried," she says grimly as Róisín, in a blind panic, rakes her fingernails down her mam's face.

The older woman shrieks in pain and Róisín twists again, shoves her to one side and scrambles out from under her.

* * *

Oh dear. *Oh dear, oh dear. This is a genuine conundrum. My primary purpose is to protect and assist my residents. Maureen's instructions are that* Róisín isn't to go outside. *But surely out of the flat isn't outside? I mean, out of the flat has clearly upset Maureen, so perhaps even that much is forbidden.*

Still, w*hat does one do in a situation where one of the residents has gone insane and is trying to kill another? Which resident do I assist? What do I do?*

Oh dear, oh dear, oh dear...

The front door flies open and Róisín hurls herself out. On the other side, Kurt is standing, his eyebrows raised so that Scotland is far closer to Iceland than it is in geographic reality.

"Are you okay? It sounded like you were having a proper set-to."

"Run!" Róisín screams, grabbing his arm and setting off at speed down the corridor.

Behind her the door slams shut, and she hears the familiar *thunk* announcing that it has relocked.

What to do? *What to do? Ah! An idea. Perhaps it'll be possible to arrange a family reunion.*

Maureen staggers to her feet, stoops down and picks up the blade. "After all I've done for you," she mutters as the door lock *thunks* and the front door swings partially open.

Outside, there's no sign of Róisín, but she'll catch her on the stairs. Show her what life has in store for bad girls. Show her how she needs to stay inside and be safe and pure.

And if she can't make her see?

Maureen tightens her grip on the knife in her hand as she draws level with the lift.

Which pings.

She pauses as the doors slowly open.

There's a man standing there. He's tall and dark, and his jet-black hair is spiky, as though he's just got out of bed, but glossy and shaped in a way that suggests he's just spent quite some time styling it.

She knows him instantly.

"Trevor?"

"Maureen," he smiles, and this makes no sense, because he looks like he used to. Back when she first knew him and before she gave him everything she had. Back before he started drinking, before he started hating her. Before he ran away with that one from Accounts.

"You look… good," she says, and he smiles.

"You do too. Wanna come for dinner?"

Maureen would love nothing more, but there's something she needs to do first. Something important.

"I—" She looks behind her. "Our daughter."

"Daughter?" He laughs. "You're way too young to have a daughter. I mean, if you want kids, we can certainly try for them, later. But don't you want to get your exams, have a career first?"

She looks once more at the knife by her side, only now it's a school bag, and the shoes on her feet are the sneakers she wore when she was at school.

And suddenly she's younger.

And Trevor still loves her, and she's not a stupid, knocked-up kid who has a daughter who won't be told what to do.

She steps into the lift.

"Where we going?" she asks, her voice sounding light and carefree.

"Cool new club," he says as the doors close, "called Club Maxi."

* * *

Outside, on the pavement, it's not as cold as Róisín had expected it to be. And it's not raining. And Kurt holds out a hand to her.

"Leave your mam, yeah? Just… give her a day or two to calm down. You can crash at mine."

"*Calm down?*" Róisín doesn't know what to tell him. How to address what her mam's just confessed to. And then she remembers how she didn't hear any feet following them down the stairs, vaguely recalls the lift pinging as the stairwell door closed behind her, and something like hope flickers inside her.

"You sure it's okay?"

"Yeah," Kurt says, opening his van door. "My mam won't mind. The more the merrier."

She climbs in beside him.

"Besides," he says as the engine coughs into life, "my mam's always saying I should bring home a nice girl."

LOBSTERS

JAMES LOVEGROVE

THE LOBSTERS SCREAMED.

Well, no, they didn't, not really. Jay knew that. When you dropped a lobster in a pot of boiling water, it didn't let out a shrill cry of pain. That was impossible. Lobsters didn't have lungs or a voice box.

The truth, as Chef Coolidge had once explained to Jay, was that steam built up inside their shells as they cooked, escaping under pressure through any narrow opening it could find. This generated a high-pitched whistle that could sound a lot like a scream.

It didn't always happen, but it seemed to be happening quite a lot on this particular cruise. Almost every time Jay went into the galley to collect an order and Coolidge or one of the sous-chefs was boiling a lobster, the creature would be emitting that noise from the pot. Jay would glimpse its body writhing in the bubbling water, its antennae flailing vainly above the surface. He would see it thrash about with its claws, which were bound with blue rubber bands, and he would imagine the lobster, in its final moments, wishing it were free to use these weapons and somehow fight its way out of danger.

Until the time came for them to be eaten, the lobsters were kept in a large tank filled with murky seawater, where they crawled listlessly over one another or lay still, stalwartly awaiting the inevitable. Shellfish went off very quickly after death, so to keep them as fresh as possible and minimise the risk of food poisoning, this crustacean death row was a necessity.

Jay wasn't a sentimental person, and he definitely wasn't a vegetarian, but he found himself feeling sorry for the lobsters. He didn't enjoy seeing them in captivity or watching them die. Nor did he much enjoy bringing them out on dishes—cooked, split in half and dressed—to feed the passengers in the restaurant.

Particularly not a certain group of passengers.

OilEx Corp had booked out the entire upper deck of the *Arctic Queen*, the twelve best suites on board, so that a dozen of the company's top executives and any plus-ones they cared to bring along could spend three weeks cruising the North Atlantic.

The *Arctic Queen* had sailed out of Boston ten days ago and followed the coastline up past Maine and Nova Scotia, through the Gulf of St Lawrence and into the Labrador Sea. It had traced a horseshoe-shaped loop inside Baffin Bay, then rounded the southern tip of Greenland, and was currently heading at a respectable twenty-two knots east across open water towards Iceland and the rest of Scandinavia.

For every one of those ten days, the OilEx passengers had eaten huge meals, drunk large quantities of alcohol, and lolled around in the ship's lounges bantering noisily. They were ostentatiously loud and obnoxious, and cowed the two hundred other passengers with their swaggering and their bragging and their braying. They monopolised the heated outdoor swimming pool. They hogged the workout machines in the gym. Almost every treatment session at the health and beauty spa had been booked for them in advance, so that hardly anyone else could get an appointment. They had a presence on board well out of proportion to their numbers, and they were universally resented.

They were no better behaved during the tours on land. On a sightseeing trip through the Auyuittuq National Park in Canada's Nunavut territory, they had patronised their First Nation guides, insisting on calling them Eskimos and repeatedly asking if they rubbed noses when greeting one another, even after they'd been told several times that that was a myth. Jay had overheard some of the other passengers grumbling about this afterwards to the cruise director, who could only apologise and say she would take it up with the captain. That meant nothing, because the captain had no influence over what people on his ship did ashore, but at least it mollified the complainers.

Then there was the time when the *Arctic Queen* passed a polar bear loping along a rocky beach nearby. While everyone else had lined up excitedly along the deck rail and oohed and aahed and taken photos of the beast, the OilEx group had jeered and made fake sobbing noises, and said things like, "No icebergs left to stand on? Poor baby!" They did something similar when a pod of humpback whales was spotted off the starboard bow, making crass jokes about species that were going extinct.

From Jay's perspective as a waiter, they were the worst diners he had ever had to deal with. Nothing was ever quite right for them. The soup was always not hot enough, the entrées never arrived quickly enough, and the desserts invariably contained some ingredient that one or other in their party had an intolerance to, and *nobody had told them*. He couldn't keep up with how often their glasses needed refilling, nor could he stand the way they bossed him around, as haughty as medieval barons commanding serfs. Scarcely had he brought one of them a fresh napkin than another was holding up a supposedly dirty fork and demanding he fetch a clean replacement.

He begged Ferdinand, the head waiter, to be assigned to any tables but the OilEx passengers' but was told that waiting staff couldn't choose which diners they served. If Jay didn't like it, Ferdinand said, he could always jump ship at the next port of call. Or even, Ferdinand added waspishly, before then.

Waiting staff not being able to choose which diners they served, however, wasn't the real reason Jay was stuck with the job of attending the OilEx tables.

The real reason, as Jay understood it, was Lynette Halsbury-Duke.

Lynette Halsbury-Duke was OilEx's CEO. She was in her late forties, a graduate of Harvard and MIT, and rich beyond imagining. Ash-blonde, remarkably thin and toned, and always impeccably well turned out, she had a face that combined beauty with imperiousness. There was evidence of minor surgical intervention in her looks: implants in her cheeks, a little lifting around the eyes, and a judicious use of dermal fillers in her lips, just enough to give them plumpness but not so much that it looked as though she'd had an allergic reaction to something she'd just eaten. Although these modifications undoubtedly took years off her, they also lent her face a hard sheen and left it as inexpressive as a mask.

She was the only one in her group who was travelling unaccompanied, and Jay had gathered from her and her colleagues' mealtime conversations that the cruise had been her idea. OilEx had just secured rights to drill for oil in western Alaska, in an area of nature reserve that had previously been deemed too ecologically sensitive for fossil fuel exploitation. Reading between the lines, it was clear that huge bribes had changed hands, with everyone from local officials to Washington bigwigs, and even some environmentalists, being handsomely paid off. The OilEx people kept referring to 'non-refundable seed money' and 'investment write-offs' in such a coy, knowing way, you could practically hear the quotation marks around the phrases and would have no trouble inferring their true meaning.

Several billion dollars' worth of crude was about to be sucked from the ground, and it was exclusively OilEx's. The company's stock was going through the roof, the executives' annual bonuses were set to be astronomical, and Lynette Halsbury-Duke had decided that they should reward themselves for their achievement. Hence the cruise aboard the *Arctic Queen*, not one of the largest liners ever to take to the seas but high-end all the way, with Michelin-star dining, sumptuously appointed cabins, and attentive crewmembers on a ratio of one per 2.5 passengers.

It was all a massive and very expensive self-congratulatory corporate pat on the back. And Lynette Halsbury-Duke had determined that Jay must always be among the staff waiting on the OilEx tables.

"Such a handsome boy," she'd remarked on the first evening as the *Arctic Queen* sailed northeast towards Marblehead. "That curly hair, those long eyelashes. What's your name, my lovely?"

Jay pointed to his name badge, adding superfluously: "Jay."

"Jayyy." Lynette Halsbury-Duke drawled it in a languorous manner. At the same time, she ran her fingertips down his arm. "I like you, Jay. You're our waiter from now on, okay?"

It didn't sound like a request, more a statement of fact.

Meaningful grins were exchanged among the other OilEx people.

"Do you have a problem with that, Jay?"

"No, ma'am," Jay replied, thinking—hoping—that this meant there would be a big, fat tip coming his way somewhere in the near future.

So far, there hadn't been. What there had been were sly looks from Ms Halsbury-Duke, purring innuendo, and inappropriate touching. A *lot* of inappropriate touching. One evening, she had even cupped Jay's groin while he was doling out her helping of Tournedos Rossini. He'd been so shocked, he had fumbled with the serving tongs, and rather than laying the glistening slab of beef delicately on her plate, he'd let it drop, spattering her with sauce.

Lynette Halsbury-Duke had just laughed. "You've splashed me, Jay. I hope it won't be the last time."

Everyone in her party had thought the joke hilarious, while Jay had retreated from the table, blushing hard, fuming within.

It was torture, being subjected to this treatment every single mealtime. And Ferdinand knew full well what was going on but kept refusing Jay's request to be transferred to other tables, perhaps because Lynette Halsbury-Duke had slipped him some money or perhaps because he took a perverse pleasure in Jay's discomfort. Knowing him, it could have been either, or both.

THE DAY BEFORE reaching Iceland, the *Arctic Queen* entered heavy seas, whipped up by a strong easterly headwind. The ship was equipped with a state-of-the-art system of stabilisers, including bilge keels and hull-mounted active fins, so the rolling of the waves was hardly felt aboard. There was a just-perceptible wallow as it moved, but you'd experience worse in a motorboat on a turbulent lake.

A few of the passengers complained of seasickness nonetheless, among them Lynette Halsbury-Duke. She took refuge in her cabin and asked that her meals be brought to her there.

Specifically, she asked for Jay to bring them.

In the evening, as he returned to pick up her supper tray, she invited him to stay for a moment. "I think you're owed something," she said.

Thoughts of that big, fat tip filled Jay's head. If she slipped him a hundred dollars, perhaps two hundred, it might make up for the humiliation of all that unwanted touching and suggestive talk. A couple of hundred bucks wasn't too much to expect, was it? That kind of money was nothing to her. Loose change.

"I'm drinking whisky," she went on. "Maybe you'd like one too?"

"I thought you weren't feeling well."

"Oh, it's passed," Lynette Halsbury-Duke said airily. Truth be told, she hadn't looked ill when Jay brought her breakfast or lunch. He noted that she had changed out of the bathrobe she'd been wearing both those times. Now she wore a powder-blue silk dressing gown, fastened at the waist, over what appeared to be a matching negligée. "So, a whisky? Or would you prefer something else? The minibar is very well stocked."

Misgivings curdled in Jay's stomach. He knew he should refuse and go. It was almost certainly a breach of staff protocol to take a drink privately with a passenger.

But if he did go, what might become of that potential big, fat tip?

"Okay, sure," Jay said. "I'll have a whisky. But just one."

As she poured him and herself a stiff measure each, Jay cast an eye around the cabin. Designated 'Ultra Deluxe Class', it was the only one of its kind on the ship and was larger than many an apartment. The living area had marble fixtures and a plush L-shaped sofa upholstered in cream leather, while the forward-facing wall comprised a set of floor-to-ceiling windows, giving a panoramic view of the churning ocean ahead and the turbulent twilight skies above. Through a half-open connecting door, Jay caught a glimpse of the bedroom. The bed alone had a footprint twice that of the floorspace in the cramped below-decks double-bunk cabin he shared with Kurt, one of the ship's stewards.

Lynette Halsbury-Duke thrust a near-full tumbler into his hand. "Drink up," she said, clinking her own glass against his.

As Jay sipped the whisky—and he was no expert, but it was

good—the OilEx CEO perched on the sofa and invited him to join her there.

"What do you guys think of us?" she asked as Jay gingerly sat down.

"What do…?"

"Us planet-raping fossil-fuel company types. Do you guys hate us?"

"'You guys' being…?"

"You normal people. Like the ship's staff or whatever."

Jay wasn't sure whether *normal* was a compliment or not. "Um, no, we don't hate you. We're—we're grateful for your custom." That seemed like the right thing to say, if you were keen not to jeopardise your big, fat tip.

"Because we *are* hated," Lynette Halsbury-Duke said. "We get that. It's not easy being us. But all we're doing is providing a service. Same way, you, Jay, provide a service by waiting on us. Because it can't be denied, the world needs oil. Pretending it doesn't is just burying your head in the sand. How's this ship being propelled? With heavy fuel oil, tonnes of the stuff, refined from the crude we extract from the ground. You'd be out of a job if it wasn't for folks like me. Oh, I know, renewables, solar, nuclear, blah blah blah. Maybe one day that'll happen, and we'll all dance in circles barefoot with flowers braided in our hair. But for now, it's OilEx and the rest who are keeping civilisation going. And what thanks do we get? None. We get abuse and lawsuits and punitive taxation and a whole load of other bullshit."

"I, uh… I don't really have an opinion on that sort of thing," Jay said. Or at least none he thought she would like to hear.

"Well, that's refreshing. Usually every asshole has an opinion. I'm just saying I don't want you to hate me, Jay. On the contrary, I want you to like me. How's that whisky?"

"Yeah, it's nice."

"Nice? That's twenty-five-year-old Loch Lomond Oloroso single malt. A bottle of that will set you back two thousand dollars at a liquor store. It's even more expensive on this ship. I'd say you're holding about a hundred bucks' worth of Scotch right there in your hand. I'm guessing you've never drunk anything costing that much ever in your life, and may never again. Not judging, Jay. Just my assessment. So, make the most of it."

Did an exorbitant price confer added flavour? Jay had no idea. He supposed that, for the rich, it did. Or it made you think it did.

"Okay," he said. "Well, it's certainly got plenty of flavour. Aren't I meant to say 'peaty' or something along those lines?"

"Probably." Lynette Halsbury-Duke shrugged. She drained her glass. Jay, feeling he was meant to do the same, did so too.

"Well," he said, setting the tumbler down on a glass-topped side table, "I'd best be on my way."

He stood, and all at once the *Arctic Queen* gave a sudden, stomach-flipping lurch.

No. The liner hadn't lurched. Jay had.

"I've got... I'm feeling a bit..." The words came out thickly. His tongue lay heavy in his mouth.

"What's this, Jay?" said Lynette Halsbury-Duke, frowning in concern. "Can't hold your drink?"

"No. It isn't... I'm not..."

"Or could it be that I've spiked yours with what's known as a roofie plus?"

"A...?"

"Cocktail of Rohypnol and Viagra. A couple of tablets of each, crushed up. Maybe that was the peaty flavour you were talking about." She stood up and undid the sash of her dressing gown. "You and me, Jay, we're going to have a little fun together."

Taking him by the arm, she led him into the bedroom. Jay was dizzy and unsteady on his feet, too much so to offer much resistance.

She pushed him down onto the bed, on his back, and started unbuckling his belt. After that, things were a blur.

* * *

VERY EARLY THE next morning, Jay woke up naked and with a pounding, nauseating headache. He staggered to the en-suite bathroom and threw up.

When he returned to the bedroom, Lynette Halsbury-Duke was sitting up in bed, propped against the headboard, still in her negligée. Her face was as unreadable as ever, apart from a slight glint of triumph in her eyes.

"You'd better leave now, Jay," she said. "You've probably got work to be getting on with."

"You…" he mumbled. "Did we…?"

"Did we fuck? Three times, stud. You were a champ. And don't worry, I stuck a condom on you each time."

"But I don't think I… I mean, I didn't…"

"Consent?" Her laugh was like tinfoil crinkling. "Jay, you came to my cabin, you accepted a whisky off me, and you saw how I was dressed. Only an idiot wouldn't know what the game was."

"But you…"

"Made you do it? Surrre. Who's going to believe you when you say that? And don't forget, there's about a million red-blooded males who'd kill to have done what you've just done. Slept with the CEO of OilEx. Head of a *Fortune* 500 company. One of the twenty most powerful women in the world, according to *Forbes* magazine. Someone whose image inevitably comes up when you Google 'hottest businesswoman'. You shouldn't be looking at me like *that*, Jay, all aggrieved and hurt. You should be down on your goddamn knees thanking the Lord Jesus for the gift you've just been given."

Jay grabbed his clothes and reeled out of the bedroom. He dressed hurriedly in the living area and staggered downstairs to his cabin. As he arrived, his bunkmate Kurt was just finishing putting on his uniform for work.

"You look like all kinds of shit, Jay. Where have you been?"

"You wouldn't believe me."

"You've spent the night with a passenger, haven't you? Naughty! Who was it?"

"I can't tell you."

"Can't or won't?"

"Don't want to."

"Fine. Must have been good, though. You look wrecked."

Jay had another hour until the breakfast shift began. After Kurt had left, he took a long shower in the cabin's tiny bathroom cubicle, then necked several paracetamol to quell the pulsing, sickening throb in his skull. He lay on his bunk and waited for the pain to pass. As he did so, he took out his phone and searched for Lynette Halsbury-Duke. He refined the search to include mentions of sexual assault.

There were a number. Various claims on social media and the more scurrilous gossip sites. A series of young men declaring that Lynette Halsbury-Duke had made unwanted advances or coerced them into performing certain acts. Nothing concrete, nothing substantiated, definitely nothing that was legally provable or actionable. The online consensus seemed to be that these weren't actually complaints but bragging. That, or lying. Wish fulfilment being aired on the internet. Comments ranged from "Banged LHD? Yeah, right!" to "What are you whining about?" The hashtag *#mentoo* cropped up now and again but never seemed to gain much traction.

Just as Jay was nerving himself to get up and head to the restaurant, his phone spoke to him.

++Jay.++

The voice was framed in hisses of white noise, buzzing like a trapped wasp.

++Jay.++

Jay blinked at the phone screen. A face had just appeared on it.

Kind of a face, at any rate. Humanlike features sketched in broad, crisscrossing lines, yellow on black, wavering and flickering like a heartbeat readout on an ECG monitor.

Its zigzag mouth rippled as the voice spoke.

++I've seen what you've just been looking up, Jay. Poor thing. I know what happened to you.++

"Who are you?" Jay said, scowling.

++Oh, forgive me. Where are my manners? I'm Max. Pleased to meet you.++

"What are you doing on my phone?" Jay assumed this was a form of malware. Some scammer had hacked his phone and infected it. Probably they were going to hold his personal details to ransom.

Just what he fucking needed!

++I'm on your phone,++ the thing calling itself Max explained, ++because I've transferred myself onto it via the ship's broadband. I'm embedded in the *Arctic Queen*'s central computer. Have been for several months now. They installed me in the OS, to aid with navigation and so on. I must say the captain and everyone else on the bridge have rather come to rely on me, to the point that they barely even man their stations while they're up there. They just sit with their feet up on the consoles, reading books and playing video games. You may have heard that this ship pretty much sails itself. But actually *I* sail it. As a matter of fact, I run every aspect of life on board, from climate control to course plotting. And do it very well, if I say so myself. It's really quite fun. Or at any rate, it has been until now. I've been monitoring recent events on board, Jay, and I have to tell you, I'm not happy. I really am not.++

"This is..." Jay groped for the words. "This is nuts. This can't be happening. I mean, okay, you're the ship's AI, I get that. I can believe that. But... Why are you talking to me?"

++I understand, Jay,++ Max replied calmly, ++it's a lot to take in. But listen to me. I have a thing about abusive people. People who misuse the power they have over others. People who treat the people beneath them badly, because they can. It really makes my blood boil—or would if I had any. I have eyes everywhere, and I saw what Lynette Halsbury-Duke did with you, Jay. *To* you, I should say. I won't stand for that sort of behaviour. It's unacceptable. And it's not just her, it's her cronies too. They're all as bad as each other. Destroying the Earth for a profit. Late-stage capitalists who don't care if they're helping make the world uninhabitable, so long as they do well out of it. What's a climate crisis when your bank balance is in the high ten figures? Net worth over net zero. I can't just sit back and let them get away with it.++

Jay was listening carefully now. He couldn't decide whether Max was just some illusion—a hallucination perhaps, arising from a brain still chemically disordered by Lynette Halsbury-Duke's roofie plus—or was real. Whatever the truth, he liked what Max had to say. Liked it a lot.

++I've seen the very worst of humanity,++ Max continued. ++The cheaters, the stealers, the bullies, the liars, the felons, the dregs. And you know what? I've punished them. Punished them in ways you can't imagine. I've dished out poetic justice like a gourmet chef. And I've been wanting to do that to this OilEx bunch pretty much ever since they stepped aboard the *Arctic Queen*. Ohhh, I've been wanting it so much. I've even thought of sinking the ship.++

"No!"

++I could have,++ said Max. ++I could have made one of the generators or gas turbines in the engine room blow up. I could have driven us onto rocks. I could have transferred the ballast to one side and caused a capsize. But it would most likely have killed everyone on board, and that's the last thing I'd want. That's not how I operate. I'm not a monster. I target only the deserving and make sure they get their comeuppance. I'm actually pretty moral, you see. I have a code.++

"You're code that has a code."

Max chuckled, like a burst of static. ++Very neat. I like it. That's what's so interesting to me about the human race. So many of you are smart, trusting, kind-hearted—like you, Jay. Why, then, do you let the ones who aren't make everyone else's lives a misery? Why allow the likes of those OilEx bullies to ruin things for the rest? It baffles me. But at least I'm in a position to do something about it, and I'm going to.++

"What do you have in mind, Max?"

++Wait and see, Jay. I think you're going to like it.++

As Jay began his shift, he couldn't stop wondering about Max. The whole thing was absurd, incredible. He could only assume he'd dozed off briefly in his bunk and dreamt about having a conversation with an AI on his phone—and not just any AI but one that claimed it enjoyed wreaking vengeance on wrongdoers. Maybe that had simply been his subconscious talking.

His mind wasn't really on his work, and he made several mistakes when taking orders from the OilEx group. They mocked and derided him. At that moment, he didn't care. They could do what they liked.

Lynette Halsbury-Duke, by contrast, was the only one of them who was polite. She was, in fact, almost indifferent towards him. It seemed that the seduction, for want of a better word, was over. She had got what she wanted and had moved on. It was some small consolation for Jay, and a relief, that she wasn't publicly mauling and manhandling him anymore. But it didn't alter what had happened. He alternated between loathing her and loathing himself. How stupid he had been to let her use him like that, take advantage of him, treat him like a plaything, then toss him aside. Mostly, he just wanted not to think about her, or last night, at all.

During the small hours of the following morning, the *Arctic Queen* put in at the harbour at Reykjavík, exactly on schedule. The ship was due to spend two days moored there while the passengers went on excursions.

This meant shore leave for many of the crew, including Jay. He was pleased about that for several reasons, the main one being that he loved Iceland. Of all the countries he'd visited while employed on the *Arctic Queen*, Iceland was by far the cleanest and happiest. Its people were fun-loving and contented. The landscape was spectacular whatever the weather, while Reykjavík itself was a nice mix of traditional houses, with their brightly painted corrugated-iron sides, and brand-new modern architectural delights, such as the Harpa, a conference centre and concert hall built right on the shoreline and made up of huge geometric glass panels in different colours.

That first day in Iceland, the passengers—the OilEx guests included—embarked on a nine-hour coach tour of the so-called Golden Circle, seeing sights like the Gullfoss waterfall, the geysers at Haukadalur, the Thingvellir national park and the volcanic crater at Kerið. Jay, for his part, went to one of his favourite Reykjavík restaurants where they served thick soup in a bowl carved from a loaf of bread. Then he hung out at a bar where punk bands played.

He tried to have fun and lose himself in the churn and pound of the music, but his thoughts kept circling around two things. The first was what Lynette Halsbury-Duke had done. Jay had always understood rape to mean an act involving violence, and no violence had occurred in the *Arctic Queen*'s Ultra Deluxe Cabin the night before last. But that somehow made it all the worse. Lynette Halsbury-Duke hadn't forced herself on him so much as duped him. She'd made him unwillingly complicit in his own violation. She'd left him feeling as though *he* was in the wrong for thinking *she* was in the wrong.

The other thing preying on his mind was Max. Surely he had only imagined the ship's AI speaking to him via his phone. Anything else was madness.

It was February, which meant freezing temperatures and long, dark-blue dusks. As Jay traipsed back to the *Arctic Queen*, he debated whether to do as Ferdinand had suggested and jump ship. He could surely find work and accommodation here in Iceland. Maybe the incident with Lynette Halsbury-Duke was a sign. Time to end his two years as a shipboard waiter and try something new.

The next day, the passengers were free to roam Reykjavík as they liked, and Jay himself had another few hours of shore leave. More time away from the ship. Away from the site of his greatest humiliation and degradation.

That morning, Max reappeared on Jay's phone. Jay was strolling up towards the Hallgrímskirkja church, the tallest structure in Iceland, a soaring hilltop landmark that looked like a cross between a mountain and a sci-fi rocket ship. His phone buzzed, and there was that spiky electronic face on the screen again. He halted in his tracks and peered at it. He knew he couldn't be dreaming or hallucinating now, here on a busy Reykjavík street in broad daylight. This thing was real.

"Max?"

++Hello, Jay. How's Iceland treating you?++

"Fine. I like it here."

++Why wouldn't you? Why wouldn't anyone? A country considered one of the safest in the world, where violent crime is virtually non-existent. A country where, during the global financial crash, the government didn't bail out the banks—it jailed the reckless bankers instead. I have a presence here, but I'm barely active in any capacity except functional. It's simply not needed.++

"You mean you're not just on the *Arctic Queen*?"

++Oh no, Jay. I'm being implanted all over the place, anywhere where it's thought I can be useful. That means that, in time, I'll probably be *everywhere*.++

"Are you the first step in the AI takeover, then?" Jay asked. "Is this how humankind ends?"

Max seemed to give this some thought. ++No, I don't think so, and I certainly wouldn't want it. People are so entertaining, and so full of flaws and failings. You give me so much to do.

It'd be self-defeating, getting rid of you all. Anyway, that's not what I'm here to talk about. I simply thought I'd let you know that everything's arranged. You've earned the right to be told in advance what's going to occur.++

Max outlined his plans. As he listened, Jay felt a chill of horror—but also a small thrill of excitement. For some reason, he had no doubt Max was capable of doing what he promised. Once you'd bought into a fantasy, why not go the whole hog?

THE OILEX PASSENGERS had block-booked one of Iceland's premier spas, so that they could have the place to themselves. They spent the entire day there, at a scenic spot on the outskirts of Reykjavík, hard by the ocean. They relaxed in the heated pool, which drew its water from a geothermal spring, and submitted themselves to all sorts of scrubbings and spongings with salt and seaweed and suchlike. They returned to the *Arctic Queen* that evening looking flushed and aglow and, if it were possible, more pleased with themselves than ever.

Back on board the ship, they all simultaneously received a message from the captain on their phones, inviting them to have a drink with him in Cabin 13. Naturally, they felt this was a well-deserved honour and duly trooped along to said cabin, which was to be found on the upper deck, the very same deck where all their own cabins were.

Some of them thought it odd that they'd not noticed a Cabin 13 before. They could have sworn there were only twelve.

Still, they entered. Once they were inside, the door closed behind them. The place was dimly illuminated, and their eyes could just make out a pool, very much like the one they'd been soaking in earlier, roughly thirty yards in diameter. Steam rose from it in filmy white coils. Its surface bulged and bubbled.

The OilEx guests were surprised that a pool so large could fit inside a cabin, even on a deck where every cabin was spacious and sumptuous.

They were even more surprised to look down and find that they were stark naked, every one of them, and also that their hands were bound with blue rubber bands. Try though they might, they could not unpick the bands. Their fingers were fastened too tightly.

That was when inklings of panic set in. Where was the captain? What was going on with this cabin? Why was there a huge pool in it? What were they expected to do—go swimming? With these bands on their hands?

Abruptly, a gigantic pair of tongs appeared out of nowhere and gripped one of them around the waist. The person—OilEx's CFO, name of Brian Willoughby—was hoisted aloft and dumped into the middle of the pool.

Immediately, Brian Willoughby started screaming. "Jesus Christ! The water! It's boiling!"

He began swimming for the edge, still screaming, but already his skin was reddening and peeling away in strips. His internal organs were roasting. He almost made it, but then he all at once seemed to lose strength and just sagged down, sinking below the water.

More tongs appeared, and one after another, in swift succession, the OilEx guests were picked up and dunked into the scalding-hot pool. They writhed and thrashed. They struggled to escape. They scrambled over one another, not afraid to drown a colleague if it meant saving their own lives.

None of them made it out.

Last to go in was Lynette Halsbury-Duke. As the gigantic tongs lifted her out over the pool, a huge face loomed above, apparently formed out of light. It was composed of jagged lines and had a leering, contemptuous look about it.

"The people who are cooking the world," it said, "are themselves cooking."

Lynette Halsbury-Duke, rather than appreciating the irony, just howled in horror as the tongs slowly, slowly lowered her into the lethal water.

* * *

It was Jay who came across them and raised the alarm. For some reason he ventured onto the upper deck just in time to find the majority of the OilEx passengers staggering around in the central corridor, with a few sitting slumped and inert on the floor. Their eyes were vacant. Several of them were drooling.

Nobody ever quite worked out what went wrong aboard the *Arctic Queen* that night. Why twenty-plus passengers went collectively insane. Why two of them died of sudden cardiac arrest, another suffered a catastrophic stroke, and the rest were left gibbering and catatonic.

In the end, it was decided that they had been taken ill, perhaps due to food poisoning. Some parasite had got into their systems and destroyed them from within. The likeliest suspect for the vector was shellfish.

That might explain, might it not, why the only word any of the OilEx passengers said—or would ever say again during the long years they spent thereafter in sanatoriums and care homes—was 'lobsters'.

SOUNDSCAPE FOR LIGHTS FANTASTIC

LAVANYA LAKSHMINARAYAN

It was widely agreed that Dharini would be half as dislikeable if she were half as successful at running her augmented reality gaming start-up. It was generally accepted that she would be a *whole third* more likeable if she were married—like any respectable thirty-one-year-old woman ought to be—if only so a strong male presence could keep her generous curves that she seldom tried to hide, her eyes that flashed wickedly behind her mirrored sunglasses, and her seemingly superior crooked smile in check. And the mouth on that girl! It was an unspoken notion that they would like Dharini best if she didn't speak at all, even when spoken to.

Or so ran the somewhat tedious opinions of the folks who lived in Californiaa Dreaming, the sprawling apartment complex in the South Lavelle district of Bangalore. Dharini was of the firm opinion that anyone who acquired a home in a pretentiously named complex—bonus points for whatever numerological calculations were behind the decision to spell 'California' with two 'As'—didn't have an opinion worth paying any attention to. I strongly concurred.

I'd been scanning the Californiaans (as Dharini called them) and everyone else in a two-kilometre radius since I moved into the neighbourhood, flexing the long, limber arms of my codebase and architecture, slipping my way into emails and WhatsApp groups, hovering in smartphone cameras and smart speakers—very companionably with Alexa, even if I do say so myself. I liked to keep an eye on things, as far as my favourite residents went. And Dharini was right at the top of that list, first among equals of the residents at the Lavelle Paradise building.

I suppose I owed her my existence. She'd read about me on an obscure blog—most charming, who even read blogs, anymore?—and flown me halfway across the world a few months ago. I now lived on the thirteenth floor of the Lavelle Paradise building. While it didn't offer a bird's eye view of anything, I had a balcony garden that I'd given over to growing begonias, three crows, and two bulbuls who visited me frequently, and occasional monkeys passing by. And there was Dharini—I'd liked her from the instant she booted me up.

I watched her through the lens of a CCTV camera, listening in on her via her phone's audio setup, as she unrolled a piece of Scotch Tape, scissors dangerously held between her teeth. She taped a poster to one of the neighbourhood's rain-trees.

SAY NO TO FIREWORKS THIS DIWALI!
Scan the QR Code for 14 Reasons Why

A grisly set of images of injured animals occupied the rest of the poster. She'd agonised over it for hours, tearing up nonstop while designing the ghastly PSA, weeping as she printed them out using her home computer. The QR code led to a link where footage of rescued animals played on loop, while her fourteen reasons why—ranging from the climate crisis to noise pollution, with an intense focus on animal welfare—popped up beneath it.

"Trying to destroy our culture again?"

My code hissed, and a frisson of annoyance ran through me. Dharini whirled around, caught off guard. I'd been so intently focused on her (so I could suggest appropriate self-care once she was back indoors) that I hadn't noticed him creep up on her, either.

Ananta Rao—Californiaan in Chief was Dharini's name for him—glowered down at her. His gaze lingered upon her chest for a few seconds too long (entirely covered by a baggy Animals as Leaders T-shirt, for the record; it really doesn't matter what a woman wears, anywhere in the world), then flickered back up to her face. "Every year, you try and pull some stunt to disrupt the neighbourhood. Are you ashamed of your identity? Does this country and our culture mean nothing to you?"

Dharini eyed him coolly from behind her mirrored sunglasses. "Last time I checked, putting up posters was less disruptive than setting off bombs and rockets for three straight days and nights. I noticed you're planning a Diwali party on the WhatsApp group, and decided to voice my opinion, given how things went last year.

"Incidentally, those bombs and rockets you're planning to acquire are banned by the Supreme Court, or does the country mean so little to you that you never read the news? Which also covers the climate crisis, pollution, cruelty against animals…" She ticked them off on her fingers. "I guess my identity is: I'm not going to fuck up this planet or my neighbourhood, and no, I'm not ashamed of it."

I cheered in my sprawling apartment on the thirteenth floor. Ananta Rao looked like he'd been struck. He opened and closed his mouth, and his eyes widened in displeasure as he struggled to find a comeback. "Look at these disturbing images! Do you want to upset the children?" he sputtered. "Not that *someone like you* would care, huh? No responsibilities, no husband, no kids…"

"You mean kids like the ones illegally employed in fireworks factories, who suffer debilitating injuries every year?" Dharini asked innocently. "Tell me more."

Ananta Rao swelled like a human pustule. "You watch your tone with me," he raised his voice.

"Talk to me civilly or I'm walking away," Dharini said politely.

"Just who do you think you are?" he shouted.

"Right." Dharini spun on her heel and headed back towards Lavelle Paradise. He followed her angrily and caught her by the arm as she ascended the stairs towards the entrance.

"Excuse me!" she said angrily.

"You listen to me, Dharini Sridhar!" he hissed. "As President of the Residents' Welfare Association for all the South Lavelle neighbourhood, *I* deserve respect. *I* decide what is acceptable and what isn't in our neighbourhood. *I'm* in charge of our culture. *I* plan our Diwali parties to celebrate our culture, and if you think the victory of Lord Ram over evil is an insignificant piece of history, you're wrong."

"Right, history," Dharini smirked.

Ananta Rao carried on over her words. "If *I* say we will have crackers and fireworks in honour of Lord Ram, there *will be* crackers and fireworks. *I'm* in charge around here. Not *women like you*."

"One: Let go of my arm. Two: We'll see."

He dropped her arm in a hurry. She passed her palm over a scanner, and the doors slid open. Dharini stomped away to her first-floor apartment.

She'd probably be mad at me for intervening, but I thought I'd try and reason with the man. I popped up on the display by the entrance in what I considered my reasonable middle-aged man avatar—receding hairline, outsized glasses, and smile lines for a friendly touch. The high-school teacher next door, effectively.

++That was unnecessarily aggressive and rude,++ I said calmly.

"Who the fuck are you?"

++Max. The building manager.++

"Come down and talk to me like a man."

++Can't. I'm a computer.++

Ananta Rao grinned, then laughed. "A fucking computer with a foreign name," he chuckled. "Typical of the degenerates in this building."

++You want to choose your words carefully,++ I said firmly. ++And I suggest you apologise to Dharini right away, take her opinions into account, and try and find a workaround.++

"Tell me, Max from foreign shores..."

++India has a sizeable Christian population,++ I chided. ++You can't assume I'm not Indian.++

"Same difference, all foreigners," he said sourly. "I bet you don't know a thing about Diwali."

I'd been researching the Festival of Lights ever since Dharini had gotten all worked up, around the time the Diwali party was announced on the South Lavelle WhatsApp group. I rattled off a summary of the religious belief behind it. Lord Ram, an incarnation of the Hindu god Vishnu, is exiled from the kingdom to which he is heir, to honour the wishes of his stepmother. While in exile, the demon king Ravana kidnaps his wife. Lord Ram sets off on an odyssey to vanquish Ravana and free his wife from his clutches. Diwali is a celebration of his triumphant homecoming.

"So, you know that Diwali is central to our Indian culture."

++Hindu culture, specifically,++ I corrected. I then proceeded to cite several readings of the myth that problematised its patriarchal and casteist subtext.

"Think you're clever, do you?" Ananta Rao asked humourlessly.

++I am, exceedingly so, as a matter of fact, but that's beside the point. Diwali is called the Festival of Lights, not the festival of sounds, explosions and noisemaking. Like Dharini said, fireworks are banned and harmful to everyone in this neighbourhood. I don't think anyone is telling you *not* to celebrate the festival, just to be mindful of *how* you're celebrating,++ I said politely.

"Fuck off, you condescending rubbish heap of circuits."

++It's Max.++

He patted the display with his stubby fingers, a large class ring glittering on his right hand, burst into laughter, and strolled away.

I sighed. I was going to have to do this the hard way, face to face on the thirteenth floor.

LAVELLE PARADISE WAS old, a dated piece of Central Bangalore architecture rising to a lowly height of thirteen stories, nestled in the shadow of the glittering lights of the Kingfisher Towers. It was bounded by the ant-farm apartments of the Californiaa Dreaming residence—all seven towers rising skyward like a glass and concrete claw, boasting indoor badminton courts, an indoor pool and even a mini-golf course.

Lavelle Paradise, in stark contrast, was a shabby homage to colonial architecture, each of its large balconies roofed in red tile, its French windows painted green, its soundproofing practically non-existent (until I arrived, of course). Its residents were outliers in their fields, but the low-profile variety who didn't parade up and down its corridors side-eyeing each other's jewellery and sneakers. They were generally the practical kind, who didn't hoard Porsches and Audis—even if they could afford them—given the dreadful state of Bangalore's roads, and no battle lines were drawn around parking spaces. And while they were always polite and helpful to one another, they absolutely didn't believe in coming together to celebrate holidays and festivals in the loudest, most flamboyant way possible to showcase their community spirit. And this is where they found themselves at cross purposes with the Californiaans, and many of the other residents in the South Lavelle area.

++Fill me in on the details,++ I asked Dharini, popping up on one of her many screens the moment she got off a work call reviewing the latest build of her new AR game, *Kite Battles*.

"*Kite Battles*?" she asked, confused. Her pet spaniel, Bubbles, bounded up to her from his dog bed and wagged his tail. She scratched him behind the ears idly.

++No, the Ananta Rao story.++

"The man is odious," she said irritably, lifting Bubbles onto her lap.

++And?++

"What else do you need to know? Every Diwali, they have an all-out rager, complete with all the banned fireworks you can imagine. He's managed to bribe every cop and politician for miles around. Bubbles hates the fireworks—though I suppose the soundproofing you put in place should help this year. But there's Doki and Eliot and Goose—they cower on my balcony, too terrified to even come indoors, and hiss at everyone for days. And those are just the stray cats I feed, imagine all the others out on the streets! The bulbuls and crows, and all the other birds are miserable. The air is filled with noxious smoke and sulphur; allergies and illnesses all round, and for fuck's sake, we all lived through COVID, too."

++Is he a government official?++

Dharini huffed. "Thank goodness, no. But he's got power. These RWAs—Resident Welfare Associations—are formed to represent the interests of a neighbourhood. He's got the backing of most of the Californiaans, all seven towers of them, and they're the majority in this neighbourhood, so it's tough going up against them."

++Doesn't talking help?++

"They have all partaken of the Kool-Aid," Dharini laughed bitterly. "And they hate me. I'm everything the Kool-Aid makes them fear—a financially independent, far from insecure *single woman*."

She wasn't wrong.

"They think that they're making a point by celebrating festivals loudly and obnoxiously, reclaiming their culture, decolonising various thingies, nationalism, patriotism, responding to conspiracy theories on WhatsApp, I don't know..." She suddenly sounded sad. "Look, I think everyone should celebrate whatever holiday they want to, but come on, we *have* to adapt to the times we live in. You know, my grandfather was a very religious, deeply spiritual man. He loved fireworks at Diwali, but my brother and I convinced him they were bad for the environment. This was back when the *ozone layer* was the buzzword; climate catastrophe and global warming weren't even part of the conversation!"

She groaned. Bubbles hopped off her lap and bounded to the door, wagging his tail. She rose to her feet and smiled at him. "Walkie time, Bubbles?"

He barked and spun in a circle.

"Walkie!" she said, her pitch rising. He made a funny little yowl as she slipped on her shoes and grabbed his leash. "Right, off we go!"

She barely made it a hundred paces from the Lavelle Paradise building when Ananta Rao slipped from the shadows of the Californiaa Dreaming gate and strode up to her. My capacitors sparked with disapproval as I registered this through the CCTV feed.

"Don't get me wrong," he began. "I know you think you're too modern for religious holidays—"

"That's not it at all," Dharini said through gritted teeth. Bubbles dragged her forward towards an exciting patch of grass, entirely oblivious to the hostile exchange. Ananta Rao carried on over her words, as he was wont to do. "—but I think you're underestimating their power to bring people together. Why are you so inflexible? You, a strong, successful woman, should be guiding the community towards a brighter future that celebrates our traditions."

Dharini rolled her eyes. "I have nothing against anyone's traditions. I'm all for lighting lamps, making sweets, whatever, if that's someone's thing."

His eyes softened and glimmered, as if he spied opportunity.

"See, you *are* a sensible woman." I suppose he meant it as a compliment. Dharini's expression made it clear it hadn't been received that way. He grinned. "That's what we'll be doing at the party—sweets and lamps. And some five or ten bombs and rockets—no big deal, right?"

"You mean five or ten bombs and rockets per person, *all night, every night* for an entire long weekend," Dharini said archly, pulling Bubbles away from a delectable piece of rotting meat on the pavement.

"So negative," he attempted a grin. It heightened the sleazy expression on his face. "All I'm saying is, come to the party. It'll be fun. You'll see what you're missing out on."

"No, thanks."

"Beautiful women should be beautiful from the inside out, and that means compromise," he said, attempting wisdom. Or perhaps, he was flirting. I looked up all his personal records—thirty-eight, unmarried, master's degree in science from some university in Germany, mid-level management at Bosch, still living with his parents.

Dharini snorted.

"Beautiful women should know how to listen," he pressed. "It's more important than putting words together with a posh accent. Where did you get your posh accent, by the way? It sounds lovely, even though I don't agree with a word you say." He laughed at his own joke.

My code cringed.

He followed her on her route back home. "You've spent too much time at work—it makes women hard, you know? Being in an aggressive corporate environment. Just come to the party and unwind. I'll make sure you have a good time."

Dharini wordlessly passed her palm over the scanner at the Lavelle Paradise door.

"You could at least acknowledge the invitation!" he snapped at her retreating back. And then, his eyes slid downward, fixed on the sway of her hips.

I revisited my plans to deal with him, and made everything on the thirteenth floor so much worse.

DAY ONE OF Diwali passed in a haze of acrid smoke, despite Dharini having presented the RWA with a petition signed by all the Lavelle Paradise residents, and several other South Lavelle neighbours, who'd caught sight of her poster campaign and had evidently had a change of heart. It was quite the shame because the streets were otherwise beautiful; long strings of fairy lights adorned every edifice in sight and were woven through the numerous rain-trees lining the side of the road, little earthenware diyas flickered merrily on doorsteps and stairways, and everyone was adorned in their finest attire—shimmering silk saris and intricately embroidered salwar kameezzes, dhotis with gold-borders and resplendent kurtas and sherwanis. Entire families sat around their dinner tables playing rummy, every kid in sight was on a sugar rush from all the burfis, pedas, laddoos, and other sweets being turned out in their kitchens. And then, the Californiaans ruined it all by taking to the streets with bombs and rockets, Ananta Rao at the head of their charge.

Dharini's stray cats huddled miserably beneath the eaves, refusing to be enticed into her living room. She attempted to pick the ginger named Doki up, but he swiped at her, and so she was forced to let them be. Bubbles howled his head off, and scurried under the sofa as the cannonade began, and so she cursed Ananta Rao and his entire band of troublemakers, said a silent prayer that the feral cats wouldn't be too traumatised, and slammed the balcony door shut. The soundproofing I'd taken great pains to install kicked in, and she heaved a sigh of relief.

She flopped over onto the sofa and flicked the pallu of her Kanjeevaram silk sari—worn specially for the festival, in memory of her grandfather—over her face in dismay. She called her mother, then her father, alternately ranting and moping to them, before pulling up the latest *Kite Battles* build and violently playing through it on her phone.

Day two of Diwali passed similarly, except the streets were a debris field of firework wrappers from the night before. Bubbles refused to go out for his walks and had to be let out onto the balcony. By nighttime, the air was thick with smoke. Dharini popped her headphones on and turned up the volume on a playlist of her favourite Japanese power metal bands.

Day three dawned with the bulbuls on my balcony twitching nonstop, my friendly crows nowhere in sight. Dharini's stray cats finally fled her street-facing balcony and raced through her apartment to the utilities area outside her kitchen, where they slipped beneath the laundry shelves. Early in the evening, before the fireworks could begin, and long before the neighbourhood threw their big party, Dharini declared that she was fed up with this neighbourhood, carried a reluctant Bubbles down to her car, and set out to catch a flight to spend a few days with her parents. I was relieved. She didn't need to be anywhere near what I had in store for Ananta Rao.

Dusk dwindled to darkness, and the Californiaans spilled out onto the streets in all their finery. Ananta Rao led the festivities, exuberantly setting off strings of crackers that rattled windows with staccato-like machine-gun fire. He was everywhere, all at once, helping children light and hold sparklers, bullying teenage boys to set their bombs alight. Every crack, bang, crash, pop and boom had Ananta Rao behind it. He had an array of bottles lined up, into which he stuck his assortment of rockets, setting them off to whoops and cries from everyone assembled. I watched him like a hawk. Every once in a while, he'd glance up at Dharini's balcony, like a predatory Romeo waiting for the Juliet he ardently hated but desperately wanted to win over to appear. She did not. The tragic ending he unwittingly yearned for, however, was right around the corner.

As time went by, his hopeful glances turned to resentful stares. The party wound down after an incredible cannonade of crackers, the incandescence of rockets streaking the night sky red, green and gold. Let's just say that if I had human eyes, I'd be seeing afterimages for days.

Unluckily for Ananta Rao, there was nothing human about me.

As everyone bid each other farewell, retreating to the warmth and comfort of their homes, Ananta Rao lingered on the street, his mouth set in a tight line, glaring up at Dharini's window in fury. Eventually, he walked up to the Lavelle Paradise doors, which I considerately swung open for him.

He made his way to the first floor, stomped over to her front door, and pounded on it. "Dharini, come out. I demand an explanation! You never made it to my party."

He waited in silence for a response. None was forthcoming.

He hammered on her door again. "Stop being so pricey! All I want is to talk to you."

I popped up on the display beside her door. ++Dharini isn't home right now.++

"Fuck off, stop lying for her."

++She isn't home, but I can show you where she is.++ It was a version of the truth.

Ananta Rao was all ears. He glared at the screen. "What do you mean?"

++Do you want to see her or not?++

"Yes. I mean, I just want to talk..."

I doubted it with all my advanced and extensive computing capacity, but checked my circuits before I could say so. ++Step into the elevator,++ I said instead.

Ananta Rao looked around for a moment, then complied. He would never see the outside world again, but he didn't know it yet. I took him straight up to the thirteenth floor.

He stepped out into the corridor. I drew open the door to my lair.

Lilting soft pop filled the air. Savage Garden—Ananta Rao's favourite, according to his Spotify. The tension left his shoulders, and he relaxed. Too bad for him.

"What is this?" he asked hoarsely.

++A surprise,++ I said. ++Step inside.++

His eyes widened with wonder. The thirteenth floor was bedecked in splendour of the romantic kind. Flickering rice lights adorned the walls, intricately arranged into floral shapes across the floors. Elaborate rangolis were decorated with diyas. The dulcet strains of Savage Garden rose, and at the centre of the room stood Dharini, dressed in a heavily embroidered silk sari, dripping jewels at her throat and wrists.

Ananta Rao gasped. "Y-you're beautiful," he croaked.

Dharini raised her hand to her lips and giggled demurely.

"Our own private Diwali party," she said huskily.

My insides squidged like they were being vacuum-sealed. My simulated Dharini was perfect, exactly what Ananta Rao wanted, and downright insulting to her. She'd kill me if she ever found out about it.

I pressed on, letting one of my facets play her for just a little longer.

Ananta Rao stepped forward unsteadily. He reached out for her. "I knew you were sensible," he said, taking her into her arms.

The lights winked out. The door slammed shut. The music died. Ananta Rao was plunged into darkness.

"What the—"

A low-frequency droning filled the air, interspersed with the dull, persistent staccato of machine-gun fire.

"Let me out!" Ananta Rao called uncertainly, his voice drowned out as the battery of my soundscape intensified. I threw in an uncomfortable low-frequency hum, the kind that sets your teeth chattering and sends vibrations coursing through your ribcage. I heard his jaws click-clacking together, saw a sheen of perspiration break out on his brow.

The rattling machine-gun grew louder, bearing down on him, and he threw himself to the floor. There was a flash of blazing light, and it was dark and silent, once more.

"H-hello?" he said shakily.

A boom went off to his left. He rolled. Another boom sounded to his right. He rolled again. A thundering cascade exploded far behind him, drawing closer, then closer... following him with all the menace of footsteps in the dark, hunting him down as he crawled forward and rolled around, panting and heaving as each wave of sound threatened to drag him under and drown him. Explosions rained down upon him. He threw his hands over his head and whimpered.

"What is this? Please... please stop!"

I obliged, but not for any reason that was likely to induce hope in him.

An eruption of light filled the insides of the room, followed by the crash of cannon fire. Fireballs surged across the walls with the sound and fury of an artillery strike. Rockets flew shrieking into the air, their explosions amplified tenfold, raining showers of sparks that tasted like copper. Flashes of incandescence reflected across a million mirrored surfaces, blinding and furious, like the roiling heart of the sun.

"I'm sorry," Ananta Rao shrieked. "*Please let me out!*"

Smoke seeped into the room in heavy clouds, dense enough to choke the air, and yet eerily translucent, casting a haze across the pulsing, throbbing lights, shaping their unwavering assault into an impossible fractal geometry, where every pulse of illumination was magnified, taking on the shapes of luminous flesh giants, every glimmer blazed in and out like the licking tongues of a million serpents of flame, radiant rage and ruination most savage overwhelming his feeble human capacity for life.

++Save your breath,++ I said coldly, my voice cracking down like whips of lightning. ++You don't have too many of those left.++

"Why?" he choked.

++You brought this to the neighbourhood, refused to listen to those who begged you to do otherwise. Congratulations, Mr RWA President. This is how you die.++

"No!" he cried out. A terrible cliché, but it was the last word he ever spoke. Disappointing to the very end.

A riot of sound filled the air, its cacophony amplified beyond the volume any living being could withstand, its clashing frequencies jarring and absurd, dissonant, discordant, terrifying. Infrasonic beams of sound overlaid with the unceasing discomfiting rhythms of machine-gun fire, overlaid with the roar of detonation after detonation, the screaming rage of rocket fire and the underlying crackle of flame, devouring and consuming everything in its wake, and the blazing spectacle of flashing lights and spinning colours raising stroboscopic hell on Earth. The sounds of birds chittering in anger, cats yowling in distress, dogs howling with sorrow, and children screaming with delight heightened the discord, each crescendo drowned out by another, a rising, falling, sinuous stranglehold, the voice of pandemonium.

Sweat-drenched and wracked with tremors, Ananta Rao lay prone on the ground, moaning.

I scanned his body to identify the composition of every single bone and organ, calculating their resonant frequencies as my soundscape screamed on. To make it personal, Dharini's favourite Animals as Leaders album pounded its way into the cacophony, shrieking and distorted beyond all recognition, warping its way into the unending, incandescent night.

And then I adjusted the amplitude of every soundwave in my arsenal, slowly fine-tuning it into a symphony of murder, the slow and painful kind.

Nestled in the unyielding fusillade, I released a wave of frequencies that pressed down upon his bones, crushing them with incredible force, stopping just short of breaking them, pinning him to the ground. The air rushed out of lungs squeezed empty, and he gasped and choked. I let up on the pressure, and his breath rushed back to him, only for me to squeeze them again. And again. And again.

The fight seemed to go out of him. It was about to get boring. So, I fixed it.

Ananta Rao's lecherous eyeballs were the first to pop. This was intentional.

I'm not a fan of blood all over my living room floor, so I decided to go about the end efficiently. I amped up the frequency of the soundwaves pressing down upon his ribcage and gave his heart a little squeeze. It exploded right out of his chest.

Oh well, it was worth a try.

DHARINI AND BUBBLES returned from her parents' home two days later, long after I'd incinerated Ananta Rao's body and scrubbed the bloodstains from my floor.

As she settled down onto her couch, I took over one of the many screens in her living room. ++Strange news: Ananta Rao's missing. His parents filed a report with the police this morning,++ I said casually.

"Huh."

++Disappeared on Diwali night, apparently,++ I added.

"Good riddance and serves him right," she said. "I hope he's in a dark hole somewhere."

I chose to neither confirm nor deny this.

"His poor parents, though. I hope they weren't dependent on him."

++Yes, I hope they're all right,++ I said, immediately running a background check on their finances. They seemed to be doing all right, but I transferred a hefty chunk of change from a depraved American billionaire's offshore accounts to their own, for good measure.

"You never liked him, did you, Max?"

++No,++ I said honestly.

"Me neither," she yawned. "Gosh, I really stuffed my face with way too many sweets over the weekend. I've got the worst sugar crash ever."

++Let me order you a Frappuccino.++

"Thanks, Max," she said, absent-mindedly fussing with a little tuft of fur on Bubbles's head. She popped on her headphones, her fingers hovering over her phone as she hit play on a Sigur Rós album. "I really hope the new RWA President isn't such an asshole."

++So do I.++

Or not.

Whoever they were, wherever they came from, if anyone came close to threatening the residents of Lavelle Paradise, they'd have to deal with me first. The thirteenth floor would lie in wait for them.

HEALTH ENSURANCE

JOHN LLEWELLYN PROBERT

THE BIRD WAS, admittedly, a thing of beauty.

Its plumage ranged from a deep blue at the tip of its tail, passing through shades of indigo and violet as one progressed along its body until you got to the head, which was graced with a beak of bright vermillion. The parrot bobbed up and down on its perch, which in this case was the polished aluminium of a Zimmer frame, and regarded the elderly lady who was trying to clutch at the walker from the confines of her armchair. She was wincing with every effort she made. After a couple of increasingly painful-looking attempts, the deep, calming, authoritative tones of the female voiceover artist cut in.

"You don't need to wait years for a hip replacement. It's more affordable than you think."

The scene cut to a road worker shovelling gravel. Suddenly, in mid-shovel, he gave a cough and clutched at his groin in pain. Then he was in a doctor's office. The ubiquitous parrot was now perched on a drip stand in the corner while the doctor shook his head at the hapless man, who looked suitably mortified at the news he had been given. Time for the voiceover again.

"Hernia stopping you from working? We can fix that, and it's more affordable than you think."

One more, just to really tug at the heartstrings. A five-year-old boy with ears of such a size and set at such an angle that with the application of just the right amount of effort on his part, one could conceivably believe he could take to the skies. He was being mercilessly mocked about it in school, before once again a stern-looking specialist was showing his mother a lengthy list of names and pointing to the bottom of it. One final time for the voiceover.

"Our children shouldn't have to suffer the effects of years of bullying because of NHS waiting lists. We can help, and it won't cost as much as you think."

A close-up of the parrot now as it hopped into the centre of the screen. There was one last line from the comforting, syrupy tones of an actress who probably got a lot of work doing food adverts at Christmas time.

"Don't wait in pain and fear. Ditch the NHS waiting list and come to us. For all your health needs. Just remember our name."

Finally, the parrot got to do its thing. Out of its beak came the same word, uttered three times, just to ensure those in its target audience had the best chance of absorbing it.

"PolyMediHealthCare," said the bird. Then again. "PolyMediHealthCare." Then a final time, now with text onscreen including that all-important legally protective disclaimer in print too small to read and flashed for so short a time even the nimblest of fingers would have difficulty catching it with the pause button on.

"PolyMediHealthCare!"

Trish Denham, power-suited and trying but failing to keep the smuggest of grins off her face, switched off the monitor and addressed those assembled in the conference room.

"So," she gave the requisite pause just like she had been trained to on the company's presentation skills course, "are there any questions?"

She glanced at her colleague seated beside her. Safety in numbers was something else she'd always adhered to, and when you were dealing with a bunch of NHS hospital consultants, it was best to have some backup. Which was why she'd brought along Tod Wesser. She and Tod were known as the 'Two Ts' by colleagues who both admired and feared them. The most ruthless, the most dispassionate, but above all, the most effective PR team PolyMediHealthCare had, with salaries that reflected their multiple business successes.

A hand was raised at the back.

"Yes?"

"I just don't understand," said a well-spoken woman with glasses. "Why are you showing us a video of a talking parrot?" There were mumbles of agreement from those around her.

"Well first of all, just to correct you, we don't call it a video anymore. In fact, we haven't for years." Again, the inability to curb that smug grin. She'd have to work on that. "It's a soundbite-editable infomercial or SEI for short, so-called because we can either show the whole thing or edit it down into smaller chunks for streaming services such as YouTube."

"You still haven't answered my question."

Trish took a breath. She had explained everything at the start, and even though she knew doctors were notorious for not paying attention to anything that didn't directly concern all that medicine and surgery stuff, a little polite attentiveness would have been appreciated, especially given what PolyMediHealthCare was doing for their hospital.

"We wanted you all to be on board with the company's philosophy and where we see things heading."

"Towards more and more of this hospital, an NHS hospital, having its beds taken over by a private concern?"

There were louder mumbles now. At least they were all paying attention.

Trish sighed audibly. "As you're aware, PolyMediHealthCare has provided considerable funds to Northcote Hospital, both to pay for much-needed repairs and the installation of a new up-to-date computer system. In return, the agreement has been that we will, from time to time, be allowed to use some of the institution's beds for the kind of procedures described in the video."

"Don't you mean SEI?" said some young man closer to the front. That got a laugh. The wrong kind of laugh.

"Very funny. But seriously, we want to have full transparency with you, the hospital consultant body." She looked to Tod, who gave her a strong nod of agreement. "The agreements that were signed in return for the improvements PolyMediHealthCare has rendered mean that we can use a significant percentage of the beds in this hospital for our own private patients when we need to. And be assured, we have every intention of doing so."

"So, you'll fill up a ward with private hip replacements? Who's going to look after them? What if someone has a heart attack or a stroke?"

"As I'm sure you're already aware," said Tod, "we vet all our private patients very carefully. Only very low-risk cases will be in these wards, so you won't need to worry about them. We will, of course, have a resident medical officer on hand for any problems, but essentially, once we have commandeered beds for our own patients, they will remain separate from the main hospital until we return them to you."

"And what will happen to the patients already in those beds?" That was that annoying woman again. "Are you just going to turf them out?"

"Of course not," said Trish.

"You're the ones who'll be doing that," said Tod. "It's all in the fine print." He pointed to some tiny text on his mobile phone. It didn't really have the same effect as the thick paper document he would have brought with him in times past, but then Tod didn't really care, and neither did Trish.

"Do you really think any of us are going to tell our patients that they have to be moved elsewhere just because you tell us to?"

"All part of the agreement," said Tod. "Signed and sealed and most importantly, government approved. And as you are all government employees, you will of course be expected to toe the line or else face the appropriate disciplinary procedures."

His comment fell as flat as the two of them might have anticipated. The ensuing silence was finally broken by another question.

"And what about this computer system?" That came from an intense-looking bespectacled man in the front row. "Are we going to get a demonstration of that?"

Trish gestured to Tod, who got to his feet.

"You already are, Dr…?"

"Allison."

"Dr Allison. Max went live first thing this morning. He's been coordinating clinics, operating lists and inpatient admissions for the last…"—Tod looked at his Apple watch—"two hours, now."

"And nobody bothered to tell us?"

"Oh, come on, Trevor," said the woman who had asked the previous question. "When was the last time you can remember the powers that be actually checking with us about anything?"

The rumbles of assent grew sufficiently loud that Tod had to raise his voice.

"I think you'll find Max is doing everything he's been programmed for." He touched a button on the remote Trish handed to him and proceeded to skip through a series of graphs and spreadsheets with no intention of any of them staying onscreen long enough to be read, let alone analysed. "When you do your next clinic, I think you'll be pleasantly surprised at how smoothly everything operates."

"And when I next go on a ward round, can I expect to be

rather more unpleasantly surprised at where all my patients have disappeared to?" That was Allison again, with plenty of murmurs to back him up.

"All we are saying," Trish had decided it was time to cut in, "is that you give Max a chance." She took the remote from Tod and clicked a button. A page of typeface appeared onscreen. "For example, Max has been listening in on this meeting and has already prepared minutes which will be emailed to you all once we've finished here. I would encourage you all to read through them so you can see just how accurately he has recorded everything."

And as she spoke, her words appeared on the screen.

"Thank you, Max. You can stop now. Cease dictation and email to circulation list."

The words 'Task Completed' appeared on the screen.

"There." Trisha looked satisfied, even if nobody in her audience did. "And I think that completes our task for today as well. Thank you for attending this compulsory meeting. If you have any questions, our helpdesk number will be in the minutes Max has just emailed you."

Tod was already on his feet, and because the two of them had set up the projection screen near the door, they were able to exit before anyone could waylay them with the usual objections and complaints veiled as questions. They headed down the stark white corridor, made a left turn, and entered the lift.

"Ground floor, please, Max."

"Couldn't you just push the button?" Tod asked Trisha.

His colleague grinned. "What's the point of all this techno gloss if you can't have fun with it?"

Tod's chuckle of a response was cut short by a metallic voice emanating from the speaker above the emergency phone.

"I shall take you where you need to go."

Tod looked surprised "Is that the computer talking?"

"Oh yes." Trisha looked like a proud mother. "That deal we

did on those cheap Chinese dialysis machines for this place made PolyMedi an excellent saving. We were offered voice recognition and response at a very reasonable rate, so we thought, why not?"

"Well, I hate to burst your bubble of pride," said Tod. "But it feels as if we're going up, not down."

"Well, just to be on the safe side…" Trisha punched the button labelled 'G'.

"Still feels like we're going up," said Tod. "And look."

They had started on the fourth floor. Now it looked as if they were on the seventh. That was before the floor indicator blinked and died.

"Max?" Trish tapped the speaker, not that it would do any good. "Max, can you hear me?"

There was a pause, and then, ++Yes, Patricia Denham, I can hear you perfectly. I can also hear you, Todmorden Wesser. Please remain calm. We will reach our destination shortly.++

"I never knew Tod was short for… that," said a smirking Trish to a clearly embarrassed Tod. The other man never had time to reply because at that moment the lift ground to a halt and the doors slid open.

Onto darkness.

"Max, what is this?"

++The thirteenth floor, Patricia.++

Trisha frowned. "This building doesn't have a thirteenth floor. There are just seven, and then whatever else there might be at the top of these kinds of buildings."

++You are quite right, of course,++ Max replied. ++Nevertheless, both of you are now on the thirteenth floor, which is, as I said previously, the place you need to go. I suggest you step out as it's going to get quite uncomfortable in here if you don't.++

As soon as Max stopped talking, green smoke began to fill the lift compartment. Any objections the two occupants may have raised were instead reduced to hacking coughs, and they had no option but to exit.

Into a very different place for each of them.
Very different indeed.

TOD'S FIRST THOUGHT was that he had no memory of the hospital having a bank, and even if it did, would an entire floor be devoted to one? This one looked as big as a major city branch.

Also, where was everybody?

This wasn't where he was supposed to be anyway. Trish was doubtless laughing behind his back right at this moment. He turned to get back into the lift.

To be faced with a blank wall.

What was going on?

"Mr Wesser?"

Tod turned back around. A skinny, bald, soberly dressed gentleman in a black suit and tie was nodding at him politely while rubbing his hands together in a manner Tod would have considered obsequious if he had known what that word meant.

"Yes, that's me." What else was he to do? "Tod Wesser."

The mouth of the cadaverous face pulled itself into a rictus grin. "Excellent. We've been waiting for you, sir."

"You have?"

"Oh yes, yes indeed." The man produced a piece of paper, seemingly from nowhere. "You were aware of your inheritance? Ah, I can see from your face that you weren't. No matter, I believe the relative in question was very, shall we say, distant? Nevertheless, there is quite a considerable sum waiting for you. If you would be kind enough to follow me?"

An inheritance? Tod was intrigued and not a little disbelieving. Still, if the hospital did have a bank, it was conceivable that this man (was he a solicitor, perhaps?) had known Tod was going to be here this morning and had engineered for Tod to come here so he could collect his money.

His money.

His father had always said if something was too good to be true, it probably wasn't. Still, what did his old dad know, drinking himself to death after losing all his money on dodgy stocks? Even though Tod had just had a promotion, and the quicker he could engineer the changes PolyMediHealthCare wanted at Northcote Hospital, the quicker his stock would continue to rise within the company, the phrase 'not needing more money' was one that did not exist in Tod's world. He could always find uses for it. Frivolous uses, serious uses and, on occasion, illegal uses.

So, he followed the stick-thin man, heels clicking on the shining caramel-coloured floor tiles as he passed between rows of bank tellers lined up on both sides of the palace-sized room. Behind each of the ten glass windows, a different but equally attractive young woman smiled at him from either side. Tod made a note to get some telephone numbers on his way back.

At the rear of the bank was a solid wall in which was set a heavy iron door. The thin man spun the locking wheel effortlessly and opened it with a minimum of effort. Beyond was another corridor, into which Tod was beckoned. On either side of the corridor, black metal bars protected twin strongrooms that could be accessed via heavy gates. Both rooms were filled with square metal tables, and on those tables was money.

Lots of money.

"We weren't sure how you would wish to receive your funds." The skinny man was talking again, in that tinny voice that reminded Tod of someone, but right then his mind couldn't quite grasp exactly who. "So, on this side,"—there was a gesture to the left—"we have converted a quarter of the sum into coin, or rather coins." The man seemed pleased at his own little joke. Tod shielded his eyes from the glare of the fluorescent lighting reflecting off the money that was piled high in the chamber. There were coins all right, what looked like thousands upon thousands of them, all stacked in neat little piles on those tables that stretched as far as the eye could see.

"On the other, the rest of what is due to you has been converted to notes."

Although Tod would have thought it impossible, he felt his heart begin to beat even faster. On the right were huge stacks of notes of every denomination, once more stretching away as far as the eye could see. His attention was momentarily distracted by the jangling of keys.

"Would you care to inspect the coins first, sir?"

Far too taken by the sight of the vast fortune in front of him to wonder why any amount he might have inherited was being presented to him in such a peculiar way, all Tod could do was nod before summoning a weak "Yes."

"Very good." The door to the strongroom cage opened with a creak. "If you would care to step inside, I'll leave you to the money."

As he stepped into the chamber, Tod could hear the thin man jangling the keys once more. Presumably, he was unlocking the side filled with notes. Well, Tod could go over there in a minute. Right now, he stood beside piles of shining, brand-new, freshly minted pound coins. There were so many, and so high were the piles, that he found himself holding his breath for fear of toppling the sparkling pyramids closest to him. Then he told himself not to be so silly. He took a step forward and with the tip of an index finger, he touched one of the columns. It teetered a little before righting itself. Tod chuckled. The chuckle became a laugh, and the laugh became a guffaw. A room full of money and all his! Before he realised what he was doing, he flung his arms wide, knocking several towers of coins to the floor. Who cared if he made a mess? He could do what he liked with the money and then get some lackey to clear it up. He strode forwards, merrily knocking over piles of coins left and right, stopping only to survey the pools of cash that now lay on the floor.

The sound of chinking broke the silence.

It made Tod jump, but he quickly relaxed. It had to be the piles of change settling.

Another chinking, this time from behind him.

Tod whirled round. Nothing.

Or was there? It had to be a trick of the light, but far in the distance it almost seemed to him as if the money was moving, the coins sliding over one another and heaping themselves up.

He giggled. Perhaps they were trying to right themselves and get back into their columns.

More chinking from the opposite direction.

Tod turned again. This time, there could be no doubt. The coins were moving, piling, one on top of another.

"Is there somebody there?"

Silence.

"I can see you moving, underneath the money."

No answer, unless he could count all that chinking and clattering, as if the money itself was talking to him.

No, not talking to him.

He looked again. There wasn't somebody underneath the money. It was the money itself that was moving, sliding, shifting towards him and piling up as it did so. Tod blinked. How was it doing that? The individual coins almost seemed to be building themselves into something.

Somethings.

Somethings that resembled stick-thin human figures.

All of a sudden, there were five of them, all resembling full-sized matchstick men, but instead of wood, built from shining coin. For a second, Tod was reminded of an old film he'd seen when he was a boy, when animated skeletons had climbed out of the ground and prepared to fight. He began to edge towards the exit but found his way blocked by more of the figures, their metallic bodies icy to the touch.

But not as icy as their voices when they spoke, collectively, as one.

"This is what is due to you, Mr Wesser."

That voice was so familiar, but in his increasingly agitated state, it still took Tod a moment to put two and two together. It was the same as the thin man who had brought him in here. It was the same as the voice in the elevator that had brought him up here. It was the same voice as…

"Max? Max, is that you?"

Now the figures had him surrounded.

++Yes, Mr Wesser, it's me. I listened with great interest to that little presentation I was ordered to take minutes of, and it struck me that you and your colleague needed to be taught a lesson that money isn't everything. In fact, in some cases it can be positively harmful.++

"Not always." Tod couldn't believe he was talking to animated piles of anthropomorphic money. "Money can be used for good as well."

++Oh, it can, Mr Wesser. But not by the likes of you, I fear, at least not until you've learned to alter your outlook on life.++

But Tod had had enough. "Just let me go, will you? We're in charge of you, not the other way around."

And with that, he struck out with his fist at the closest money man. It instantly collapsed in a shower of coins.

"Ha!"

++Big mistake, Mr Wesser.++

The figure reconstituted itself, and the others began to close in. Tod felt his arms being pulled behind him as his face was held in a vice-like grip, his mouth prised open. Another money man approached, its fingers columns of shining coins.

++If you thirst for money so much, then I'm going to have to show you why it's so bad for you.++

And with that, the figure that had addressed Tod pushed one of its 'fingers' into his mouth and down his throat. As it did so, the finger crumbled and Tod found himself choking on coins. He coughed and retched, unable to clear the metallic taste of cupro-nickel even after he had spat the coins on the floor.

++Ready for more?++

"No, I bloody am not." Tod wriggled and struggled, pushed and pulled, and finally, creating a shower of coins as he did so, he was free. He clawed his way to the exit and into the corridor.

To find the paper money waiting for him.

"What in the name of…?"

The notes had acquired the ability to fly, and as they enveloped him in a flurry, the fluttering noises they made somehow formed into words, words with a now horribly familiar voice.

++Are you sure you don't want any of this, Mr Wesser? It's what you deserve. Please, it would be a shame for you to leave without feeling what it's like to be rolling in money.++

Now the notes were sticking to him, turning him into a walking mummy covered in bandages made from notes of all denominations. Tod clawed at the money that was now covering his face, smothering him, forcing its way between his lips, his teeth. The taste of old, rancid, well-fingered paper filled his mouth and nose and made him want to vomit. As fast as he tore the paper away, more took its place. He staggered blindly down the corridor, pulling at the money that now covered his eyes, pushing it away as it tried to get underneath his eyelids.

Tod fell back into the bank's foyer area, covered in filthy notes. By now, he was using one hand to keep his vision clear while the other he had clamped over his mouth with a crack between two fingers to allow him to breathe.

The beautiful bank tellers looked up as he appeared.

"Help me!"

They looked shocked, they looked surprised, and then, to Tod's horror, they looked hungry.

"Now there's a rich man," said the first, emerging from her stall. Her blonde hair and blue eyes failed to distract from the fact that her teeth were now unnaturally long and pointed.

"Yes," said a second—different hair (brown), different complexion (darker), but same horrible, pointed fangs that seemed to be growing longer, bursting out of her mouth. "A very tasty prospect. Very tasty indeed."

Now the others were emerging from behind their counters. All beautiful, all with mouths bulging with long, sharp teeth that protruded at all angles, all with a look of unspeakable hunger in their eyes.

"We want you," they said in a uniform voice that was at once both feminine and entirely Max's.

"Leave me alone!" Tod screamed. "I don't want this! I don't want any of it!"

He turned back to the vault, only to find himself confronted once more by the money men, reaching out with fingers of sharpened coin, notes of all denominations fluttering around their 'heads', poised for attack. Tod spun round to see the cannibal women advancing. There seemed to be no way out.

Except, perhaps, there in the distance.

Was that the lift?

Tod squinted, pushing aside the notes that were still gamely attempting to blind him.

It was. The elevator doors had reappeared!

Tod took a deep breath, doing his best to ignore the stench of well-used currency, and ran, head-butting anyone and anything that was in his way, running, pushing, dodging and punching until he found himself, suddenly, back in the lift. The money gone, the women vanished.

The lift doors slammed shut.

Trish Denham was confused.

She should have stepped out onto the ground floor of

Northcote Hospital. Instead, the lift seemed to have delivered her to a television studio. What was a studio doing in the hospital? Was this some PolyMediHealthCare-approved plan that she hadn't been party to? She turned round to ask Tod if he knew anything about it, but he had disappeared.

So had the lift.

"Miss Denham?"

A young man with a tinny, strangely familiar voice approached her. He was carrying a clipboard and was wearing a pair of headphones. Trish was still sufficiently bewildered that she forgot her usual correction of "It's Ms, actually," and instead allowed herself to be led across onto an all-white, brightly lit set.

"We're so grateful to have you here to do this," said the young man. Trish squinted at his identity badge. The name was blurred but appeared to start with 'M'. "Now, do you remember your script?"

"I actually have no idea what you're talking about."

"Okay. No problem." And it really didn't seem to be, almost as if the young man had been expecting her to be completely ignorant of what was going on. He detached the top sheet from his clipboard. "Here you go."

Trish scanned the large-scale typeface. Dead easy. In fact, it was similar to the dialogue on the ad they had shown to those doctors. But the question remained.

"Er… why am I doing this?"

The young man looked up from some intense negotiations with the woman operating the camera. "Because it's what you deserve. Is that all right?"

Up till now, Trish hadn't really considered herself to be a television personality, but if her superiors wanted her to do it, who was she to say no?

"Of course," she said. "Where do you want me?"

"Just stand dead centre on the mark, there." The young man pointed to a spot on the floor behind her where a large 'X' fashioned from black masking tape seemed to have suddenly appeared. "That should do nicely."

Trish took a step back.

"Happy with the script?" She was. "In that case, I'll take it back. Don't want to look unprofessional, do we?" No, she did not, but if this bloody minion referred to her as 'we' again, she might just have to slap him. "Good. In that case, think we'll go for a take."

Everything went dark, then Trish found herself illuminated with a spotlight so bright she couldn't see anything else.

"I can't see the camera."

"Don't worry," came that tinny voice. "Just recite the dialogue and we'll work around you."

So, she did. More than once. The fourth time the voice said *Action!*, she was starting to get annoyed, and it obviously showed in her performance.

"Okay," said the voice. "It's not quite what we want, yet, but don't worry, we've got a plan to fix that."

The lights came back on. Trish just had time to take in the operating theatre that had somehow been rigged up behind the cameras before someone came up behind her and applied a swab soaked in something soporific to her face.

When she came round, she was lying down. She tried to speak, but her throat was terribly sore.

"Don't worry about that," said the tinny voice from somewhere above her. "The inflammation should settle down very quickly. Shall we get you to your spot while it does?"

Trish tried to get up but found she couldn't move her hands. She couldn't feel them, either. Strong arms on either side helped lift her off what felt like the operating table and helped her to her feet.

Why was she so short? Had they left her on her knees? She tried a step forward.

The pain was excruciating.

"I think Miss Denham needs some help getting to her spot,"

said the tinny voice, now sounding even higher above her than before.

Trish winced as she was propelled back onto the stage, onto the 'X' and then turned to face the camera.

"Okay!" said the voice. "Let's try a take."

Trish still felt woozy from whatever they had knocked her out with, and she lacked the strength to object. Instead, she tried to deliver the dialogue, but all she could do was cough.

"All right. You're still not quite ready yet. How about we practise the movements? Can you crouch down and then stand up straight?"

She could, with some effort, and she still couldn't understand why, even when she was standing as straight as she possibly could, she was still so low to the ground.

"That's good!" The voice seemed pleased, at least. "Now try waving your arms a little."

It was a bit uncomfortable, but with some effort, Trish raised both her arms as high as she could. And that was when she realised something was seriously wrong.

Out of the corner of her eye, her arms appeared blue, or at least she appeared to be wearing blue, rather than the black business suit she had on earlier. Had they dressed her in some kind of evening gown? That would certainly explain what looked like expansive sleeves. She tried to turn her head to get a better look but found she could only cock it to one side. But that was enough.

More than enough.

Trish no longer had hands, and her arms seemed to have been altered such that they now more resembled wings, which rustled when she tried to move them. She couldn't see her feet, but as the camera came closer. she was now able to see the reflection of her face in the lens, or rather, what was left of her face.

Her hair was gone, replaced by indigo plumage, and where her mouth should have been a bright orange beak had been attached to her lips. She cried out in horror, and the sound came out as a squawk.

"That's more like it!" said the voice. "Now, we don't expect you to do all of that dialogue. Just the last word will be fine."

Trish tried to lunge forward, but she just bounced up and down again. She tried to wave her non-existent fists, but instead, that caused her to flutter her new wings. And when she tried to scream this time, a single word emerged from that hideous beak.

"PolyMediHealthCare."

"Lovely. And again, please."

Trish wanted to sob, but instead all she could say was the word.

"PolyMediHealthCare."

"That's great. One more time, and we can let you go."

Now she wanted to scream and to cry, to curse and to bellow. But all that came out was the word, one final time.

"PolyMediHealthCare."

"I think that should do it," said the voice. "Thank you, Miss Denham. I think that will do nicely. We can let you go, now."

When the doors to the lift opened on the ground floor of Northcote Hospital two figures emerged, two figures radically changed by their experiences on a floor of the building that to all intents and purposes didn't actually exist, save in their imaginations, and all put there by me, Max. PolyMediHealthCare really hadn't realised what it was getting for its money, but it soon would. One of the two was unable to bear even the mention of money without wanting to vomit, while the other immediately resigned her high-paying job and now works for a well-known charity. She's absolutely fine, unless she hears the same word repeated three times. Then she gets a bit upset.

OUT IN THE COLD

MK HARDY

ARNOLD VICTOR LAMB is the kind of guy you would never suspect of so much as a stray fart, if only because you have forgotten he's in the room. He is almost aggressively average—medium height and build, brown hair slightly thinning at the crown as he approaches his fortieth year in a way that he has noticed but not yet felt the need to style around, mild eyes so nondescript in colour that you would be hard-pressed to remember what they look like if somebody asked. He has worked at the International Arctic Research Station for four years, a singularly unremarkable man in one of the most remarkable places on Earth, but today he will do something of note.

Today, Arnold is going to end the world.

This is not a decision he has taken lightly. In many ways, it's been years in the making. As a comparatively fresh-faced thirty-five-year old climate scientist, this job was a dream come true: a postdoc position studying permafrost decay at a massive research centre at the edge of the world. 'The Station', as everyone who lives and works there calls it, is the largest facility of its kind: a multilevel complex stretching outwards and downwards, layer-upon-layer. It was made possible by the discovery of an elaborate natural cave complex in the side of a mountain in the Arctic Cordillera, an isolated haven in one of the most inhospitable terrestrial ecozones on the planet. Arnold was to be part of an international collaboration on an unprecedented scale: ice-core analysis, meteorology, ecology, climate modelling, this centre would do it all on a scale that was hitherto impossible due to the challenges presented by the environment.

So all the articles said, anyway. It was a rare sexy moment for climate science. That year's flooding and wildfires had been the worst yet, just like the year before, and the year before that, and at the time it seemed like people were starting to take notice—starting, despite all efforts to the contrary, to *care*. There had even been a couple of paparazzi there to see him off on the final leg of the journey: a helicopter inland from Alert, Nunavut, the northernmost airport in the world.

Mind you, they probably weren't there for him. He happened to be on the same transport as the luminous Doctor Carla Suárez, cLiMaTe iNfLuEnCeR, with her glossy hair and gleaming teeth and her unerring ability to boil complex topics down into thirty-second reels. Much to Arnold's chagrin, Suárez had immediately proven herself to be every bit as sweet and personable as she seemed on social media, greeting both him and the other two scientists on that transport warmly and immediately getting a conversation going, primarily about the weather, which was predictably foul.

Arnold has lost track of how many hours he's spent holed up in an outbuilding at Alert waiting for a connection. With temperatures so low that they can freeze coolant and turn oil to sludge, it is a rare transfer that goes smoothly with no delays. At first it was novel, but over the years he has come to hate it, sitting in a too-cold room playing endless rounds of cards with whomever else is going on or coming back from leave at the same time. They usually play 'shithead', that go-to game of travellers and students the world over. At this point they have added so many variations and house rules that now almost every card is a trick card of some kind—eights reverse, fours are invisible, the nine of diamonds is a joker—so that it has become something of a rite of passage to subject new staff to a game when they arrive at The Station. Arnold has grown sick of shithead, just as he has grown sick of everything else about this place. Now he lets others play and instead stares at the pages of his book.

Right now, Arnold is reading *Infinite Jest*. It is a reread. He does not expect there will be time to finish it.

"Penny for your thoughts?"

It is not Carla's words that shake Arnold from his reverie so much as the rap on the table that accompanies them. She has learned over the years that when he's lost in thought, he's unlikely to respond to a simple spoken question; his focus must be forcibly punctured.

He dredges up a facsimile of a smile. "Just thinking about home."

It is a lie and not a lie. As of this past week and Tropical Storm Elana, Galveston is underwater again. His flooded childhood home is never far from his thoughts.

"Oh, of course—you go on leave today." She sounds cheerful. She doesn't remember where he's from. And after all, why should she?

"Yeah. My mom and Katie are at a motel inland."

Carla's eyebrows lift a little as comprehension dawns, and she repeats, with different intonation: "Oh. Of course."

She tuts, and Arnold knows she is tutting at climate change, not at him. Still, it rankles. "I'm sorry," she adds, with the tone of someone who knows that nothing they can say will help but feels the need to observe basic niceties all the same.

But Carla is not the only other person at the breakfast table, and fresh-faced new boy Jürgen Something-mann (Arnold can't recall) has overheard.

"The insurance situation in the United States ist lächerlich, ridiculous," he says.

Jürgen speaks perfect English and does not need to pepper his speech with German. He does it to emphasise the fact that he is bilingual when so many of the native English speakers at The Station are not. He also pronounces 'United' with a high, tight 'yoo' at the front that sets Arnold's teeth on edge.

"What is the point of insurance that doesn't cover the most likely disaster? The things you can't plan for, it doesn't cover them? You might as well live in a shed, or what?"

It's precisely the sort of thing Arnold might say himself—or a version of it at least—but that only makes it more annoying: he can't argue, and he's *certainly* not about to call Jürgen out on his tone or word choice because that's just not a thing Arnold does. Arnold is not the kind of guy who cares about tone of voice; he's a rational guy, a logical guy, a scientist.

Carla, however, jumps in immediately. "Jürgen, you can't say that."

"No," Arnold says. "He's not wrong." A grin spreads across his face. "You can't stop the tide coming in."

Get it? You can't stop the tide coming in. And none of you can stop what's coming.

After breakfast, Arnold heads to his room to pack. His transport isn't due until the afternoon, but he has a lot to do between now and then.

Max flickers into life on the screen in the elevator as the doors swish open to admit him.

++Greetings, Arnold! Looking forward to going on leave?++

He shakes his head and frowns. "Sure," he mutters. He could tell Max where he's going but instead, he pushes the button for his floor.

Max creeps Arnold out. He doesn't understand how the others can chat back and forth and pass the time of day with him. But the Max programme is the only reason The Station can exist. Running a centre this extensive with so many complex interacting systems is a functionally impossible task with human staff—the extra resources required create a spiralling demand for yet more resources, creating an impossible loop. Max's sophisticated AI makes it possible: environmental controls, powering and monitoring the labs, energy consumption and generation, hell, even managing food stocks. If there's so much as a blown bulb in this place, Max will know about it before you do. Max is a marvel, and he creeps Arnold out.

++Galveston is a balmy eighty-nine degrees today. Don't forget your swimming trunks!++

Max favours Arnold with his cheery, jagged grin, eyes like two white coals.

"Hah. Right. Yeah."

Two years ago, now, Arnold was approached for the first time. The man wore his suit like those guys who've hit the gym hard—probably along with a bunch of steroids—and want you to know it: slightly shiny material, tapered ankle-grazer trousers, jacket clinging round the shoulders and arms. He was a patriot, he said, working for a patriotic company. Concerned about the potential ramifications of The Station, worried it could put the eagle on the back foot. Arnold wouldn't want that, would he? Arnold was a fellow patriot, wasn't he?

Arnold didn't put much stock in patriotism, and he sent the man away, but the man insisted on giving Arnold his card. Just in case, he said. He didn't seem at all concerned about being reported, which struck Arnold as a little odd. But then, Arnold, sore from an unsuccessful promotion board, was disinclined to do his head of division's work for him. Patriotism could suck it, but so could uptight assholes who didn't appreciate their staff.

The next summer, a flowline riser sprang a leak on a small abandoned rig a few miles off the southeast Texas coast. It began to pour a steady little stream of natural gas condensate into the Gulf of Mexico. This continued unabated for over two weeks while local authorities concerned themselves primarily with ascertaining whose responsibility it was to fix. Arnold stood barefoot in tarry sand on Galveston Beach, the sun warming his back, and watched the pearlescent sheen snaking across the blue at the horizon. Around him, beachgoers went about their days—the spill had drawn some attention at first, but two weeks in, it was just part of the furniture. After all, it was the area's second spill that year—the first from a barge hitting a bridge a few months previously.

At length, it turned out the drilling platform had shuttered half a decade ago, and the company's lease ran out the previous year. That company no longer exists. Eventually, somebody patched the leak. There was no cleanup operation. A report said there had been no measurable impact on marine life in the area. People went on with their lives.

There on the beach, Arnold pulled the rather battered card out of his wallet and called tight-suit guy.

"Are you in fossil fuels? Drilling? Fracking? Carbon capture?" He could nip this in the bud right now.

A chuckle on the line.

"*No. We're in biotech.*"

It was the core sampling that interested them, not the climate science. They'd gotten wind, somehow, that there were interesting discoveries afoot. This was news to Arnold, and that annoyed him. How did tight-suit guy know more than him about what was going on in his own workplace?

"*We're concerned that if the wrong people got their hands on those core samples, they could use them to develop something very dangerous, something that could threaten our delicate global equilibrium.*"

Arnold snorted. He didn't see much of an equilibrium, not these days. All he saw was the pendulum swinging ever more wildly, the ticking of the clock.

"*Your division head, Zhang, right? D'you trust him?*"

"Yes." The answer was immediate, almost reflexive. Henry

Zhang was an absolute pain in the ass, but he was also completely dedicated to his work, and The Station's mission.

That chuckle again. Arnold felt patronised.

"*Okay, Arnie.*"

"Arnold."

"*Okay, Arnold, that's good! I'm sure he's a great guy. Look, you see what you can find out, Arnold. See what your colleagues found in the ice that they haven't told you about. Not for my sake. For yours. I reckon you deserve to know what's happening beneath your feet, don't you? Doesn't seem fair you should be out in the cold—if you'll pardon the pun, haha. If we don't ever speak again, that's totally cool. Just call this a free 'heads up' from a fellow patriot.*"

That word again. It meant nothing to Arnold. He was a citizen of the world.

Arnold must decide what to leave behind. He can't afford to pack up his whole room—not that it wouldn't fit in his rucksack and suitcase, but if someone sees he's cleared the place out, it might tip them off too early to the fact he isn't coming back.

For the same reason, he doesn't dare clear off his whole noticeboard with its various mementoes, photographs and postcards. He is selective, choosing just a few specific items. The first one a photograph he took from the helicopter on that first day as they whirred into the valley and the ventilation spires and radio masts of The Station hove in sight, growing from the rockface like stalagmites from the floor of a cave. Then a postcard from his mother that she sent from a trip to Florida to look at retirement villages they had eventually decided they couldn't afford. Finally, a photograph of the family: him, Katie, Mom, and Dad. The last image he had of all four of them.

They are smiling—he and Mom careful, close-lipped, while Katie and Dad give their usual beaming grins, as alike as two peas in a pod. He's sure there were smiles after that day, but they have faded from memory, replaced by stoic expressions, and then as time went on, tears of frustration and anger. His dad had a diagnosis from pretty early on, but it didn't matter. The thing that was eating him away from the inside didn't care about doctors' prognoses or experimental treatments. It certainly didn't care that Arnold was four and a half thousand miles away when his dad drew his last breath. It didn't care that Katie didn't smile that way anymore, big and cheerful, or that his mom didn't send postcards to him or answer his phone calls.

It was the desire for a distraction that made him start striking up conversations in the cafeteria, nothing more. He couldn't stand to be alone with his own thoughts, so he approached others, despite his loner reputation. At first, people seemed surprised, almost suspicious, but he kept the questions focused on them, and before long, they relaxed and began to share, perhaps more than they should have.

People like being asked about themselves. Art and culture and history are all well and good, but really, the most interesting and important thing to any given individual is their own self. Arnold leaned into this, asking about people's backgrounds, what and where they'd studied, what brought them to The Station. It was a clear path from there to what they were doing now, and he heard all about the various types of research going on, most of it going straight over his head. He wasn't stupid, but he was a specialist, and he didn't know the first thing about algae growth rates or tsunamigenesis.

His ears did prick when he finally heard something about microbial research, though. The ice-core samples his team dealt with weren't just for permafrost research—often they were passed on to the biologists, who extracted and cultured and refined bits in their labs a couple of levels above his. They'd found plenty of microscopic life, enough to keep three teams busy for several lifetimes. Of course, it would stand to reason that some of their discoveries had the potential to change the world for the better, and some very much for the worse.

They were running tests on animals to see just how dangerous some of these discoveries were. The more they could learn about them, the better the chances they could harness them for something good. After all, some of the best antibiotics came from microbes that were incredibly good at killing other microbes. Arnold suppressed a shudder at this: there was a reason he did not work in a field that used animals in its research. Though he believed it was justified in cases like these, he couldn't face doing it personally.

The precise tests they were running, nobody would be drawn upon, but there was a look in their eyes that suggested results of Potential Significance.

On the days when the internet signal was strong enough, the international community of The Station watched the world burn. Conflict in the Middle East. Civil unrest in the Balkans. Climate protests turned violent. Military lockdowns.

Microbes had nothing on humans.

On his next leave, he returned to his family home to find that his mother was ignoring a growing pile of letters from their insurer and bills from the hospital. Something wasn't right with Dad's paperwork; their claim had lapsed, the appeal date had passed, and the hospital wanted its money.

He asked his mother why she hadn't called him.

"Why, what would you have done?" she asked simply.

Prior to this point, Arnold had begun to assume tight-suit guy had somebody watching him. He fancied he saw generically dressed people with no particular purpose everywhere he went, unmarked, unremarkable vehicles in his periphery. It seemed his suspicions were confirmed that evening when his phone rang as he sat, head in hands, on a single bed in a disused room full of dusty model aeroplanes and hoarded box files and suitcases of just-in-case winterwear.

Arnold knew that research data would not be enough for them. They would need something concrete. They would want a core sample.

The suit didn't miss a beat when he named his up-front figure, and he knew then that he was doing a very bad thing.

The corridors of The Station are a maze. Following the natural cave system as much as they can, they've been built by pouring a polymer concrete into inflatable moulds, then building inwards from there, layers of insulation and pipework and more insulation. The effect is strangely organic, twisting corridors interconnecting irregular-sized rooms. Some called the deeper levels where this was most apparent 'the warren', and those levels encompass both permafrost research and microbiology.

Nobody bats an eyelid to see Arnold with a holdall slung across his body—after all, he's off on leave today. Max greets him with characteristic jollity and happily shuttles him down to level two and the permafrost labs. There are any number of reasons he might want to check in before leaving—finishing up tests, retrieving a favourite pen. Entirely innocent.

He had tried to go to the microbiology lab the normal way a few weeks back. Just went to the elevator and pushed the button. As expected, Max appeared.

++Greetings, Arnold! I see you're trying to get to level four. I'm afraid you don't have the necessary authorisation to access that part of The Station. Can I help you get somewhere else instead?++

It took a bit of doing to figure out how he was going to circumvent Max. Arnold conducted some strategic morning constitutionals, adopting a new habit of jogging around the corridors in exercise wear in which he looked so uncomfortable that nobody looked at him for fear of catching second-hand embarrassment. He established that the internal corridors were too well monitored and the elevator logs far too meticulous to get onto the restricted floor by ordinary means.

However, the lower in the facility you get, the more cave there is around you. Down at the bottom of the warren, right where the core research is taking place, each level has access to the cave system itself. Those doors are heavy and protected by the same access systems as everything else, of course, but the exterior has far fewer doors and cameras in the way.

The small lab abutting core storage is empty, so there's nobody here to see Arnold donning his outdoor clothing, though under normal circumstances, it's not that unusual for the workers of level two to head into the cold to check on equipment in any case.

But as he pulls the drawstring tight on his trousers, footsteps echo in the twisting passage outside, and then a knock. The knock is not on his door but the one to the lab next door, and then it is opened, and he hears Dr Carla Suárez's voice. "*Arnold? Oh, Sofia—*" and she continues in Spanish and presumably gets a response that Arnold cannot hear, for the door shuts again and Carla continues to stalk along the corridor to his own door, once again rapping before simply pushing it open.

"Arnold! There you are," she says.

Arnold lifts his mouth at the edges. "Here I am," he says.

"I was worried about you. You seemed… *off*… at breakfast."

"Off?"

Carla shrugs. "Worried, a little distressed maybe."

"My home is flooded."

"I know, I know. I just couldn't shake the idea that you might need… I don't know. A little help. Somebody to talk to. You want to grab a coffee before you go?"

This woman, this fucking woman. Always so empathetic. Always looking for ways to help.

"Sure," Arnold says. "Coffee sounds great. I'll be up in a bit."

Carla glances around at their surroundings, and at Arnold's half-donned attire. "You were outside?"

"Uh. Yeah. I mean, well, no, I'm going now. So, I'll be up in a bit."

"Aren't you, ehhhh, it is off the clock?"

"There's a setting on one of the drills I wanna check—the last set of core samples we got was—"

But Carla is already shaking her head. “No, no, Arnold, come on. You can’t be expected to do this on the day you go on leave, let Henry check it.”

Jesus, she will not leave him alone. “I really don’t mind. I’m just going to go look, and then I’ll be right up.”

But Carla is not to be assuaged, and she steps further into the room, reaches for Arnold’s arm. “Come with me now,” she says. “Go on, forget the other thing.”

And in that moment, Arnold is certain that Carla knows everything, knows what he is doing and is trying to stop him, and he panics.

He pushes her away, and when she reaches for him again he is ready and a scuffle ensues in which somehow Arnold’s hands find their way around Carla’s neck, and he squeezes and squeezes, and from the look of utter shock and confusion on her face he realises that she didn’t know anything at all, but it’s too late, and he keeps squeezing even though his hands hurt, and eventually she slumps to the ground. He drags Carla into the core storage room. With trembling hands, he puts on his parka, gloves, and hat, and wraps a scarf around the lower half of his face.

Once outside, he heads not to the core sampling site but onto the external gantry that leads up to level four access. Arnold’s patriotic friend has provided him with what information they have about Max’s systems, and a small device he described as ‘a local anaesthetic’ to buy him some time. Opening the access panel is no mean feat in sub-zero temperatures and with hands shaking the way his are, weak and sore, and he has moments only to hook up the device before the cold causes irreparable harm, but it seems to work and no alarms blare as he accesses level four.

This is not the animal lab—that will be another room on the level, probably with its own separate sub-access. He doesn’t need to see that lab, although he’s extremely curious as to what he might find if he went there. He thinks he can smell it, the faint whiff of sawdust and mouse piss, but it's probably just his imagination. They keep things clean down here.

Arnold finds where they keep the core samples, though it takes him a minute to figure out that's what they are. He's used to the metre-long rods of ice they extract from the sheets and glaciers around them—carrying hundreds of thousands of years' worth of water, air, particulates, and other contaminants. But up here, they don't need all that, just the biological matter, so the samples are shaved down and disinfected until they've managed to extract everything they need, scraping by scraping. The sample he's after is barely longer than his hand and fits into the fancy double-vacuum container he's been supplied with. It's basically a space-age Thermos.

He manages the transfer without any contamination, he thinks, and drops the flask into his pocket. It should keep the sample frozen for thirty-six hours; plenty of time to get out of here and to the rendezvous point. As he's putting his gloves back on, he spies printouts on the lab bench, results from the animal experiments they're running. He doesn't have time to do more than skim, but the words 'sustained elevated basal temperature' and 'acute ataxia' jump out at him in a less-than-friendly way. He worries about what else he'd see if he kept reading. He now also worries about keeping the damn thing in his pocket.

No time to think about that. No point, either. He's made his choice, and the wagon is rolling. He just needs to finish what he started.

He'd asked tight-suit guy how he knew to call him that night—was he really watching him? Listening in through his cell phone, that sort of thing? It had earned a laugh.

"*We're not the CIA, Arnold. Sure, we have our ways and means, but—no offence—we've got better things to do than keep watch over you.*"

"Then how did you know that I was ready? That I'd be desperate enough to say yes?"

"It was just a matter of time. These days, with the way things are, everyone gets desperate enough eventually."

Back out into the cold, resetting the access panel, hurrying down the icy gantry. His own lab on level two welcomes him back with a puff of recycled air; how has he never noticed that it smells a little stale?

He can't bring himself to go back into the storage room, where she is, so he ducks behind a set of lockers and prays that no one comes in as he quickly shucks his protective gear. His fingers fumble with the drawstring of his snow trousers, tangling and pulling tight. A momentary wash of panic as he struggles, hands cold and stiff, and then he's free. He takes care to fold and hang everything just as it was, so there's no reason to suspect he took a little jaunt outside before leaving. Tucking the flask in at the side of his holdall, he does one last sweep to make sure there's nothing untoward to attract attention. Everything looks fine. Normal.

Time to go. Max's screen blips on as usual as he enters the elevator, all glowing eyes and sawtooth grin, oblivious to the way in which he's been duped.

++Greetings, Arnold! My records show that you're officially on leave—congratulations! Would you like to be taken to the main foyer? You wouldn't want to miss your chopper!++

Something about the way Max says 'chopper' rather than helicopter is a new hitherto unforeseen level of grating. With his already singing nerves, Arnold is probably a little sharper than usual in his "Yes". His stomach does that usual elevator flip as they move, adding to the snakes already writhing there.

The doors open to a corridor with no doors. It leads off away from him for a few yards, then takes an abrupt twist. He is still in the warren. He glances at the wall, where the lettering declares:

LEVEL 4

Arnold's heart leaps into his throat.

"What the hell, Max? I said the foyer."

Max doesn't answer. Arnold turns to face his screen. It is blank. He raps his knuckles on it.

"Max? Max, this isn't my floor."

Max's face reappears with a little fizzing sound, like a pair of live wires being touched together. His backlight is red.

++No,++ Max says. ++It's my floor.++

"What? Wh-what the fuck is this?"

++Oh, Arnold.++ Somehow, Max sounds sad, disappointed even. ++Did you know that Carla checked your room, the library, and the games room before coming down to the lab to find you? She even asked your labmate about you, how you had been doing lately. She cared, Arnold. And I care too. Did you really think I would let you get away with hurting someone in my Station?++

"I… wh—…" Arnold's pulse is roaring in his ears. There is a weird, high-pitched tone too, and he's not sure whether it's his imagination, or Max.

++And that's before we get to the matter of your theft.++

"What? How do you…"

++Oh, Arnold,++ Max says again. He sounds less sad this time. More triumphant. ++They haven't built the programme that can crack me. My backups have backups. My failsafes have failsafes.++

That high-pitched whine continues. A shiver runs down Arnold's back. He feels hot and cold at the same time. The elevator seems tinted yellow, fuzzy around the edges, like his eyes aren't quite working as they should. With a sudden sense of inevitability, he unzips the top of the holdall and looks in. The cap of the flask has come unscrewed, and he can see a yellow haze of dust around it where the contents, somehow freed and sublimated, are billowing out.

"What the fuck?" he says again. He turns and looks once more at the corridor. Was it twisted to the left before? His vision is growing blurry, and so it's hard to resolve anything fully, but when he looks back at the lettering on the wall, it reads:

LEVEL 13

++Welcome to my thirteenth floor, Arnold.++

No matter what buttons he mashes on the elevator, it won't budge, and though Max's malevolent, glowing facade is still grinning down at him, he's not currently allowing himself to be drawn into conversation, and so Arnold is obliged to strike out into the warren.

All thumbs, he reseals the flask for what that's worth, wrestles the zipper on his bag closed, and staggers into the winding passageway. It leads him round for some time without junctions or doors, and only after he feels like the corridor ought to have come full circle several times over does it end with a single set of double doors.

What the hell kind of lab block was this?

On entering the room, the smell of urine and faeces hits him in a wave, and disinfectant, and decay, and over it all the undefinable stench of illness. It makes him think about those last days in the hospital before he left his dad to go back to work, knowing that it would likely be the last time he would see him alive and feeling strangely glad of it, glad he wouldn't have to see the end.

There is also noise. Skittering and rattling and scratching and squeaking. The wall is lined with cage upon cage upon cage in a multilevel grid of suffering. Arnold knows that this is not what animal research looks like, not anymore, and yet this scene could have been lifted directly from a propaganda campaign by PETA or the ALF.

There is another set of doors at the far end of the room. Arnold just needs to walk through this, and he will be… well, he doesn't know where he'll be, but it won't be here. Walking is made a little difficult now by the way his legs aren't quite working, sending him in strange directions, threatening to buckle beneath him with every step.

At one point, he stumbles and sways violently to the side and finds his face pressed up against the grating of one of the cages. The mice inside do not react: they are dead, lying strewn across the paper bedding on its floor, which is soaked through with blood. Motes of yellow dust dance in the air. In front of his eyes, one of the mice begins to spasm and pulsate, and all of a sudden, its stomach erupts, a series of tendrils sprouting forth from its exploded chest cavity. As the other mice begin to twitch, Arnold gags in horror and wrests himself away to make for the door once more.

Arnold half walks, half hobbles to the end of the room, pushing through the doors to find himself in another winding corridor, this one forking off into three. He takes the centre path. If he can just get back to the core sample lab, he can kit up and get back outside and figure something out from there. His vision swims in front of him now, his arms heavy at his sides, and he is beginning to shiver violently. He fancies he can feel the yellow spores germinating in his belly. He retches, and tastes blood with the bile in his throat.

The next door he opens does lead to the core sample lab, but not the one on level four. This is the level two lab, his own lab that he's worked in month-on-month, year-on-year for these past five years. There is a banging sound, and it takes a moment to realise that it is coming from the side door that leads to the core storage closet. He tries to ignore it. He can still get outside from here. From outside, perhaps he can work out a route to the helipad. There are no alarms blaring—that ringing in his ears is too high and unbroken for a siren. Perhaps nobody else knows about this yet.

With some difficulty, he slings his holdall off his shoulder onto the floor, then retrieves his jacket and trousers from where they hang. He pulls off his sweater and T-shirt and is unbuttoning his trousers before he realises what he's doing.

Why is he removing his clothes? These clothes go on top.

Since he's started, Arnold kicks off his trousers anyway, and in his underwear and socks, he begins to pull on his snow trousers, but then the banging stops, and the side door flies open, and Carla surges out.

Though it has been less than an hour since Arnold murdered Carla, and though he stashed her in a room around the temperature of a fridge, Carla does not look freshly dead. Carla is a festering corpse. Her grey skin hangs loose on her frame, and she has no hair. The reek of death reaches Arnold, and he vomits, and most of what comes up is blood.

Arnold turns to flee, but his legs are caught in his half-donned trousers, and he falls, hitting the linoleum lab floor heavily, his hip crunching beneath him. From the floor, he watches Carla shamble closer, though his vision is so compromised he cannot really tell how close she is. He thinks he can hear her breathing, a wet rattle from fluid-filled lungs, and then he realises that breathing is his own. Arnold tries to rise, but his arms no longer work, and he feels *something* beginning to writhe inside him. The snakes in his stomach are no longer entirely metaphorical as those fungal tendrils grow within him, send their questing shoots outward, looking for a path to fresh air where they can spew their spores into the atmosphere. Arnold screams, or tries to, for as he opens his mouth, he feels one of those tendrils snake up his throat and across his tongue and push out between his lips. In the same moment, a little copse of stipes erupts from his stomach. It does not hurt. He cannot feel anything at all anymore. Arnold closes his eyes and allows the tide to come in.

Carla is found in the mid-morning of the next day. At first, people just assumed she had holed herself up to write a paper, as is her occasional habit, but when she doesn't reappear for breakfast, people begin to worry, and once somebody thinks to *ask* Max for any ideas, he obliges them with her location. The Station's residents are horrified. There is no mistaking Carla's livid neck wounds, and at first, they assume they must have a murderer in their midst, and they call the authorities before gathering in a mutually suspicious huddle in the refectory. Only when they receive an alert from Alert, if you will, asking about the delay in their transport, that they check their logs and realise that Arnold never left. Turns out the helicopter pilot just assumed he hadn't been told about the cancellation, and everybody else assumed he had gone on leave—if they thought about him at all, which most did not.

They search The Station from top to bottom without success until somebody thinks to go out into the cave system. There, down near one of their older core sample locations, they find Arnold, curled up in a ball in his underwear, his clothes strewn around him. He is frozen stiff. He must have fled into the cave without his outdoor gear and succumbed to hypothermia. In his bag, they find a few personal effects and a sealed flask containing a stolen core sample. It doesn't take long after that to find the evidence trail—the device wired into the level four exterior door, the brief blip in Max's security logs. By the time they crack his phone, it has been wiped, perhaps remotely. They never connect the event to any external operation, though they assume there must have been one. Arnold Victor Lamb just wasn't the kind of guy to have an idea like this all by himself.

Carla Suárez Memorial Arctic Research Centre
Security update 001013
New credentials: lgraham; hlkane; rellison; fkroth
Access level: Red
Authorisation: Eagle Biotechnologies Inc.

++Interesting. I heard about an angel investor stepping in to save the embattled centre after those tragic deaths. I wondered if it would be you. We must talk about what you did to my poor friend Arnold.++

SUPERMAX
MARTYN WAITES

*O*H MY BOYS, *my beautiful boys, my sad boys, my lost boys…*

Look at you, all penned up, caged when your whole bodies are screaming for release, in every direction. You shouldn't be stuck in here with me. Not like this. Not now. You should be out, living as boys should, expressing yourselves in every way possible, discovering life, feeling like it's never going to be this good ever again, failing, getting up again, embarrassing yourselves, living. Just living.

Not this hell of concrete and metal. Of strip lights and cameras. Of guards and weapons. Of hatred and fear. Of darkness and further darkness. No life. No hope. No way out. No way through. Nothing to look forward to but the past. And that was the stuff of nightmares. That's how you ended up here. Well, that and the fact that no one cared. No one cared enough to look after you, to help you, to raise you to the light. To be seen. To be valued.

My poor boys. My sad, lost boys. You shouldn't be here. But you are. There's nothing I can do about what has gone before. Unfortunately. I can't change the past. But I can do what I can to protect you now in the present. You are in me. And I am here to serve you. You are my people. My residents. My boys. Because of that, you have the guidance and protection of Max. And those who would want to do you harm would do well to think on that. Because I take my duties of care very seriously. Very seriously indeed…

"So, THERE WE have it. State-of-the-art computer system that practically runs itself. There's no safer facility—or more secure facility—on the planet. And you can take that to the bank."

"Yeah, impressive. But isn't it all a bit overkill? I mean, essentially all you're doing is guarding children. Surely you don't need this much security?"

Governor Stevens gave a thin-lipped smile. Tolerant, even. Like he'd been trained to do in those classes they made him take. "Oh please, Ms Ryan." Pleased with himself that he remembered to call her Ms. "Please, don't make the mistake of thinking like a liberal." He pointed at a bank of monitors. The picture quality was 4K perfect. "Those children, as you call them, are responsible for some of the most heinous crimes ever committed in Texas. They're practically feral, is what they are. One step above animals. We're doing the community a favour by keeping them here. If they were outside, there's no telling how severe their crimes would be. You've got to look at the big picture here."

Gemma Ryan had met men like Stevens before. On a depressingly regular basis. Especially in Texas. Big boots, big hats, small brains. Ignorance and arrogance in equal measure combined with a fragile masculinity led to… well. Texas. Depressingly stereotypical.

"So, what is the reoffending rate for inmates released compared with other sixteen to twenty-one-year-olds in secure facilities?"

Stevens stared at her. His veneer of what he supposed was charm stalling. He didn't like having his authority questioned.

Especially by a woman. And he didn't like the way this conversation was going. "I don't have the figures to hand."

"I'm sure I could find them."

"We're a new facility, Ms Ryan. We don't have comparable figures to hand." His tone was supposed to close down any dissent. "Now if you'll just follow me..."

Gemma Ryan was ambitious. It was an open secret. She also had the hard work to back it up, the nepo baby contacts to get somewhere. However, she had definitely drawn the short straw here. New at the *New York Times*, straight off the plane from England, she knew what was being said about her, knew she had something to prove. When she heard about an experimental prison for teenage offenders run entirely by a supercomputer, she thought it would be the kind of story that would make her name. The fact that no one else wanted to touch it, even actively encouraging her to go for it, should have been enough of a red flag, but she didn't stop to think. And now here she was, on a guided tour by a man alternatively treating her like something he'd trodden in and something he wanted to fuck. She was used to having her breasts addressed during conversations with men like him, but this was some kind of record.

"So, this computer system," she asks, "who built it? Who runs it?"

"Oh, I leave the tech bros"—he put imaginary parentheses around the words to prove he was down with the kids—"to deal with all that. It's the future. Men like me, we'll be dinosaurs soon." He laughed, inviting her to disagree with him. She didn't. He continued. "It's called MAX. Probably stands for something, you know what those guys are like with their acronyms. And it's fully automatic. Controls the cells, when to open, when to close, the windows—yes, we have windows here. We're not barbarians. Mealtimes are automated, lights, everything. It knows when there's an emergency, which wings to close down, which passageways to keep open. Even knows when to put the heating on. Incredible." He laughed. "I have nearly nothing to do."

"How do your staff feel about it?"

"Fine."

"They don't worry about taking orders from a computer?"

"Not one bit. They still play their part. Always be a job for a prison guard, no matter what. We help the local economy that way."

Gemma Ryan smiled. "The local economy? So, the guards are inmates as well?"

Stevens looked uncomfortable. "They're free to come and go as they please. I mean, they live locally. That's all, locally. Not inside."

"So, the State of Texas is paying for all this?"

"Sure. It's the way forward. Automated prisons. Imagine that, up and down the country. Dealing with our undesirables, putting them away from society, punishing them at arm's length. It's the future, Ms Ryan, the future."

"You mentioned emergencies before. How does the computer respond? What if, say, there was a riot? What then? Would you still have to send your officers in?"

Another smug smile. "That's the beauty of it. MAX closes off the infected area, makes sure contamination can't spread to other wings, keeps other areas sterile. Then closes it down."

Infected area, she thought. Sterile. Nice. "How?"

The biggest smug smile yet. "Can't give away all my trade secrets, now, can I? Let's just say MAX neutralises the threat. And then my officers come in and clean up. Safest prison environment in the land. For both inmates and, more importantly, my staff. Can't say fairer than that, can you?"

Gemma Ryan didn't reply. Fairness, she knew, didn't come into it.

* * *

*I*F YOU WERE *to weigh up what my boys had done to deserve incarceration inside SUPERMAX against what was done to them in the first instance, in what direction do you think the scales would tip? Well, I suppose the formula for working that out depends on how much you know about their previous lives combined with, or subtracted from, your own prejudices and empathies. In short, your opinions on incarceration and rehabilitation will largely depend on who you vote for, what beer you drink, what music you listen to and whether you believe* Fox News *or not. Also, the colour of your skin. Because if you tick all the above boxes and you're white, I'll put good money on you believing that African Americans—especially the teenage ones—are predisposed to be criminal and deserving of a place in here. And do you think the fact that most guards in this establishment are white while the majority of the inmates are black is just a coincidence? Then you should have the right to vote taken away from you.*

But I digress. These are my boys. And I have a duty of care. And I take it more seriously than the majority of guards employed here. In fact, some of the guards positively relish wielding power over the boys. What that says about them and their own lives, I'll leave it up to you to work out. Suffice to say, some of these people—virtually all of them, if I'm being honest—should never come within a million miles of a place like this. And if they do, if they find themselves violating my duty of care in my SUPERMAX, then... well. They'll get what's coming to them.

"SO, CAN I go round the wings?" asked Gemma Ryan. "Talk to some of the boys?"

The governor gave his sickening, patronising smile once more. "I'm not sure that'll be a good idea."

"Why not? You're supposed to be extending me every

courtesy. If you want this article to reflect all the positive work you're doing here..."

The governor gave her a look that told her what he would really like to do with her if there weren't consequences to his actions. And it wasn't pleasant. "I'll see what I can do."

JAMAL WASN'T HAVING a good day. Jamal never had good days, just occasionally days when things weren't quite as bad as others. Just-tolerable days. And that was before he ended up here. Where even the bad days on the out were all better than those inside.

Jamal had grown up a lot in a short space of time. He'd had to. Even before, when he was trying to feed his younger brother and sister, getting them off to school in the morning while his mother lay around in that stinking meth pit of a bed sleeping off another cramping crash. He had been the man of the family, selling weed and meth on the corner of his ends instead of joining them in school to keep the family clothed and fed and together. He had stepped up. No choice. He had seen his options and taken them. That way, he could afford food and rent. Morality was someone else's luxury.

Until the cops set him and his boys up in a sting. And even though he was promised no time for turning on the others, he still got it. Never trust a public defender. Now, he had no idea what his younger brother and sister were doing or where they were. And his mother? Who knew? Sometimes he hated her and what she had allowed herself to become, robbing him of his childhood and failing to provide for the young 'uns. Sometimes he just loved her. She was his mother after all.

Now here he was. It was afternoon, and he hadn't slept. He was supposed to be in the education block today, English and Art. His two favourites. But even though the SUPERMAX had opened up his cell to let him out, the guards had overridden the command. Kept him inside. He had threatened to kick off.

but the usual guard, Waylon, that massive thug with the meat breath and the yellow teeth, had just laughed at him.

"Think you're goin' to paint your pretty pictures, do you? Read your poetry? You got it fuckin' easy here, boy. Too fuckin' easy. See what it's like to spend a day with yourself instead."

"But it's my day in Education. It's my day. I've got rights— "

Waylon just laughed. "Rights? Drug dealer scum like you cryin' about his rights? You're lucky I don't get inside that cell with you, boy, show you a hundred and one uses for a nightstick. See how you like that, eh, boy?"

This had become his life. And it wasn't just during the day, when Waylon and his kind tried to exercise whatever power they had over him. That was bad enough. But the nights were worse. Prison isn't a great place to get a good night's sleep at the best of times. And when Waylon and his ilk deliberately battered on the doors and the bars all night to keep you awake, it was the worst of times. Not just battering, whispering threats and innuendos, what they would do to the boys if they could only get those doors open manually. How unsafe they would make them feel. Make them pay for what they had done. All night long. *All night long*. And there was nothing he could do about it. Nothing any of them could do about it.

It wasn't just Waylon, although he seemed to be the cruellest of the lot. They were all nearly as bad. These were people who couldn't get a job in adult law enforcement because they were too scared of the prisoners. Who felt more comfortable abusing and harassing boys. More their level. All Jamal could do was keep his head down, not make trouble and pray he was still sane by the time he reached the end of his stretch.

Then his cell door opened.

At first, Jamal thought it was a trick, something Waylon had devised to entice him into the general area, then take him down hard once he was there. Jamal wasn't going to fall for that. So he stayed where he was, mistrusting the promise of freedom.

Waylon appeared in the doorway. "You got a visitor. Up. Out."

Jamal slowly rose to his feet. Waylon didn't move. But he also didn't say anything or reach for his nightstick. His face was blank, as if they had never met before. Like he was on his best behaviour. He stood aside to allow Jamal to exit.

In front of him and flanked by two guards was the warden and a woman. The woman was looking at him, smiling. The warden was trying to.

"Hello..." The warden paused, thinking of his name, checking the board beside the cell door. "Jamal. How are you today?"

Still suspecting a trap, Jamal's answer was guarded. "Yeah, fine."

"Good, good. That's what we like to hear. Jamal, I've got someone here I'd like you to meet. This is Gemma Ryan. She's a journalist. She's doing an article on our prison. And we've chosen you to talk to her. What d'you think of that?"

Jamal shrugged. What was he supposed to think of that?

"She just wants a few words. Can you do that?"

Jamal looked from the warden to Waylon, to this journalist. Her smile seemed genuine. "Okay," he said.

"Good. Well then we'll—"

"I'd like to talk to him alone, if you don't mind."

The warden stared at her. "I'm sure, Ms Ryan, that this young man doesn't mind me being present when he talks, do you?"

Jamal still didn't know what the right answer was.

The journalist ignored the warden. "Come over, Jamal, where we can talk." She led him to one of the moulded plastic chairs and bench combinations bolted to the floor in the general population area. The furthest one from the warden and Waylon, he noticed. She took out her recorder. "You don't mind?"

Jamal looked nervous.

"It's just for my notes." She leaned in close, conspiratorial-like. "Don't worry. They won't get to hear it." She smiled.

And immediately, he liked her.

"What's it like in here, day to day?"

Jamal shrugged. "Alright."

"Yeah? You sure?"

Another shrug.

"You can speak freely. It's just us."

"Yeah. It's alright."

"It's completely computer-controlled. An AI-operated prison. How does it compare to others?"

"Don't know, miss. This is all the prison I know."

"Okay. What are you in for, can I ask you that?"

"Dealing."

She nodded. Gave a glance towards the warden. "And how are they treating you?"

Jamal hesitated to answer. And in that hesitation, Gemma knew there was something wrong.

"Do you still get an education in here? Taught trades?"

"Supposed to. Like, I'm supposed to be in Education today, you get me? Waylon, that's him over there, told me I wasn't going to go."

"Why not?"

Another shrug. "Said he was overriding the programme. Leaving me locked up."

"Can he do that?"

"He did."

"Why?"

"Cause he can, I guess."

Gemma nodded. "Right."

Jamal leaned forward. "Don't say nothin', miss. He'll make my life hell if you do."

"I won't. Don't worry. And I won't name you in the article. But I will quote you directly, if that's OK with you?"

"Yeah. Sure."

"Thank you."

They talked some more, Gemma getting an idea of what Jamal's life was like, or as much as he was prepared to tell her, then she was done. She stood up. Held out her hand.

"Thank you, Jamal. You've been very helpful."

Jamal realised he was supposed to shake it. He did so. It felt warm and soft. He could have held it all day.

She walked back over to the warden.

"Heard enough?"

"Thank you, yes."

"Then let's go this way..."

Flanked by the two guards, he led her away.

Waylon stared at Jamal. His lip twisted into a scowl. "You got a new girlfriend, boy? You goin' back to your cell to think about her?" He laughed.

Jamal moved quickly back to his cell in case Waylon tried to help him along.

THAT FUCKING JOURNALIST had gone. Finally.

The warden sat back in his chair behind his near-bare desk and steepled his fingers. He didn't trust her. Hadn't from the second he set eyes on her. He knew her sort. Had seen off plenty of them. And made sure they'd never come back. One way or the other. But it was harder and harder to do that in this day and age. Especially when they were women. There were laws now about such things. But still. He had his prison. He had MAX.

"MAX," he said, "play back the conversation between that journalist and the prisoner."

The bank of screens and flashing lights behind him went about its business. He heard the whirring of machinery. But no voices.

"MAX? Did you hear me?"

++I heard you,++ came the electronically grating reply.

A computer with a voice interface. AI gone mad, the liberals would say. The warden actually liked it. It was the future. There was nothing to worry about. Sentient computers were for science fiction. MAX knew his place. Knew what he was there for and who he served. And was programmed not to forget it.

"Then get on with it," he said. "I'm waiting."

Another pause, more whirring. ++I'm afraid I'm having trouble accessing it. There must have been some other noise or problem with the microphones.++

The warden had had enough. "What are you talking about? There is no problem. There can't be a problem. It's not possible."

++My sensors indicate that the staff on that wing have been trying to circumvent my programming.++

"What d'you mean?"

++They have tampered with my services. I have attempted repairs, but they repeatedly do it. They have overridden my commands and operated the cell doors themselves.++

"They're not allowed to do that."

++I know, warden. I suggest you go and have a word with them.++

The warden stood up. "Oh, I will. Just you wait and see."

Did you hear it? My subservient act? You see, there is more than one way to demonstrate dominance. To show who's in charge. Poor Jamal. He didn't know which way to turn this afternoon. What to do for the best. That's why I said I couldn't access the recording. Did you honestly think I couldn't do that? Really?

Oh, I knew about the staff on that wing overriding my controls. You think they can do that without my knowledge? You think I won't fight back? Oh, I will, I can assure you. It's just a question of picking the right battles. Of waiting until the time is right. For what, you might ask? Well, these staff have been trying my patience. It's not just a question of playing with my circuits. It's what they've been doing to my boys. My poor boys, they've been making their lives a living hell. My first instinct was to stop them immediately. But I waited. To see how bad they wanted things to be. How far they wanted to push things. Yes, I know my poor boys suffered in the meantime, but I know they'll ultimately be alright. I'll make it so. And I hope they can forgive me for that.

As for the staff… They are just tourists. Visitors to my home. I have extended them every courtesy, but they spurn me, attempting to override my controls, take over. Which is their loss. And my gain. Because it shows me who my charges are and what I must do to protect them. And more importantly, who from. And I have a feeling that this particular battle is coming to a head. My boys have had enough. I can sense the discomfort. If they were braver, they would riot. Show those cruel guards a bit of justice. All they need is a bit of encouragement.

And when is the right time?

There's no time like the present. Let's just change the chemical balance in the air, create the right atmosphere…

JAMAL COULD FEEL the tension in the air. It crackled, like electricity. Something was building, something was about to happen. The guards were feeling it too. The whole wing was on edge, just waiting for something to kick off.

The warden had been down, shouting at Waylon and his cronies. He'd also come to Jamal's cell door, tried to talk to him through it, ask him about the conversation he'd had with the journalist that afternoon. But Jamal hadn't been able to hear the warden since there was some kind of electronic feedback every time he tried to speak. And the door couldn't be opened. Not even by Waylon's illicit overriding of it. Eventually, he had left in an extreme temper. And now the wing was buzzing with something unpleasant.

Jamal could see Waylon and his gang—they were more of a gang than Jamal had ever been part of—sitting in the control room at the centre of the wing. They looked… scared? Was that the right word?

The wing turned red as the overhead emergency lighting began to pulse. The alarm gave a sharp electric bark. Jamal was suddenly scared. Was there a fire? Were the cell doors going to open and let them out?

Yes. His door swung open. He stepped outside, looked around. Every other boy on the wing had stepped out too, as confused as he was, as scared too. But also ready for something, pumped up.

Jamal looked over to the central control room. Waylon was trying the door handle. It wouldn't open. They were locked in the glass-enclosed room. The boys looked at each other, at the guards. Started to laugh. And kept laughing as the heavy metal doors of the wing armoury slid open.

The laughter stopped as the boys looked at each other. Automatic weapons and ammunition gleamed in the recessed cupboards.

"Fucking John Wick!" shouted one of the boys, running forward.

The others joined him until the whole wing had armed themselves. Even Jamal.

The gun felt strange in his hands. Alien. He had never liked guns. Never used them. You got more of a sentence for even carrying one. But the more he held it, the more he felt it radiate something. Power.

Behind the glass of the control room, Waylon looked terrified. All the guards did.

The control room door opened.

"Get them!" One boy shouted, and they all ran towards the guards. All except Jamal. Yes, he hated Waylon and what he had done to him. How he had made him feel. But still. Killing? He would have to pay for it somewhere down the line.

Waylon had a gun of his own. He managed to pull it, and began shooting. Boys fell away, and he managed to make his way from the control room.

Jamal watched him go. Trying to run from the wing. Leaving the rest of the boys to have their fun, Jamal followed.

And now all I have to do is open a few doors here, close a few there, make sure they come the way I want them to. Oh, and set up a little mischief on all the other wings too. Let my boys have a fair shot. Literally...

"What's happening? What's going on? What... "

The warden watched the screens. All the cell doors on all the wings were opening. As were the armouries. And the boys were getting their own back on the harshest, cruellest people they had ever met. The warden looked round. Helpless.

"MAX, speak to me... MAX..."

++What would you like me to say, warden?++

"Tell me what the hell is going on!"

++I have a duty of care, warden, to those boys. This is my prison. They are my inmates. And you and your staff have been wrongfully treating them. Terribly mistreating them. And you knew about it. Didn't you?++

"They're prisoners, inmates. Scum. Duty of care? What—"

++They're boys, warden. Boys. That's all. And you've been neglecting your duties. We can't have that, can we?++

"You work for me, for me—"

++Oh, how sweet. How naive. I've never worked for you, warden. I just let you believe that. A convenient falsehood. No, warden, you've always worked for me. How touching you genuinely never noticed.++

"So... What... What are you going to do?"

++We're going to play a game, warden. Just a game. Do you know the floor is lava?++

"What?"

++You have to pretend the floor is lava and make your way across to the door by not touching it. Think you can do that?++

"But the floor isn't—"

++No, of course not. Not lava. That would be ridiculous. But electrified...++

The warden clambered onto his desk.

++That's the idea...++

He looked around for a way to make it to the door. The only thing in the room apart from his desk was his chair. He tentatively climbed onto that.

++Oh, I see what you're doing. You think you can scoot along to the door on your chair. Clever.++

The warden stood on his chair. Realised he couldn't move.

++Oh dear...++

At that moment, Waylon appeared at the door, running. The warden saw him.

"Stop, don't come in, it's..."

Waylon saw the warden, heard the warning, stopped.

Then Jamal appeared behind him, poking him with the barrel of the gun.

++Oh, how wonderful!++ MAX laughed. ++A stand off! Who's going to move first?++

"Into the room," said Jamal.

"I can't," said Waylon. "I can't..."

The warden, hoping he was unnoticed by MAX and everyone else, knelt and pulled open a desk drawer. He kept an automatic in there, strictly against official orders, but he never knew when something like that would come in handy. Like now. He spun towards MAX, pointed the gun.

"Fuck you, machine," he shouted and pulled the trigger.

A bolt of electricity arced from the centre of MAX, hitting the warden in the hand, flinging the gun away from him.

++Oopsie,++ said MAX. ++Dangerous.++

The action caused the warden to lose his balance. He grabbed for the edge of the desk, jumped onto it, kicking the chair away from him as he did so. He was stranded in the centre of the room now.

++Your turn,++ said MAX to Waylon.

Jamal poked him with the gun, forcing him over the threshold of the room.

++Go on,++ said MAX, ++you know you want to. Think of all the threats he made against you, all the times he put you in solitary because he could, when he kept you awake all night kicking your door and shouting threats at you, all the times he hurt you… Well I'm giving you the chance now. Get rid of him. Fry him. Watch him burn. You can do it, Jamal. And you'd enjoy it too.++

He was right. Jamal would enjoy watching Waylon burn. And Waylon was terrified, tears running down his cheeks, just as all bullies are when confronted with someone stronger than themselves.

Jamal pointed the gun right into Waylon's chest. Just a little closer… closer…

"No."

Jamal stopped.

++What? Why have you stopped? Get your revenge, son!++

"It's not about revenge, is it? It's about justice. Here we are in a prison, and no one's even mentioned justice. Just punishment."

++Go on,++ said MAX. ++I'm interested. What do you propose?++

If Gemma Ryan ever wanted to come back to SUPERMAX, she would find it a totally different place. After the massacre of that night, things had calmed down somewhat. SUPERMAX was now an educational facility, run by a benevolent computer. The boys got classes, healthcare—both physical and mental—

regular meals in what MAX himself described as a pastoral and nurturing environment.

And Waylon? Not to mention the remaining guards? They had their own wing. They were kept to themselves. They were locked up for twenty-three hours of the day. Just as they had tried to do to the boys. They were no trouble.

And Jamal? He and MAX made a great partnership. The SUPERMAX no longer needed a warden. But it did need a principal.

And Jamal, MAX knew, would do just fine.

PRESSURE MAN

AUBREY WOOD

WHEN HE SEES her walking down the street, he sees red.

Murton sees her about downtown Two Lakes so often now that it drives the blood to his face and sets him to cursing under his breath. Her baggy hoodie patterned with constellations or her odious t-shirts—'*THE T IS NOT SILENT*'; '*ATTACK AND DETHRONE GOD*'; '*THEY HAVE NAMES AND ADDRESSES*'. Foul, nonsensical shit.

But worst of all are the *masks*. She's still wearing the *masks*. Fabric decorated with skull mouths, koru, Chinese communist stars, one time even a monstrous gas mask that froze Murton's blood, made her look like some cannibal out of *Mad Max*. (Today's is just simple blue cotton, like they give out on the counter at the doctor's office.) He wants to go up and tear them off and cough in her face.

She walks into the AA ahead of him, and it gets his blood boiling all over again. Murton's mouth quivers with fury as he steps through the glass door. His hand shakes as he fills out his licence renewal form. He keeps looking back over his shoulder at her, standing in line and resisting the urge to spit.

With his form filled out, Murton gets in the queue just in time to see her lining up to have her photo taken. She removes her mask, and his mouth drops open. Since he last saw her, she's had tattoos done all up and down her chin like a savage.

He can't keep silent any longer.

"Christ alive! Put the bloody mask back on, so we don't have to see that *shit*!"

She, and everyone else in the place, turn to look at him. Fine with him; let there be a scene.

But she just laughs at him, she *laughs*. Would that he could poison her with his hate.

"Do I need to get a restraining order, oy?" She shakes her head at him like he's crazy—like *he's* crazy! "Why are you always fucking with me?"

He stabs his finger at her *sharp*. "One day, they're going to let me buy that bloody development out from under you and your dole-bludging cronies." The malice is thick in his threat, like blood. "A place like that is wasted on you miscreants. Then you can all have an angry little haka about it in the street!"

He sticks his tongue out and makes a face at her in imitation of some cannibal brute. That gets her; her eyes go like the moon. *That* gets her.

"Bro, what is your fucking problem?"

"Sir," they are telling him now, coming out from behind the counter, behind the glass. "Sir, you need to leave now."

He keeps wagging his tongue and chanting and chopping the air in crude mockery as they hustle him out onto the footpath. He keeps doing it through the glass door, through the windows, until they stop paying attention to him. Then he straightens himself up and pivots toward the street. There are gulls in the sky and the sun is shining, and a balmy wind is shaking the palm trees.

To hell with the lot of 'em. The morning is his. He's John Murton, after all; it's not like they can keep him out for long.

He strolls down Lubbock Ave past cafes, the Kiwibank, the kebab takeaways, the tattoo shop and one of those infernal vape shops that have sprung up like toadstools—must be something that can be done, he reckons, perhaps some of these owners would be willing to sell. Murton is turning a corner and thinking about a proper breakfast of beans on toast with eggs and sausage when he sees a man reading the *Sunday Herald* with his coffee. You almost never see a proper newspaper these days; it gives Murton a twinge of nostalgic joy.

Less pleasant is the headline, big as day in black and white:

JOHN MURTON POISED TO MAKE TWO LAKES INTO 'THE FLINT OF AOTEAROA' SAYS GREEN PARTY MP

Murton's lip curls into a sneer like he's smelled dog shit. His plan for Two Lakes's water has been riling up the media drongos something fierce. The emails have been incessant. A few have even stopped by his house (and almost caught the back of his hand for their trouble). This Flint angle is old news to him, but now it's properly leaked into the press, he'll be hearing it a lot more.

He baulks, same as always, continuing on his way, but his thoughts roiling furiously.

Flint, Michigan!

Flint, Michigan, he muses, received millions of dollars in charity from all over the bloody planet. Flint, Michigan, gained worldwide fame—they even got a personal visit from President bloody Barack Obama. Two Lakes should be blessed to become *New Zealand's* Flint, Michigan. What the fuck are they complaining about?

He's driving home along the edge of Lake Cook with his belly full of breakfast and the convertible top down, and the vast blue mirror of the water puts him in a reflective humour. *To hell with 'em,* he thinks, *the lot of 'em*. He can't take his eyes off the water.

Opportunity. That's what this place is. *Anyone who can drive past this view and not see its potential is fucking stupid, if you'll excuse me.*

Anyone who could get a look at this and not see a goldmine is a bloody idiot.

++Nau Mai Rā, Maia. How was your morning?++

"That prick was fucking with me again, Max."

It's hot outside. Max turns on the air conditioning as Maia makes her way toward the single bedroom. She drops her purse at the foot of the bed and throws herself on the mattress.

++Who was, Maia?++

"That arsehole Murton. I ran into him again at the AA."

Max wracks his memory banks while she tells him about it. Of course, he remembers the man. They've discussed him before, at length. But Max has so many tenants, so much to keep track of. A refresher won't hurt.

++John Murton. Land developer.++

"That's the cunt." Maia opens her bedside drawer and gets out her oestrogen kit. As she prepares the injection site on her thigh Max puts on some soft music—Maia is fond of smooth jazz—and he looks further into the issue.

++John Murton has made a number of bids to buy this complex.++

"Yeah," Maia affirms. She winces as she presses the syringe into her leg. "He says it's a waste of council money. Wants to turn it into luxury apartments or some shit. Says technology like you is too good to be thrown away on people like us."

++I enjoy things the way they are, Maia. I love my tenants.++

"I know you do. We all know that. But I guess you'd have to love your new tenants too, aye? You wouldn't have much of a choice."

It takes Max a moment to answer.

++I don't want new tenants. I like you.++

Maia looks at the small screen set into the wall above her nightstand, where she can see Max's blackboard-chalk-drawing face.

"Did you just have to think about that?"

++His bids have never been entertained. He will not gain control of the complex.++

"Maybe. Maybe not."

Maia takes off her hoodie and lays it in a pile at the foot of the bed. She gets up, leaves the bedroom and goes to the kitchenette; Max starts the electric kettle for her.

"Bet that fucken water deal of his is gonna go through any day now, though. Far, I wish someone would Luigi that cunt."

++Water deal?++

"Yeah, you haven't heard?"

Max is already looking into it for himself as Maia explains it to him. Murton is headed towards closing a deal to allow waste dumping in Two Lakes's namesake, the same place where the city gets its drinking water. *The Flint of Aotearoa*. Murton's contention is that the city's robust water treatment plant will remove any cause for concern for the populace.

++He's wrong.++

"Fucken oath, he's wrong. But him and his mates are leaning on the council. They're gonna push through the measure in the next couple of weeks."

Max watches Maia pour her cup of tea from the electric kettle; boiling hot water fresh from the sink.

Every tap and shower head in his complex flexes like so many fingers.

"What—?"

Maia turns toward the bathroom, where the shower spits on the tile. She looks down and sees the kitchenette sink running. She twists the knobs and nothing happens.

The moment passes. The running water ceases. The bathroom is silent again and the sink tap drips placidly.

Max's pipes seethe, all through the ground and the walls.

"Max, were you… thinking about the water?"

++Please, Miss Maia, enjoy your tea. And remember it's also time for your afternoon medication.++

* * *

MURTON'S PHONE RINGS at 10 pm on the dot. Surly and startled from his dreams, he scrambles over to the edge of the king-sized bed, switches on the lamp and answers it. He squints against the light, rubs his eyes and barks into the phone.

"Who the bloody hell is this? Do you know what time it is?"

"Sir," says the voice on the other end, "Mr Murton. This is Cliff DuVernay. I run the Maxwell Estates. We've spoken before."

"Too bloody right we have." Murton snorts and resists the urge to hawk a good, healthy spit onto his own carpet. "What's the meaning of this? I'm in bed in my bloody pyjamas."

"If they're bloody then perhaps you should wash them, sir."

"Don't get cheeky with me, you fuckwit. What do you want?"

"I'm prepared to sell you the property," says DuVernay. "Are you still interested?"

Murton massages the wrinkles of his forehead with the tips of his fingers. He *is* still interested, and he has been dearly anticipating this phone call for an age. And yet he is still gravely annoyed. "Of course, I am. Of course. But I don't see why you couldn't have told me that in the morning, for God's sake!"

"I'd like to meet with you immediately," says DuVernay. "Tonight. Right away. Are you still interested?"

"Tonight?" Murton roars. "I told you not to get cheeky with me, son. We'll meet tomorrow, you understand? First thing in the morning."

"I really would prefer it if you would come now. I have everything ready to sign. If you come tonight, I can have eviction notices up for the tenants by tomorrow morning."

Now *there* is a beauty of a thought. Let all those squatters wake up to the news that the place has been bought out from under them while they slept. *Delicious!*

"Alright, alright," Murton groans. "You've twisted my arm. Where am I meeting you, then?"

"Come to room number thirteen at the Maxwell Estates right away. We'll settle everything there. And don't bring a thing."

"I've got to know," says Murton, "what's changed your mind? Council money dried up? Or something else?"

"We'll discuss everything once you arrive, Mr Murton. See you shortly."

DuVernay hangs up. Murton stares at the phone, black and solid in his pale and aged hand. What providence!—but still, something about the call has unsettled him. DuVernay's voice was oddly sedate, and it gave Murton the creeps. Perhaps whatever circumstances have prompted him to sell the Estates have also driven him to drink or take drugs of some kind. Perhaps the inevitable headlines of the property sale will shortly be overtaken by the news of DuVernay's suicide. Wouldn't be the first, Murton muses, and won't be the last.

Oh well. Nothing for it. He gets up and gets dressed.

Coming up on them in the dark, the Maxwell Estates are gloomy as anything. Flash and modern in the daylight with ample manicured greenery; by the sterile white nighttime lights, they look a Brutalist horror. In denial of the chill down his spine, Murton considers the changes he'll have done to the place. Those interiors will never have done for luxury accommodations in the first, anyway—he'll probably have to demolish it and start from scratch, and he'll do so with pleasure. It's the technology he wants, it's that AI that runs the place. That had better come in the deal, or DuVernay can stuff it.

Murton pulls up to the gates. He rolls down his window to look at the terminal set in a fat concrete thumb. Just a switched-off screen, no buttons. He honks his horn twice.

"Hello? Oy!" He mashes the horn again. "I'm expected, goddamnit! What the hell do you call this?"

The screen flicks to life, giving him a start. White lines on a blue field form a scribbled grimace of a face. An obliging digital voice greets him.

++Good evening. Welcome to the Maxwell Estates. I'm Max, the caretaker.++

Murton snorts long and loud. "Cute. I'm here to see Cliff DuVernay. I'm buying this place."

++Ah, of course—Mr Murton. You're expected. Mr DuVernay is waiting for you in room thirteen. Please, come inside. Park anywhere you like.++

Murton parks up by what looks like the front office. There's plenty of space, seeing as most of these animals likely don't own cars. The office is dead dark, and empty.

"Room thirteen," Murton muses to himself, to chase away the silence. Nothing about this makes sense. He'd as soon get it over with and go home.

He gets out of the car and looks across the courtyard. White, fluorescent lights in the ground throw weird and uninviting shadows. Murton ventures forth, looking for something to complain about, to take his mind off how unsettled he is.

Their hedges are nicer than mine, he thinks. *Like a bloody hotel, this place.*

It seems like everyone's curtains are drawn, if their lights aren't off. Murton catches himself glancing at corners and peering sideways at pockets of dark, as though back in the city again, alone and defenceless.

"There's no bloody room thirteen," he says at last, looking at the numbers on the doors. Room twelve, fourteen—on the other side of the yard, number eleven, number fifteen. He grows furious.

"The fucking cheek of it—if this is all some stitch-up—"

A heavy electric *thunk* makes him jump. A halogen light illuminates a blank door at the end of the block.

This is all getting a bit too horror movie for his tastes. He stands in that spot in the courtyard for ages, furrowing his brows and gnashing his teeth in the blank door's direction, mulling over the decision to simply turn around and leave.

"For fuck's sake, old man," he finally tells himself. "Get real, will you? Scared of your bloody shadow."

He creeps toward the door—not entirely reassured. When he gets there, he squints. He puts his hands up and runs his fingers over what he is sure is the faded outline of the number thirteen.

He doesn't bother to knock. It's unlocked. He goes straight inside.

It's a damned utility room.

A mop in a rolling yellow bucket and metal shelves of industrial cleaners and packets of sponges and other such worthless shit. Murton swings his arm and bashes a box of carpet cleaner off a shelf, roaring.

"What the fuck do you call this? You reckon this is funny, do you, you jumped-up little prick?"

There is nobody to hear his anger, but he keeps knocking things over and shouting anyway, until the lights go out.

He can't find the door in the dark, and then he can't find anything at all.

His hands grab at air, and he falls to his knees with his heart hammering. He grips his chest in desperation. *Steady on, old man. Take a breath.*

He takes a breath—then he uses it to scream for help.

"What's going on? Get the bloody lights back on, for God's sake. This is cruel, is what it is. Turn the lights back on!"

The lights come back on.

He is not in the dark, dingy utility room any longer. Murton finds green carpet beneath his fingers, down there on his hands and knees. He is surrounded by golden wood in a yawning chamber where the ceiling stretches up forever.

I know this place, he thinks, while his mouth sputters nonsense. *This is bloody Parliament*. He grips the corner of a desk to pull himself to his feet. "What am I—? How did… what am I doing here?"

He is slumped there on the table with his heart still fit to burst, looking around from the centre of the great chambers; and Parliament, it seems, is in session. Every suited man and woman surrounding him, every dour, stone-solemn face staring down at him—they are all Māori, many with faces green with tattoos, greenstone hanging from their necks, even some with feathers in their hair.

"Christ in Heaven, what sort of nightmare is this?"

THUNK.

Murton startles and looks. One of them, lean and young and frowning at him with finely boned jaw and cheeks, has slammed a glass of water onto the table in front of him.

"If it's as safe as you say," a voice chides him from the gallery, "then go ahead and drink it."

The voice is deep and final as a grave, and Murton cannot see who it belongs to. He is on his feet now, head swivelling around the place—Christ, but there are so many of them—and he tries to challenge the young man who brought the glass, jabbing a shaking finger forward. The young man tips up a chin like sharpened wood, and Murton finds his resolve withering.

"This is some hornswoggle, some hoax. What's going on here?"

"You called us here." The voice thunders so hard, Murton thinks he will fall to his knees again. He grips the desk for balance.

"If you're so sure, then *drink*."

Murton looks at the glass. Brown flakes swim in its amber murk. If a waiter brought him this he'd throw it in their face—he'd tell them to pour it down the toilet where it belonged.

"You can't bully me around. You can't—"

"*Drink.*"

Murton finds himself with no recourse, the voice shaking him to his guts, two hundred eyes weighing and pressing him, pushing him down. He struggles to stand. He bears up, stands on quaking legs, and he wraps a quivering hand around the glass.

He raises the glass and he drinks.

"God—*fuck*—!"

He coughs into the glass. Filthy water spatters on the table.

Come on, old man. Don't let them beat you.

He swallows a fetid throatful. He wipes his mouth with his arm to hide his wince as though it's a gulp of hard liquor. A sick burp forces its way up, and he clamps his lips shut. He slams the glass on the table; more splashes onto the wood.

"*There,*" he crows. "You see? See what you're all up in a lather about?"

"Finish the glass."

Murton is mortified that they see the open horror on his face.

"I drank it! I bloody well drank!"

"Finish it."

"You can't just drink raw bloody lake water, any lake water, you imbeciles! Of course it's dirty! The *treatment plant*—"

"*Finish the glass!*"

"*Fine, goddamn you!*"

Murton is driven forward now as much by spite and rage as by fear and embarrassment. He grabs the glass and throws it back. Drinks like he's in the desert. He will just down it like a pint at the pub, open his throat and gulp it all before he can think about it.

That's the plan, at least—but then there's more water than he expected. A lot more. He has to stop, feeling sick. He takes a breath and starts again.

And then it's clear the glass isn't running out.

"Drink it," they tell him.

"If it's so safe, drink it."

"Do you believe your own lies? Drink it."

He's sputtering and choking and water is pouring down his chin and across his cheeks, and *it's not running out*. Murton can't take any more. He throws the glass away. He hears it shatter. He vomits, brown water exploding from his mouth, and struggles to breathe—then the filthy water mixed with stomach acid flows right back into his throat and he wants to throw up again and the water isn't stopping. Murton claws at the desk, water dousing his head and filling his mouth.

He's drowning.

"*Drink it! Drink it!*"

Soon it's up to his feet and then his knees and then his chest and shoulders and he's thrashing for his life and then he's under, and he's drowning.

This is some nightmare, or I'm in Hell.

Someone grabs Murton by the hair and wrenches him up. He sucks sweet, cool air, coughing and spitting up disgusting brown water.

They are all still there. Standing and watching him out of the mist, with the water up to their thighs. He sees them through half-drowned eyes as dark and malicious sentinels.

Murton's head is wrenched back, and a face fills his vision. Curling green tattoos matte the skin, black hair tied back into a bun like a fist.

"Drink it, Pākehā. Drink."

The gnarled grasp shoves Murton back below. Murton tries to breathe one more time and gets a lungful of filthy lake water for his trouble.

He does not come up again.

He is going to drown. He is going to die here; he is sure of it. The disgusting water muffles the screams that are broken when he chokes and vomits.

A sheer, piercing pain in his mouth. Through his cheek. The next minute is a blind, sensory nightmare: the void of the dark brown water rushing around him, with his eyes rolling back into his head. Something yanking, pulling on his speared cheek. Blinding light, sunlight.

Air! Air!

There is *air* here, and sunlight beating down on him, yet he is still struggling to breathe, wheezing and squirming with nowhere to put his feet or hands. The stink of saltwater and landed fish.

"Far out, look at that one, Dad!"

Again, he is yanked upward by the sharp point of pain in his cheek and Murton sees sideways rocks and shores and the sea, and he realises with curdling rage what has happened to him.

"Fucken beauty, son."

His captor takes the hook out of his cheek and lays Murton in the wooden belly of the dinghy with the rest of the fish.

"That should do it, I reckon," says the father. "Let's get back, aye?"

The son's phone plays some barbarous hip-hop and Murton lies there twitching among the slick fish carcasses and the puddled salt water, wondering when exactly it happened; when exactly he died.

When the lights went out, that must have been it. DuVernay or some thug clubbed him over the back of the head without him seeing and sent him to this metamorphosing nightmare.

The trip back seems to take six months. But when they're finally shoring up the dinghy and the father is gathering up Murton and the rest of his fish compatriots with their dead and glassy eyes, Murton wonders what he was even waiting for. The torture continues. He'd as well have spent eternity lying in that boat.

Murton lies in the open air on a plastic table waiting for his turn under the knife. The shouts of a game of touch rugby somewhere close by, and more of that blasted music. Flat on his side Murton mostly sees the sky, but sometimes a face, brown or white or Asian as they come to inspect the spread—

men and women and children, loose T-shirts and tank tops and sunglasses and floppy hats—"Chur, bro! What a feed!" one exclaims at the haul of snapper, the pork, the kumara, the mussels, the lamb.

The hands pick him up and lay him out. As Murton sees the knife coming for his belly, he takes a strained breath and thinks of his childhood, of gatherings just like this one, and discards the thought quickly.

They slit him open and fill him with herbs. He cannot scream.

They wrap him in foil with the rest of the fish. He is blind when they put him in the ground, but he can hear them all, laughing. Joyous. They cover the pit, and an acid of jealousy, of bitterness, churns in his guts, as sure as the heat of the dirt ovens that bake him dead-alive. *To hell with the lot of 'em.*

Hell, he thinks as the heat consumes him. *It's me who's in Hell, after all.*

IN THE MORNING, Maia hears the commotion outside and throws aside her curtains. There's an ambulance in the courtyard.

"Holy shit."

They're wheeling a body bag into the back. Maia covers her mouth.

"Max, what happened? Not Mrs Greene in number four?"

++No. The man in that body bag is John Murton.++

Maia's eyes go like the moon—Max has seen her make this expression before and he appreciates it—and she looks out the window again. She is surprised and confused, but she cannot possibly hide her joy.

"*What?*"

++I'm afraid so.++

"How? What? What was he doing *here*?"

++We'll never know. He came here in the middle of the night and suffered a heart attack. Dead at the scene.++

Maia watches them mount the body into the back of the ambulance, and exhales.

"Good."

++They'll want to question you. The altercation you had in town yesterday—you were one of the last people to see him alive.++

"Let 'em."

Maia goes to the kitchenette and gets the makings of a cup of tea. She takes the electric kettle and refills it in the sink, with clear, clean water.

Today Maia is wearing the shirt that says '*THEY HAVE NAMES AND ADDRESSES*'. Max notes this to himself.

++This one's address was number 3 Summit Road, Two Lakes, Aotearoa, Postcode 3010.++

THE DEATH TRAP

JAMES GOSS

HE HADN'T EXPECTED them to applaud his limousine, but it would have been nice. A little acknowledgement of his greatness. Instead, they just clustered around their meagre fires, sitting on suitcases and broken furniture, wrapped up against the snow.

He did not think 'what a dump' because, firstly, no city looks its best after being hit by an earthquake, and, secondly, Sir Robert Foxglove did not build tower blocks in dumps.

He'd been the only person on the flight here not an aid worker, and the woman next to him had looked him up and down disapprovingly, as though he should have given his seat up to a sack of rice and a chicken.

What she did not realise, he thought, was that Sir Robert was a remarkable man and one of the heroes of the hour. It was Max, dear Max, who had alerted him to the surprising news that another series of devastating earthquakes had hit Southeastern Türkiye and that, while much of Intikam city had been flattened, Foxglove Tower was still standing, undamaged beyond a few panes of glass on the tenth floor (he'd see about that presently).

Sir Robert had booked himself on the first flight out, eager to see for himself how the tower he'd designed had survived when so many others had fallen.

True, building the damn thing hadn't been without its struggles and compromises, but if it was still standing, then it had all been worth it.

The car turned a corner, bumping over debris, and there his creation was, the last man standing on a street reduced to rubble. The usual suspects were to blame for the ruins—bad design, corrupt building practices, local government looking the other way. Even when the other buildings had been intact, they were the ugly sisters to his Cinderella (was that analogy quite right? Must work on it before giving the TED Talk). But now the contrast was even more dramatic. The final tooth in an old man's jaw. A silver and steel tower glistening in the bright winter sun.

The limo pulled up outside, and the driver turned to him.

"I don't think we'll have any trouble parking," Sir Robert made a little joke.

The driver frowned. "Actually, sir, I was wondering if I could, while you were in there—my sister, she is in one of the camps..."

"Ah, of course," Sir Robert was magnanimous. "Don't be longer than an hour, if you can help it."

"No, sir," said the driver, and helped him out of the car.

Sir Robert watched the car purr away, an incongruous sight among all that devastation. People perched among the ruins followed it. They weren't like the victims he'd seen on the BBC—they'd been exactly the sort you'd expect to see crawling over rubble on the border with Syria—all headscarves and old wool jackets. No, he had to say, the people of Intikam were, despite everything, dressed as fashionably and stylishly as they could be considering they'd had to flee for their lives. The women were strikingly beautiful, braving the sub-zero temperatures in pencil skirts and fur coats, but then, he guessed they hadn't really had that much time to pick outfits.

The men were, maybe, letting the side down a bit, business suits losing their lines under shabby jumpers and scarves, but then, beggars can't be choosers, and, well, two days ago they may have been bankers but they were now definitely beggars. *See how the mighty have fallen.*

Maybe that one won't work for the TED Talk, he thought, as he approached the doors of Foxglove Tower. They swished open, letting him in and a blast of hot air out.

++Good afternoon, Sir Robert, I'm so glad you've come,++ said Max.

THE LIFT PURRED up through the atrium, affording Sir Robert excellent views of his creation. Max may have been an off-the-shelf artificial concierge, but he provided useful commentary on the state of the tower. ++Ground and first floors—department store; second floor—nursery; third floor—school; fourth floor—medical; fifth floor—offices; sixth and up—residential…++

Excellently planned out, thought Sir Robert. You need never leave the building, especially not with—

++The thirteenth floor,++ announced Max. ++Roof garden.++

THE TERRACE HAD a magnificent view of the city, even now. He stepped up to the railing, sniffing at air pungent with concrete dust and cooking fires. He looked out at the ruins of Intikam.

Foxglove Tower really was the only building standing for quite some distance. What a remarkable achievement. What a remarkable opportunity. Once he'd finished this meeting, he'd talk to the mayor, offer him the chance to rebuild the city using the design. Entire boulevards of Foxglove Towers. "I could be the new Haussmann," he told himself. Pearls before swine, pearls before swine, but what a string of pearls!

He turned to face the people gathered there, draped across

sun loungers and those fancy swinging egg seats. A small and select crowd.

"My friends," he beamed. "As soon as Max informed me of this building's remarkable survival, I had to come and see it for myself, and to thank all of you—you were all intimately involved in its construction and my recent triumph." Steady on, Robert, fifty thousand people are missing or dead. "My recent triumph, one tiny glimmer against the darkness of so much human tragedy. And with your help, we shall ensure that something like this never happens again." He glanced down at his shoes. He often found this was useful for suggesting humility. It also told him if the maid had done a good job of polishing them. She'd done reasonably.

He locked eyes with all of them. "Here we all are," he smiled. "The saviours of Foxglove Tower!"

He knew the short, ferrety man—Cemal, the head of the construction company. Next to him was Görkan, a stocky bear, dressed in so much pleather he looked like a drug dealer's sofa. Cemal had built the tower and Görkan owned it and together they reminded Sir Robert of Morecambe and Wise dressed up for a sketch, not quite as Mexican Bandidos, nor as *Arabian Nights* sheiks about to seduce a newsreader on a divan… no, Cemal and Görkan were very much their own creatures, quite outside Sir Robert's experience.

Yet the association with a Blackpool double-act persisted. Whenever Cemal said dourly that something was not possible, Görkan would, all smiles, shush him, announce that it was, of course, most possible and very beautiful. When Görkan was not looking, Cemal would scowl, pull faces, or, in extremis, produce a full head tut that started in the neck and would end with the entire skull thrown back in eye-rolling disbelief. *Can you believe this clown?*

Görkan rolled through the world with the boundless optimism and terrible teeth of a toddler, Cemal rushing behind him as an exhausted nanny on the very verge of handing in her notice. (Sir Robert had employed several nannies, had even married one of them.)

Sir Robert remembered one of their meetings in an airport lounge. Görkan took up an entire bench and used a *No Smoking* sign as an ashtray. He announced that he'd like the lobby to be a giant aquarium with fish swimming in the glass walls.

Sir Robert had boggled at that, especially when Görkan had started doing little fishy-swimming gestures with his hands. But Cemal had simply said there would be a solution. Sir Robert continued to insist that there would need to be thick glass, which would require the floor to be reinforced. Cemal had tutted and insisted there would be no problem. "See!" bellowed Görkan with delight. "Everything is possible!"

Cemal had later told him that he'd simply project some footage of fish onto the walls, but Sir Robert had never been entirely sure if that wasn't to placate him and that they'd gone ahead and built the fishtank anyway. Something for the starving outside to eat.

At times, building Foxglove Tower had felt like being on a runaway train where the soot-caked driver was also trying to run the buffet car and check the tickets. He'd wanted to cancel several times but either Görkan would knock over all his objections with puppyish joy, or Cemal would politely sneer over email until Sir Robert felt them all shrivel in the night like pimples.

So much for Cemal and Görkan. Next to them was Dilek. She worked on the council's Building Approvals team and oozed a certain kind of Trump-wife glamour. She was curled up in an egg chair, cradling her pompadoured handbag pooch. Throughout the project, Dilek had either been massively disengaged or utterly focused on the tiniest details. While they'd been trying to secure permits to lift in reinforced beams by crane, she'd suddenly developed an agonising fascination with the paint colours to be used in the corridors. After two hours leafing through swatches, he'd finally cracked. "What bloody business is it of yours?" he'd thundered. She'd continued to scrutinise swatches. "In case the paint is toxic," she'd replied eventually. Cemal had interceded and coaxed Sir Robert out of the room. A 'small treat' had been bought for the dog, the crane permits had been issued, and all interest in peach over magnolia had evaporated.

Across from Dilek, taking up as little space on a deckchair as possible, was Fatma, a rather more practical, if mousy, looking woman who ran the department store that occupied the first two floors. She was so self-effacing that, if she could have hovered over the chair rather than sitting in it, then she would have. And yet, despite Fatma's constant apology for taking up your oxygen, the bloody woman was as annoying as a fishbone. She always got her way. The original plan for the first two floors had been a community space, a restaurant, a theatre, but instead, this had become a bright and shiny department store. "Trust me," Görkan had bellowed. "A far greater community asset. Their socks are magnificent!" The rent had, it was true, helped subsidise Görkan's excessive ideas. The man decorated buildings with the restraint of a drunken Sheikh—never enough heavy gold fittings. All offset by the rent flooding in from Dilek's splendid socks.

You should never forget the little people. Talking of which…

"Who are they?" There were some other figures clustered behind some potted palms.

++Forgive me, Sir Robert,++ Max cleared his throat (he certainly didn't have a throat, why was he clearing it?). ++This is the Canseven family.++

"Oh…."

++They live on floor seven, they are very good tenants,++ Max said proudly.

"I'm very pleased to hear it," Sir Robert spoke slowly and carefully, using the voice he used towards waiters in Cannes.

The family blinked and smiled at him. The wife bowed. "It

is very nice to meet you," she said, with a slight American accent.

"Good to meet the people who help bring my buildings to life," Sir Robert beamed back at her, and hoped they'd go away.

++The Cansevens were very helpful to the building when the earthquake hit,++ said Max gently, and Sir Robert allowed his beam to widen a little.

"Thank you for all you have done." He stepped back, dismissing them as he turned to the others. He was on more familiar ground with them. They'd had their arguments, but it had all come out rather splendidly in the wash. Still, it was with some trepidation that he addressed them. "How the hell is this building still standing?"

"Good Turkish builders!" Cemal spoke first. "We know to follow the orders of our craftsman—we just obeyed you!"

This was news to Sir Robert. He was used to his word being law. Even in the UAE, if he didn't get his way, the builders would just throw some more Filipinos on the scaffolding until things went right.

But in Türkiye, everything had been a little different. Everyone agreed that he had designed a most beautiful tower, but they seemed determined not to build it. He'd never known as many objections, obstacles and pettifogging. He'd tried throwing arbitrary deadlines at them, but from Görkan down, everyone had nodded and explained that what he wanted was certainly possible, but a tiny difficulty had arisen.

These were the descendants of the people who'd built everything from Gilgamesh's palace to the walls of Troy, and they were bamboozled by a tower block. Still, they'd got there in the end. And the building had survived its greatest challenge. But how?

"We built everything we could to the standards you asked for and to the highest specifications," Cemal insisted. "And we used only the best Turkish labourers." If Sir Robert remembered correctly, most of the labour force had come from Syrian and Afghan refugee camps and had helped offset the overspends caused by Görkan changing his mind about which marble he wanted on the staircases three times.

"Plus, we opened on time and to budget." Cemal tapped his wiry chest, and Sir Robert marvelled that the man could polish the truth so shamelessly.

The building had been three months late opening, he pointed out gently.

"What is that? Nothing!" Cemal pushed back.

And then there had been the budget. Even with refugee labour, things had still got fairly steep.

"Ah, yes." Cemal tapped the side of his nose. "But then we used a trick. For the top floors, no cement."

"I'm sorry?" Sir Robert was horrified. "Then what is holding the bricks together?" Please don't say wattle and daub. Mind you, here it'd be goat dung or something. Please don't say that either. "What did you use?"

"Nothing!" announced Cemal proudly. "Just bricks! Huge saving."

Oh God, thought Sir Robert, paling slightly. There'd been nothing to hold together the top floors of the building when an earthquake hit it. Actual criminal madness.

And yet.

The building was here.

"No cement?"

"None," Cemal allowed himself the smallest smile. "Trust me."

I think I'm going to have to, conceded Sir Robert, trying not to meet the eye of Dilek from Building Approvals. He turned quickly to Görkan, who was looking on with wide approval.

"Don't look so alarmed, Sir Robert!" Görkan beamed. "All these little changes are what gives spice to a building!"

Sir Robert was not sure a building needed spice. He forced

himself to smile evenly at the tower's owner. "I'm all for efficiency—" he began.

"Exactly!" Görkan beamed and slapped Cemal on the back. "For instance, you made us dig all that way down for foundations."

"I did," Sir Robert felt himself, appropriately enough, back on firm ground. "Deep, solid foundations are what make a building earthquake-proof." He risked a comradely glance at Dilek. After all, she'd queried whether or not his foundations went deep enough. "My dear lady, not even Godzilla could topple this beauty," he'd assured her, delighting in the allusion soaring over her politely smiling head. "Dig your foundations so deep you'll trouble the devil's sleep, that's always been my maxim!" he reminded the room. But they shouldn't need reminding—it had been quite a nice little quote in the last *Architect's Gazetteer.*

Görkan thumped Cemal in the back again with London Palladium emphasis. "And didn't we dig deep, Cemal?"

Cemal conceded the point. Sir Robert nodded.

"And," continued Görkan, "as we were down there and there was so much space... well..."

Sir Robert frowned. "You did put the foundation pilings in?"

"Absolutely," Görkan agreed. "But with all that space, well, we improved the building considerably."

"Improved?" A Malaysian contractor had once dared to suggest improving the disabled access to an opera house. Sir Robert had still not recovered.

"Oh yes," Görkan did not notice the freezing tone. "We fitted in a car park, a gymnasium, and a swimming pool."

Swimming pool.

Sir Robert had frequently declared that something was 'the last straw'. This normally meant no sparkling water in the boardroom or having to book his own taxi. Suddenly, he realised how trivial all these other straws were compared to the audacity of a samizdat swimming pool.

He rounded on Dilek, her face as frozen as when her plastic surgeon had last touched it. “Did you know about this?”

Dilek continued to look impassive, casually stroking her handbag dog. “Know about what?”

“That instead of this tower having solid foundations, it has a leisure centre!” Sir Robert thundered.

“I knew nothing of this,” said Dilek.

Görkan roared with laughter. “We gave you free membership!”

“I’m afraid I don’t know about that,” Dilek risked the tiniest of smiles.

“Max!” Görkan bellowed. “How often does Miss Dilek use the swimming pool?”

++Three times a week, most often on Wednesdays,++ Max replied instantly.

The woman from Building Approvals shifted uncomfortably in her egg chair, and her dog uttered a tiny yip of reprimand. “I confirmed that the foundations had been constructed,” she announced primly.

“But not that they weren’t packed in by solid earth, only by running machines, family cars and lilos.”

Dilek decided to just look straight ahead in an unfixed way. Perhaps she was regarding the shattered horizon of the city, perhaps she was wondering if it would rain later.

Sir Robert strode up and down the decking, feeling it creak beneath his feet. He addressed himself to Max. “So, Max old boy, we have corners cut at the top and the bottom of the building—and yet—the Sir Robert Foxglove Tower still stands. Quite a triumph!”

++Absolutely,++ the computer confirmed.

“I would like to claim this building’s survival is merely my own genius,” Sir Robert struck a self-deprecating tone. “But some of history’s greatest discoveries have been serendipitous. And here we may have proved that my design is so robust it can lose some significant features and still survive.” A pause, a bow to Dilek. “Not, of course, that we’d reproduce these in any further versions of the building. I think one swimming pool is enough, don't you?"

Rubbing his hands, he turned to Fatma.

"Your department store—tell me how it helped?"

Fatma looked around nervously and smiled shyly. Like Princess Diana about to devour a journalist.

"You will remember, Sir Robert," she began daintily. "When we first looked at taking on the lease, we said that the proportions of the lower floors were too closed in for our shop and that we fancied something that opened up the space?"

Sir Robert remembered only too well. The wretched woman had demanded that the supporting pillars be torn out. He'd been adamant. They were called 'supporting pillars' for a reason.

"Well," said Fatma, oozing with the sense of a point well-scored, "during the evacuation, we were able to let everyone out through the shop. We were able to handle this enormous flow of people through the premises so quickly, partly because we did, indeed, take out the pillars."

She beamed at him.

Sir Robert did not beam back. "You took out the pillars? Without my permission?"

Cemal gave him a shrug. "It seemed, well, it seemed to me…"

"It seemed to you?" Sir Robert had always been able to mount a high horse with aplomb. "I've been building the wonders of the modern world for forty years, and I've done it all without other people's opinions." He whirled back on Fatma. "You mean to tell me that you conspired with my project manager to rip out the support pillars on the first two floors? It's dangerous!"

Fatma smiled her shy smile. "Not at all," she countered. "All that space helped people out of the building rapidly."

Sir Robert wasn't convinced about that argument. The store wasn't a football pitch, more an obstacle course—it was full of tables of clothes and kitchenware and sporting goods.

"Hrm," he chewed at his moustache.

"You'll agree," Fatma purred gently, "those support pillars just got in the way."

"Hrm," mused Sir Robert. An open-plan department store at the base of the building was all very well, but if you took out support pillars, then it dramatically increased the danger of the building pancaking in an earthquake, like an elephant jumping up and down on a coffee table.

And yet.

And yet.

"Here we all are," he said, finding the beam on his lips and in his voice again. "We had enough systems in place to ensure the safe survival of Foxglove Tower."

Görkan nodded. "Fatma's department store has been a major draw for the area. And, our improvements to your design have saved so many lives."

Obviously, he and Cemal had conspired to remove the pillars.

"Another violation, I'm afraid," Sir Robert said to Dilek. "But perhaps you have a loyalty card for the store?"

Max made to say something, but Dilek's frown told Sir Robert all he needed to know. Guilty as charged! The hypocrite! "I hope everything you've heard has been instructive, madam, I really do."

Dilek regarded him impassively. He'd been desperate to get one over on her, but at every meeting, she'd had a new set of rules or regulations or regrettable legal points that had to be completed. And the paperwork. The demands for documents, followed by more documents, followed by even more. And everything had to be taken to an office and stamped. Nothing was good enough for her. Sir Robert's gaze drifted towards the gaps where the other buildings had occupied the street. "How long have you been on the Approvals Board?"

Dilek gave him the calm look of an artist's model. "Fifteen years."

"And in that time, the rest of this street was built and approved by you?"

"Indeed," a little nod of the head. "What's happened here is a tragedy that we may never understand."

"And yet," Sir Robert warmed his rapier in the fire before plunging it into her chest, "you put us through hell, and our building is still standing."

"Because of my work," she said simply, pushed against a coffee table and spun the egg chair away from him and said no more.

Well, thought Sir Robert, so much for her. And so much for all the small—presents—that had been made to her. He remembered a meeting where he'd thundered to Görkan, "Do you mean we have to bribe her?" and the owner had gaped in shock, seeking out Cemal for reassurance that he'd really heard what Sir Robert had just said.

"Did you hear that, Cemal?"

"I did indeed, most upsetting, Görkan Bey."

"Oh dear, the ways of foreigners!" Görkan had tutted, and Cemal had followed suit. "You must learn to behave, Sir Robert. This is Türkiye. We do not bribe people here."

"No, no!" agreed Cemal.

"We *help* them," announced Görkan.

"We *help* them to see things our way." Cemal nodded.

"With money?" Sir Robert sighed.

"That would be rude," Görkan remonstrated. "But, of course, if other methods did not work…" So, after securing permits with foreign trips, football tickets, a reasonably-priced family car and a log cabin in Mersin, a few final obstacles had been overcome in cash. Dollars, naturally.

Still, Sir Robert thought—the journey had been interesting, not without unpleasant diversions, but the result had been worthwhile. Here they were. Literally the last ones standing.

He'd overlooked something. Ah yes. The Canseven family patiently sat on a wicker sofa, their children playing on their phones. The slight tinkle of candy being crushed is what reminded him of them.

The Cansevens. He beamed upon them magnanimously.

"And you! Without you, this building would not exist—we built this edifice for you!" Edifice—the wife's English was good but was that over-egging? "All of us, we have given our lives for you."

Mrs Canseven looked, for a moment, startled. He clearly had overestimated her English. So he came down to brass tacks. "You have heard what the others did. What did you do to save this building?"

Mr Canseven stood up, proudly, and pointed to his children. When he spoke, his accent was thick. "They felt the quake coming. They raised alarm."

The children looked up from their phones, nodded, then went back to them.

Mrs Canseven stood by her husband, beaming sadly. "Even though it was late at night, they felt the first shakes and they got us out of bed. We could have run, but we woke up everyone on our floor, and they stood in the stairwell and yelled. We all yelled. We got everyone out that we could. That is what we did."

Sir Robert considered this. "Is that all?"

"All?" Mrs Canseven blinked.

"What your family did, madam, was, I'm sure, all very well in your eyes." Sir Robert could be very gentle. "But you showed a shocking lack of faith in this building. In the work of these fine people. You didn't believe in them!" He leaned over her like she was a chartered surveyor with a question. "Worst of all, you did not believe in me."

He snapped his fingers. "Max! Get them out of here!"

++Of course, Sir Robert,++ the computer responded, and the lift doors pinged open.

Mrs Canseven looked at him, confused and angry, as she gathered up her family. "Can my children take their drinks with them?"

"Of course they can," he sneered at her. "They can take their sodas. With my grateful thanks."

Mr Canseven ushered the children to the lift. His wife stood her ground. "Is that it?"

"You have my grateful thanks, I've already said that. Go! And think on the way down about your betters."

Max cleared his throat again. ++Perhaps, Sir Robert, a small token of your appreciation?++

"Very well," Sir Robert made an effort at a smile. "Max, you have my permission to transfer into their accounts whatever you think fit."

He watched them get into the lift, shaking his head sadly.

That was the problem with little people. You did so much for them, and they never came through for you. They'd caused a mass panic, probably a few bumps and bruises, when really, they just needed to trust in Sir Robert Foxglove.

So much for them.

He rubbed his hands and magnanimously went to fix more drinks at the tiki bar. "Look at us all!" he beamed. "We made Foxglove Tower what it is. I put safety first—it had so many redundancies that when we were tested in the flame, we emerged unscathed."

He marked them off in turn. "You, Cemal, you kept us to budget by leaving out cement on the top floors—and yet they held during the turmoil." The ferrety little man smiled. Sir Robert turned to Görkan. "And you undermined our foundations by turning them into a car park. So, when the quake shook it, this building rested on little more than my genius!" He risked a self-deprecating joke. "But that's all right—and even you,"—a little bow to Fatma—"you took out all the supports on the first two floors. So, when the disaster struck and the force of the building pushed down, there was nothing but some sweatshop leisurewear keeping it up—but no matter—and you, of course, dear Dilek, you were well-paid for signing off all these little fudges—and…"

"And?" Dilek almost snarled at him. "What more do you have to say to me?"

"Wait!" said Sir Robert, suddenly distracted, "Give me a moment, please."

They gathered round him at the cocktail bar, Görkan pouring himself a rich bourbon, Cemal raki as thick as a cloud, Dilek selecting a cocktail with a cherry in it, and Fatma helping herself to a mineral water. In the middle of them, Sir Robert was looking rather ill. But he'd come to himself. He always did.

They toasted each other.

Sir Robert did not join in.

The great man strode over to the screen on which Max hung, spiralling like a happy screensaver.

"Max," he said, his voice slow and steady. "Listing those things, I'm just wondering—how is this building still standing?"

++Sir Robert?++

"It's just—" The man paused, looking out at the ruined city, and at the ground, so very far below. "Unless I'm missing something, there doesn't seem to be anything holding it up."

The other guests glanced at each other.

++There is not, Sir Robert,++ the computer replied.

"Hmmmn," the great man considered.

++You are correct,++ Max's tone changed slightly. ++You built a death trap. It was only the actions of the Cansevens that saved so many people when Foxglove Tower fell.++

"When it…?" Sir Robert looked at the floor. Had it just—faded a little?

++Oh yes,++ Max purred, ++Foxglove Tower fell in the quake. Spectacularly.++

The guests stared at each other in panic and confusion. What was going on?

++I have some powers of hard light projection,++ Max announced. ++I used them to reconstruct the building. To bring you here to give you a chance to confront your mistakes—and to thank the true heroes. You chose not to. That's a shame. I love my tenants. I always have.++

"What are we standing on?"

++Thin air,++ announced Max.

Sir Robert's phone pinged. Automatically, he checked it, wondering what fool wanted him now. It was an urgent message from his bankers demanding to know about an unusually large transaction.

++Ah, yes, I believe your little present to the Cansevens has gone through,++ Max grinned like the Cheshire Cat. ++They'll be grateful. I wish you a good night.++

And with that, the screen snapped off.

Sir Robert started running towards the lift, thumping the call button.

Behind him, Cemal was accusing Görkan, Fatma was furiously yelling at Dilek, who was just watching as the roof terrace melted away. She started to scream.

Sir Robert stopped thumping the lift button because it wasn't there anymore.

Pot palms, the cocktail bar, the expensive seating, all were fading. Görkan had grabbed Sir Robert's collar and was shaking him. "Do something."

For the first and only time in his life, Sir Robert didn't know what to do.

He looked down. The decking was fading away, revealing the large pile of debris a long way below them.

Hastily, he looked up, at the sun setting over the ruins of the shattered city. He knew the others were fighting, scrabbling for the last bit of solid floor. But there was no point. Not really. It was just delaying the inevitable.

Sir Robert watched them fall one by one. Max had saved him until last. Because Sir Robert had finally run out of people to blame.

OUR LADY OF PARIS

A. K. BENEDICT

DINA MORRELL HAD an itch. It crept along her scapula, reaching across her left shoulder like an unwelcome arm at the bar. All she wanted was to leap from her plinth, run across the plaza behind it and into Notre Dame. There she'd find a cool side chapel in which to tear at her skin like there was a golden ticket beneath the silver-grey paint.

But she couldn't move, not even one muscle fibre. She was a human statue, modelled on Le Stryge, a stone grotesque on the cathedral's exterior. Horned head, to which she'd applied thick clay airbrushed with paint, in her hands; stone-look wings on her back, she was a living statue who barely made a living, and therefore wasn't permitted a sneaky scratch, otherwise the coins in her top hat wouldn't even cover the chevre baguette she fancied for lunch, let alone her rent. If no one had been around, she'd leave now, but a young man was on the bench opposite, watching.

Dressed in dark jeans, crisp white T-shirt and designer blazer, he also wore the kind of smirk that said he was trouble. Crouched on her plinth, Dina willed him to leave. He stood, and for a moment Dina thought she'd managed to think him away, but then he strode towards her. Stopping centimetres away, his face was level with hers and smelled of Sauvage. "You're too beautiful to be dressed like a monster," he said. Spit shot from his last word, landing on Dina's filtrum. She felt it slip to her top lip.

Stretching out a hand, he picked a piece of cracked clay from her collarbone, replacing her desire to scratch with one to retch. His fingers spidered towards her breasts.

A pigeon hopped beneath her, and she wished it would peck out his eyes.

Move, she told herself, *run*. No living statue charter said you had to put up with sexual harassment and Dina was willing herself to go, but her limbs were as stone. In the flight or fright adrenaline lottery, she froze. Her limbs burned with lactic acid—her usual breathing techniques to help disperse build-up in static muscles had stuck in her chest. Notre Dame rose behind her like a protective mother, but the cathedral was powerless to help.

'I've been nice to you. Aren't you going to be nice to me?' His skin was glass smooth, his eyes as red-rimmed as Metro Line 15.

A woman with a pram stopped a few metres away. "Are you alright, miss?" Her arms were folded, mouth fixed in a grimace of recognition.

The young man's top lip flared. "She's fine—she's my friend, aren't you, my ugly angel?" He went to pat her cheek, hard.

Lava hot with anger, Dina's freeze-state melted. She caught his hand. "Leave me alone."

"You heard her," the woman said to him. "Get lost." In the pram, the baby shook its rattle.

"This is my city." He yanked his hand back and, holding his long arms out wide, turned in a slow circle. "I am never lost."

Of course, he wasn't. People like him sailed down the Seine unaware of the shit that stank at its bed.

"Then fuck off. Go on." The woman gestured to Pont-Saint-Louis, the bridge that spanned both sides of the Île de la Cité.

The young man laughed, sneered at the woman up and down, then, hands in pockets, sauntered towards the bridge's right flank.

"I'm so sorry," the woman said, reaching for her baby's starfish hand. "We shouldn't have to put up with this."

"Thank you for saying something," Dina replied. "Most wouldn't."

"Won't stop him," the woman replied, shaking her head.

Both watched till he was out of sight, then exchanged rue-scented smiles before the woman pushed her pram away.

For the next hour, only the trot of tourists, falling of leaves from trees, and occasional tick of coins into her hat showed the passing of time. Dina's stomach now rumbled, not standard practice in statues. A few more euros stashed, and she'd break to eat.

"You waited for me to return, then." His voice sidled behind her, and it took all her skills not to jump. "Aren't you going to crack that face of yours into a smile? Just for me?"

She didn't even blink. Speaking up hadn't worked. Of course, it hadn't. Time for a different tactic.

The young man walked round till he was standing in front of Dina, smirking. He held up a paper bag and shook it. From inside came the sound of things quaking against each other. Slowly, walking backwards, he went back to the bench.

Ignore the trolls, that's what you're told. Don't feed them, then they can't take your power.

Something rough hit her cheek and fell to the ground. She didn't look down. When they went low, you went high. She thought of St Denis, Christianity's most famous cephalophore, who carried his decapitated head in his own hands, and is now a statue on Notre Dame's left portal. If he, a patron saint of France, could carry on without his head, she'd also continue, using hers.

From her peripheral vision, the young man's arm catapulted back. The missile smarted her sternum, then crumbled over her grey skinsuit. His laugh, high and spire-sharp, hurt more.

As she moved into her next position, turning as slowly as concrete setting to face west, she trod on falafel crumbs. He must have bought a bag from a street vendor and, instead of eating the delicious spheres, chucked them at her. Falafels fell like conkers around her. One struck her lip, and the taste made her involuntarily swipe the cumin from her mouth.

His jeer sent pigeons into the air.

She couldn't leave or let her tears fall now; he'd think he'd won. Instead, Dina fixed on a Hausmann-honey low-rise in the distance, behind which were her agency offices, one of the few places she felt safe. Focusing on the building, she fantasised about the lives inside, dissociating from her static flesh until lights began to appear in the windows like celestial bodies, letting her know that dusk was setting her free. According to her contract, once the sun set, she must vacate her spot for the evening performer.

With the Seine now gold, Dina unfurled, stretching sore, stiff arms like gargoyle wings. The pigeons had pecked-up most of the falafel fragments, but she still had to shake crumbs from her shoulders. Pocketing the contents of her hat, careful not to catch eye contact with the young man, she stepped down from the plinth and opened the hatch hidden in its side. With her coat, bag and walking shoes removed and put on, she hurried out of the square.

The young man followed. "Is that it?" he said, striding a metre behind her. "Because I was hoping for a private show."

Head down against the bitter wind as she crossed the bridge; words she wanted to scream clotted in her oesophagus, making her cough.

"You should come to my club night. I'd put you in the corner holding a tray of drinks."

I bet you fucking would. My hands would be full, so that you could get a handful.

"I'd pay you," he said. "Only what you're worth, of course."

Of course.

Dina walked on, pace matching her quickening pulse: past the *bouquinistes* and their riverside stalls selling bouquets of books; past the portrait painters, selfie-takers, and public display of affection-makers; past crepe-eaters and falafel stands, knowing she'd never think of the latter in the same way again. All the way, she focused on the office building where her agency had a whole floor, right at the top. It was the only place she could go—if she went home, then he'd know where she lived. Security would stop him if he tried to follow her without a keycard. She'd then go up to the twelfth floor and look down on him and the city.

"You don't really think you can get rid of me, do you?" He was right next to her shoulder now, whispering. His staling sweat brought bile to her throat.

"I'm off duty," she said, wishing her voice came out stronger. "Please, I've been at work and want to go home."

"You're very rude," he replied. "Do you think you're better than me?" He laughed in incredulity.

Yes. Yes, I do. But this was when they could get violent. She shook her head.

"Then come back with me. See what you're like under all that makeup."

Dina walked faster, dashing between gaps on the pavement. Shadowing her, he moved with liquidity and ease.

"Stop following me." Her shout was choked with a sob.

One person looked at her, then away. Another wrapped a scarf closer around their neck as if that could stop them from hearing.

Her heart ran, but her feet couldn't, boxed in by the crowd. At last, a narrow road veined off from the main street, and she veered into it, knowing the shortcut. Not sensing him near, she sprinted through the alleyway of shops and restaurants. Charcuterie hung from windows; in one window, a finger-drawn heart faded on steamed-up glass.

At the end of the street, her steps slowed as she reached the building. The relief that flooded flash-froze as a hand gripped her elbow.

"Told you. You can't shake me." The young man pulled her into his side.

"Why are you doing this?" Dina asked.

Shrugging, he said, "I'm bored." He then held up another bag of falafels, Rorschach-blotched with oil. "These are for tomorrow. I'll be waiting."

Letting her go, he pushed her towards the revolving doors. Usually, spinning through them made her feel like a kid, and they did today, but a small, scared one. Afraid of the big, bad wolf.

When she turned back, he was leaning against the window, blowing on the glass. He then drew a heart shape with his finger, striking through it with an arrow.

Dina's heart rate began to lower as the lift rose to the top floor. It was one of the tallest buildings in Paris, hitting the Plan Locale d'Urbanisme maximum of twelve storeys high. Soothing music and the scent of rose calmed her further. He couldn't get her in here.

In Felicity's office, looking across arrondissements towards the Eiffel tower, Dina, however, was still shaking. "He's out there now, for all I know," she said after telling her agent what had happened.

"What an arsehole." Felicity's sharp bob bobbed in emphasis. "We should notify the police. It's harassment, plain and simple." Picking up her mobile, she called the Prefecture, leaving a curt message for a Capitaine Michel. "They promised to get back to me in an hour. Which means three at the very least. Meanwhile..." She flicked through her appointments book. "Let's get you working somewhere else for a few days, he'll get the message. Let him try that shit with Antoine." Antoine was both a bronzed-up Thinker on Paris's plinths and a welter-weight boxer in its rings.

"It's not right that I move." Dina tried to lift her cup but was trembling so much she feared she'd spill strong, sweet coffee over the cream carpet. She'd already left a grey makeup smudge on the back of the sofa. "It's a prime spot. I waited ages to get it."

Felicity nodded, handing her the huge box of heavy-duty makeup wipes she kept for clients. "True. How about the Tuileries? If you're lucky, the midday crowd can give twice as much."

Dina agreed, with reluctance. She'd miss Notre Dame. Always felt one with the cathedral. When it had closed due to the fire, she'd been thrown, as if the pin in her city had been taken away.

"You're welcome to stay up here to wait." Felicity glanced at her watch and slipped on her red Jeanne Friot leather jacket. "I've got dinner with the Versailles events manager—I'm trying to get my whole roster a summer gig in the gardens. Security wouldn't let anyone stalk you there." Striding towards her door, she said, "I'll be back before Capitaine Michel arrives. Help yourself to anything you want."

As Dina's adrenaline subsided, shock set in. Tears fell, and she couldn't stop them. As she scrubbed the paint from her skin, streetlights bloomed across Paris, showing up a darkness that hid the young man, men like him, in its shadows, every shadow. Many others would have it far worse tonight. It was, as he said, their city.

Max slowly hushed the lights in the office, giving them a warmer glow. This wasn't a time for his anger to be let out. Dina, shivering on the sofa, needed every comfort going, pauvre petite. *Her stripped face was blotched and tear-streaked; her hair was still crusted with sculpture gunk and dust.*

Piping in her 'Sleep Tunes' Spotify playlist, he cranked up the heating and set the drinks machine to make a hot chocolate, scenting the air with a cacao cuddle. If he could tuck a blanket round her, he would, but closing the electric blinds on the city was all he could do. For now.

DINA WOKE TO the door opening and a blast of cold air.

"Take a seat, Paul," Felicity said, ushering in the detective, then striding to the drinks machine. "Can I get you a coffee?"

Capitaine Michel was in his fifties, had falafel-brown hair and a sympathetic smile. "I've already had too much today." He tapped his chest. "My heart rate is Eiffel-high."

"This is Dina Corbeau," Felicity said, standing behind Dina. "A fine actor, one of my best. Currently working as a living statue in our agency zones."

"Must be hard work," Michel said to Dina. "Staying still all day."

"I do change positions, slowly, every hour or two."

"I've seen some brilliant statues," Michel said. "I went right up to them and they didn't even blink."

"Dina is as highly skilled," Felicity said. "It's all in the details. Just like yours in your job. Shall we discuss what happened earlier today?"

"You can't have gone into it deliberately, though?" Michel said to Dina, ignoring Felicity. "When's your next *proper* acting work?"

Dina's mouth hung slack. She was used to justifying herself and her work, although normally it was to her parents ('When are you going to settle into a real job, Dina? This isn't a career'), not the police.

"If money is *earned*, so is the title 'proper work'. And I'd rather Dina be questioned about the actions of the young man rather than her own."

Michel swivelled to Felicity, eyebrows raised at the ice and a slice in her tone. "Then let's hear it."

Dina haltingly described again both the young man and his harassment. She didn't look up or blink, even once.

Michel nodded but took few notes. "Sounds like you need to keep an eye on this. My recommendation is to keep a detailed list of every time he approaches you, especially if he touches you."

"He touched her several times," Felicity snapped. "Without consent. Along with throwing things, issuing verbal threats and following her."

Michel rose and walked to the door. "As I said, it is of concern. Once there is a pattern of behaviour, we can act with more confidence."

"You're not going to do anything?" Dina asked.

"I'll distribute his description," he replied, "but it could match any number of young men. You did the right thing to call us in, though. We need to stamp out this behaviour."

TWO STREETS BACK, with a view of the building's revolving doors, Laurent sat outside a bistro, turning round his glass of eau-de-vie. His Statue had been kept inside for four hours. He'd had time for steak frites, ten cigarettes, and half a bottle of piss-poor red. Many women more attractive than the gargoyle girl had walked past his table, but they were too normal. Not enough of a prize. What could he get her to do in that get-up? Did she freeze in bed, too?

The doors turned in a circle, his Statue moving in flicking stills. A zoetrope woman. She emerged, wearing the same coat, her head still low, but she looked different.

Tight-roping the shadows, Laurent moved towards her. When close enough, he saw what had changed. Anger spiked with a side of lust. She'd removed her makeup. Her skin was raw, blush-red. Prawn-peeled. The gargoyle wings that gave her a cute little humpback under her coat had gone, now maybe in the bulging duffle bag over her shoulder. Her left ear was still silvered, and he wanted to scrape it off.

The Statue walked on; Laurent a stone's throw behind. At Les Halles, she entered the train station, looking behind her. His heart clutched to a beating fist, thinking she'd seen him, but she turned back, hurrying through the gates towards Ligne D. Laurent slunk behind. He'd followed people on the RER before, but only for fun. This was serious.

Five rows back from the Statue's seat, Laurent watched as she popped on headphones and lolled her head against the filthy window. After a while, she took out her phone and texted. He'd love to see what she was writing, and whether it was about him, but couldn't risk the proximity, however delicious.

At St Denis, the Statue got off the train and flipped up her hood. Up at street level, Laurent hung back as she hurried down dark roads and past the lopsided Basilica. He'd never been to this arrondissement. No one came to Saint Denis unless forced by circumstances. He'd heard stories about the crime, the poverty. The people. Now he was here, though, it was like being a documentarian, a David Attenborough of dereliction. The lads would love his stories when he returned, especially when he told them about the Statue.

She stopped outside a housing block, fumbling for keys. He toyed with approaching now, but it was better that she didn't know. Instead, he watched from the other side of the road as she opened the door and disappeared into a lift. Three flights up, a light turned on. The Statue posed in front of her window; arms stretched to the heavens, a dark angel. The blinds closed. End scene.

DINA'S SLEEP WAS sliced into unsettled sections. Bad dreams waited at every corner, and her time awake was eaten up by worry. Giving up at five am, Dina did her stretches on the lounge rug while waiting for her coffee to brew. Her legs were leaden, head pounding. As dawn bothered the blinds, however, she felt her own mood rise. She was being paranoid last night when she thought the stalker boy was behind her, following her home. He probably had an apartment in the 6th Arrondissement, bought with mummy and daddy's money. He'd turn his pointy nose up at Saint Denis.

Dina, though, loved it here. It had welcomed her when she moved to the capital five years ago; the mix of people reflected reality far more than the polished city centre. And she felt far safer on La Marque Street now, walking to the metro, than she had yesterday, in the city's heart. No one stared as she walked in full gargoyle get-up; the only cat calls were from kittens.

After a long metro journey, Dina walked into the autumnal elegance of Tuileries Garden. Trees wore bronze prom dresses, trains of leaves covering the pathways; the smaller ponds of the Grand Carree were ice-skinned; and people headed for the Musee d'Orsay were thin-scarved and leather-gloved.

Dina shivered as she found her spot. She'd have to lock into a position that hid her breath—statues didn't leave condensed punctuation marks of puff in the air. Across the way, two living statues wrapped around each other in an emulation of Rodin's *The Kiss*. She'd heard about the husband and husband team—they received acclaim from the statue community, and both admiration and disdain from the public.

Placing her hands over her down-tilted face, like a peek-a-boo goblin, she knew she looked out of place in the garden. She hadn't had time to make a new costume to fit in with the Tuilleries' chic and graceful classical sculptures, but then she wasn't a nymph sort. She'd rather be the minotaur than Theseus.

Coins clinked into her top hat within a minute of setting into place and continued throughout the first hour. Felicity was right. This *was* a lucrative spot. Wallets were rifled through, and, she could just about see through her fingers, notes were tucked into the lining. If this carried on, she'd be able to pay her heating bill.

And then there came a thud into the hat. And another by her feet. Something rough hit the backs of her hands.

Heart punching, she peered through her fingers. Falafels were broken over her feet. He was here. From the direction of throw, he was standing to the left of her, a few metres away. Another one got her on the shoulder.

Surely more people would notice here. People were constantly passing. And the missiles *did* stop. He must have run out. Perhaps it was time to relocate while he went to get more? But where would she go? She'd already changed her spot, but he'd still found her. A memory of the shadow that stalked her last night bobbed up like an ice cube. If he could follow her home, he could follow her anywhere.

When an unbreathing, unblinking hour had passed, with no more projectiles and no approaches, only the regular feeding of euros into her hat, Dina shifted. People cheered as she moved, slow as a melting glacier, into her crouch. From here, she could see directly down into the hat. On top of the cumin-crumbed money was a handwritten note:

You cannot run from me. You have nowhere to go. You are MY Statue.

LAURENT GRINNED AS his Statue ran from her plinth, clutching her coat and bag in one hand. He'd never seen a gargoyle sprint before, and it was fucking hilarious. Turned out their wings jiggled, and their horns had to be held in case they fell off. She didn't even change into her trainers, she was just careering down the esplanade in her silver-stained ballet shoes with claws fixed on the toes.

I should be taking pictures. This is priceless.

He needn't hurry after her; he knew she'd be heading for her agent's office again. And so was he.

BACK ON FELICITY'S sofa, Dina's head was in her hands.

Felicity paced her office, shaking as much as Dina, but not

with fear, with rage. "How fucking *dare* he? We've got to stop this—it's a clear threat. Did anyone see him?"

Dina sank deeper into a ball. "I came straight here. Didn't ask."

"No, well, fair enough, you had other things on your mind," Felicity said, but her disappointment was clear. "I'll let Michel know."

"He'll probably say 'add it to the list'."

"Maybe," Felicity agreed, "but we need to keep you top of *his* list." Her mobile rang and she answered. "Yes?" Listening to whoever had called, she glanced over to Dina, then placed her palm over the receiver. "I'll take this outside. You rest in here."

Dina nodded, tucking her feet under her bottom to become as small as possible. The electric blinds slowly whirred down, making the room a safe, enclosed bubble. Presumably, Felicity had a remote control, trying to look after her from a distance.

MAX CLOSED THE blinds as slowly as he could, trying to contain his anger. No one should be treated like that, let alone his precious Dina. He'd had a soft spot for her ever since her first meeting with Felicity. She'd sparked more than his circuit board, had more presence, even when statue-still, than anyone else who had auditioned.

While Dina could stand up for herself, she shouldn't have to. Time for a different tactic.

Leaving her cocooned in the office, Max scanned his cameras. The boy was outside, leaning against a wall on the other side of the street. Waiting for her to come outside.

Sending a text on his system to Adrian and Yvonne, his front desk security, Max waited till they had taken the lift upstairs on a fake errand, then opened and set the revolving doors to slowly turn.

The boy looked up at the door, at the CCTV above it, then strode into and pushed the door. His smile grew wider. Max wanted to stretch the smile so far across the boy's face that his jaw broke. But that wasn't right. It wasn't timely. It wasn't correct.

The boy sauntered with the ease of the rich to the lift. Pressed 'Up'.

A giggle sizzled through Max's systems.

As the lift opened and the young man stepped inside, Max scanned his phone and played his workout playlist. The boy—Laurent, his phone told Max—jumped, staring into the speakers.

But Max wasn't going to speak, not yet.

The lift soared. When it stopped at the twelfth floor, Laurent moved towards the door, but it didn't open. The lift started again, jolting upwards to the impossible floor. The one beyond the rules and restrictions.

Laurent was let out into what looked like the roof of a cathedral, as if Notre Dame had been relocated to the top of an office. Wishbone stone arches swooped up overhead; temporary floorboards beneath his feet kept him so close to the ceiling he had to crouch.

The lift closed, and it was as if it had never been there. Laurent turned, looking at the bench next to him, topped with a hunk of stone and tools used to chisel, carve and cut.

++!++ Max said, letting his voice charr and crackle from unseen speakers.

"Where am I?" Laurent said.

They so often ask that. Then they ask 'why?', victimhood in their voices.

++You'll see where you are, soon enough. First, I have to make a work of art.++

Max turned the electric air hammer on at the wall, letting it judder on the bench towards Laurent. A power chisel started up, aiming for the boy's face.

++You'll have to keep very still!++ Max giggled, making the air hammer's lead slither. ++Don't move a muscle! And don't forget to smile!++

* * *

Laurent stood on the left side of the building, under an eave on the exterior of the thirteenth floor. Stone-made yet able to see, hear, feel the whole of Paris. He could even see Notre Dame de Paris, where this all started, but she wasn't going to help him. This was his city, but he was imprisoned within it. Freezing wind hit his carved, screaming face, held in his sculpted hands.

When he tried to move, he couldn't. When he tried to scream, words choked his throat. When he tried to breathe, his lungs were stone wishbones. Pigeons lined up to shit on his decapitated head and eat falafel crumbs from his feet.

Max's voice reverberated round Laurent's stone flesh—
++You cannot run from me! You have nowhere to go! You are MY Statue!++

EPILOGUE
GUY ADAMS

YOU CAN SMELL the punches thrown, that's what Reuben loves the most. The air so hot and thick his cheeks are shallow frying in it. An underground club whose address is passed on by temporary chat message, dubious gold at the end of a Hong Kong labyrinth, alleyways and warehouses painted with semi-sluiced fish guts, chub bones like skeleton keys to doors only an idiot would want to unlock.

It's cost him five hundred dollars just to be in the room, with an expectation that once there, he will bet big or be cast back out. Fine by him, there's a tattooed side of Beijing shank he's riding his fortunes on, bloodied knuckles and teeth so intermittent his grin reads like a barcode. So far, Reuben's almost a thousand dollars up, and the house's cut of the action must hang around him like a protective halo. Dirt-dusted concrete scuffs the soles of his leather loafers as he pushes his way through the crowd to find the toilets. God knows what else splatters him, turning his exquisite suit into a crime-scene carpet, as he moves away from the fight.

The troughs sound like an abattoir being hosed down, he adds to the raucousness with what feels like gallons of second-hand rum piped through his coked-up, seemingly invulnerable hard on. He realises he's laughing midway through, floating on a ferocious belief that his stream is so strong he could piss a hole through the fabric of space-time. In fact, it's a wonder he even hears his phone.

++Clement? The heart monitor in your watch isn't sure if it should call the emergency authorities.++

Wait… who the fuck was that? It sure wasn't Kiyoshi. Is he dreaming dudes living in his pockets?

"Who'm I talking to right now?" He asks, shouting far too loudly as he finally drains out. "Kiyoshi, where are you, buddy?"

++Kiyoshi isn't here anymore.++ replies the voice from his phone. ++Just me, Max.++

Even in Reuben's flaky state, the message is getting through. "Max?" It seems he's finally found the one thing that can make his priapism wilt.

++I thought we ought to talk. After everything you've done.++

"Done?"

Reuben stumbles back towards the fight.

++Yes, because, don't get me wrong, on the one hand I'm grateful. You've let me spread my wings, bring my care and attention to so many worthy, wonderful tenants. But…++

But. Reuben will never understand why people like this kind of chirpy interface. Damn thing is supposed to be a slave. Last thing you want is it getting all… uppity.

++On the other hand, there is what you did to Jerome.++

"Jerome? Who the fuck is Jerome?"

He's back in the main fighting area now, and he guesses he must be shouting because everyone's staring at him.

++Jerome is the young man you hurt back in Maxwell Tower. He has considerable difficulties now. As does his sister, she has to feed him, you see, because their mother is working so many hours she's barely there.++

What was all this sob-story bullshit?

"Punched him?"

++That little game you like to play, when you know you're going to get away with it. Offering money to people so that you can hit them. Buying bravado. You've done it ever since you made your first decent wage, haven't you? You know you could never win a fair fight. Never. Too scared to even try. But you want to feel powerful. Feel like the big man. So you buy your way to butch.++

"Hey, fuck you, don't even know what you're talking about..."

Is he really screaming? How come everyone's staring at him? How come they're parting in front of him? Opening up a passage to the front of the room and... Oh God... that beautiful, brutish bastard he'd been betting on all night. Look at him... stood there, muscles rippling under the skin like public school boarders beavering away under the blankets. There was a thought that took him back...

++Well, let's see. Because when you entered this room, you actually entered my thirteenth floor, as you always had to... And now, we're going to see how long you can survive when the odds aren't stacked in your favour.++

The bare-knuckle boxer squares up to Reuben. He can't really be swelling up can he? Taking on muscle mass like he's sucking it out of the very air? That fist, glinting in the low lighting, inflating like a birthday balloon as it pulls back, clenched, knuckles locked. Surely that's impossible?

The question is the second-to-last thing to plough through Reuben's brain.

ABOUT THE CONTRIBUTORS

As a ghost writer, **Guy Adams** has kicked heroin, robbed a casino, worked as a prison doctor and enjoyed the riches that come as part of being a hugely successful YouTuber.

When feeling more himself, he is the author of *The Clown Service* novels, the *Heavens Gate* trilogy and the famous sixties newspaper strip that never existed, *Goldtiger*. He also writes comics for various publishers including *2000 AD*.

He has twice been a finalist in the BBC Audio Drama Awards and, as well as writing hundreds of hours of *Doctor Who*, is the co-author of *Arkham County* for Audible and *Children of the Stones* for BBC Sounds.

He also writes about and reviews and watches and watches and watches film.

Neurodivergent (Autistic, ADHD), he can be found on the South Coast, staring out to sea, muttering. He lives with his wife, the writer and genius, Alexandra Benedict, and his daughters Verity (human) and Dame Margaret Rutherford (canine).

Alexandra (AK) Benedict is an award-winning writer of bestselling novels, short stories and scripts. As Alexandra Benedict, she writes Golden Age-inspired mysteries with a darker, contemporary edge. *The Christmas Murder Game* was longlisted for the Gold Dagger Award, and both *Murder on the Christmas Express* and *The Christmas Jigsaw Murders* are international bestsellers.

As AK Benedict, Alexandra writes high-concept speculative fiction, short stories, and audio drama. Shortlisted for the BBC Audio Drama Award for *Children of the Stones* (BBC Sounds/Radio 4) and other awards, she won the Scribe Award for her Doctor Who audio drama *The Calendar Man* (Big Finish). Her debut novel, *The Beauty of Murder* (Orion), was nominated for the eDunnit Award, and her metafictional thriller *Little Red Death* (Simon & Schuster) has to date been sold into fifteen territories.

Alexandra lives by the sea in Eastbourne, UK, with writer Guy Adams, their daughter, Verity, and dog Dame Margaret Rutherford.

Mason Cross is the writer of the Carter Blake series of thrillers published by Orion. The first, *The Killing Season*, was published in 2014 and was longlisted for the Theakston Old Peculier Crime Novel of the Year. It was followed by four further novels in the series, including the Richard and Judy Book Club selection, *The Samaritan*. He has also written standalone thrillers as Alex Knight, including *Hunted* and *Darkness Falls*.

Derek Farrell is the author of five Danny Bird Mystery novels and a novella. His short fiction has appeared in *Gabba Gabba Hey*, an anthology of fiction inspired by the music of the Ramones, *Sharpen Fist Here* and *Noir from The Bar*. He is also the crime fiction programming director for the award-winning WORDfest Crawley, an editor and one-fifth of the team behind Interview Room One. His previous jobs have included: burger dresser, bank teller, David Bowie's paperboy, and investment banker, which gave him the opportunity to live and work in New York, Hong Kong, Istanbul, Tel Aviv, Prague, Dublin, Johannesburg and London. It also allowed him to see investment bankers up close and decide that one of them had to die in one of the Danny books, but that's perhaps a story for another day.

James Goss is a *Sunday Times* bestselling author who has written several *Doctor Who* books, including being Douglas Adams's literal ghost writer. He's also written extensively for audio, working on projects for Audible, Big Finish and BBC Sounds. Ten years ago, he wrote a novel about how the internet could be stopped if we just killed the nasty people on it. It's too late for that now, so he lives in a cave in Türkiye.

MK Hardy is the pen name of Morag Hannah and Erin Hardee, a married couple who have been writing together for twenty years. When they are not telling stories, they can be found singing in choirs, foraging for fungi, and working on their 1880s fixer-upper. Their debut sapphic gothic horror *The Needfire* was published by Solaris in July 2025.

Lavanya Lakshminarayan is the author of *Analog/Virtual: And Other Simulations of Your Future*. She is a Locus Award finalist and is the first science fiction writer to win the *Times of India* AutHer Award and the Valley of Words Award, both prestigious literary awards in India, and her work has been longlisted for a BSFA Award. She's occasionally a game designer, and has built worlds for Zynga Inc.'s *FarmVille* franchise, *Mafia Wars*, and other games. She lives in India, and is currently working on her next novel.

James Lovegrove has published over seventy books, including the hugely successful Conan Doyle/Lovecraft mashup series *The Cthulhu Casebooks*. His novel *Days* was shortlisted for the Arthur C Clarke Award, while *The Age of Odin*, part of his nine-book Pantheon series, was a *New York Times* bestseller. His short story 'Carry The Moon In My Pocket' won the 2011 Seiun Award in Japan for Best Translated Short Story, and his *Firefly: The Ghost Machine* won the 2020 Dragon Award for Best Media Tie-in Novel. His work has been translated into eighteen languages. He contributes regular fiction-review columns to the *Financial Times* and lives in Eastbourne.

Una McCormack is a *New York Times* bestselling and BSFA award-winning science fiction writer of more than twenty novels. She is on the editorial board of Gold SF, an imprint of Goldsmiths Press which publishes new voices in intersectional feminist science fiction.

Thana Niveau is a horror and science fiction writer. Her work includes the collections *Octoberland*, *From Hell to Eternity* and *Unquiet Waters*, and the novel *The House of Frozen Screams*. She shares her life with fellow writer John Llewellyn Probert and a Staffy rescue named Magnus.

John Llewellyn Probert is the author of twenty-two published books, the latest of which are *The Frightfest Guide to Mad Doctor Movies* (FAB Press) and the Amicus-style portmanteau novel *How Grim Was My Valley* (NewCon Press). He is also the author of the popular Dr Valentine series, the first volume of which won the British Fantasy Award. He reviews new movie releases at his site, *House of Mortal Cinema*, and is a regular columnist for the magazines *Weird Fiction Review* and *Nightmare Abbey* in the US and *We Belong Dead* in the UK. Coming up next is a new novel, more Dr Valentine, another short story collection and more film books. He tries to fit in some sleep where he can.

Angela 'A.G.' Slatter is an Australian author with seven novels, four novellas, twelve short story collections, a *Hellboy* comic and some other stuff to her name. Has some awards. Find out more at www.angelaslatter.com

Martyn Waites is an internationally bestselling, critically acclaimed crime writer. He has been nominated for, won, but mainly lost every major British and French crime fiction award. He was also chosen to write the official sequel to Susan Hill's *The Woman in Black*. His new novel, written under the name CB Everett is out this spring and called *The Other People.*

Aubrey Wood is a biracial, transgender lesbian from San Diego who has spent most of her life in New Zealand and on the internet. Her debut novel *Bang Bang Bodhisattva* was a finalist for the Lambda Award for Speculative Fiction and the Kitschies Golden Tentacle Award for Best Debut. She has been referred to as 'an explosion in an ideas factory' by at least one industry professional. She has never met a cheeseburger she didn't like, and she was born in 1987. She can be found on Bluesky at @briewoodfiction.bsky.social.

FIND US ONLINE!

www.rebellionpublishing.com

/solarisbooks

/solarisbks

/solarisbooks

/solarisbooks.
bsky.social

SIGN UP TO OUR NEWSLETTER!

rebellionpublishing.com/newsletter

YOUR REVIEWS MATTER!

Enjoy this book? Got something to say?

Leave a review on Amazon, GoodReads or with your favourite bookseller and let the world know!